Once Bitten

*The adventures and misadventures of a young
veterinary surgeon*

By Nick Marsh

Once Bitten

By Nick Marsh
©2016

ISBN-13:
978-1533106247

ISBN-10:
153310624X

Cover art and design by Jim Mcnulty of JMC Design & Motion Ltd.
Some chapters of this book - Seen and Not Heard, The Mutts Nuts, Dog #86324, Breeding Difficulties - were first published (as slightly different versions) in the *Veterinary Times*.

www.nick-marsh.co.uk

Once Bitten

For Kerry
(for keeping me sane)

And for Viv, Lee, Helen, Alison, Amelia, Cyndie, Mark, Fin, Neil, Elliott, Paula, and of course, Heather – this couldn't have happened without you. Thank you.

Nick Marsh

Prologue: Indestructible Alien Mercenary

When I was a child, my parents were intense holidaymakers. Not for them package flights to the Algarve or the Costa del Sol; no, they didn't feel a holiday was worthwhile unless it involved a tremendous amount of planning and work. They would spend months scrutinising maps of northern Europe, patiently plotting points, measuring distances and noting places of interest and fuel way-stations. Entering our kitchen in the weeks leading up to a summer holiday was like walking into Fighter Command during the Battle of Britain.

My parents were both teachers, and they were determined to make the best of our long summer holidays, which meant that the trips usually lasted three and sometimes four weeks – an eternity when I was ten. Large sections of my childhood holiday memories consist of the image of the back of my dad's seat rest in our old Nissan Bluebird, which I watched while I wondered how much farther we had to go to reach the next marked spot on my parents' much pored-over map.

The monotony of these long trips was occasionally leavened by my parents pulling into a lay-by beside the autobahn and swearing over that map whilst my nan, my brother and I quietly drank orange juice from pre-packed cartons[1]. These diversions were the exception rather than the rule, though, and for the rest of the time it was good to have something to occupy my mind - something to read. Therefore, my personal preparations for these epic holidays involved meticulously choosing which books I was going to take for the journey.

I must have been at a particularly impressionable age during the holiday that stands out in my mind because I packed two books that had such an impact upon me that they affected the entire future trajectory of my life.

---

[1] I know they meant well, but the taste of warm cardboardy orange juice slurped down in autobahn lay-bys was enough to put me off drinking it for fifteen years.

The first book was called *Deathwing over Veynaa*, by Douglas Hill, and it was about an indestructible alien mercenary from the planet Moros.

The second was *Every Living Thing*, by James Herriot.

When I'd finished them, I knew that was it for me. I knew exactly what I wanted to do with the rest of my time on Earth.

Unfortunately, I soon discovered that it's incredibly difficult to actually become an indestructible alien mercenary, so I settled on trying to become a vet instead.

*

The Legionnaires of Moros were mercenaries, but they were ethical - they never joined a fight that wasn't morally right, and they never did it just for the money. Their quest was to make the galaxy a better place, one job at a time. Back on my Earth, there were a disappointing lack of alien battalions to fight, but I felt I could still serve my galaxy with honour. If James Herriot had made me want to be a veterinary surgeon, the Legions of Moros had made me want to do it right. Which is why, fifteen years later, when I stood in a marquee in a field at the Langford Veterinary School in Bristol University, dressed in black robes and reciting the oath of the veterinary surgeon, every word of it came straight from my soul:

'I promise above all that I will pursue the work of my profession with uprightness of conduct, and that my constant endeavor will be to ensure the welfare of the animals committed to my care.'

In that marquee at Langford, I stood up to speak the words as an apprentice, but I sat down as a legionnaire. The oath was my own Quest. I was going to make the galaxy better, one animal at a time.

Like many brave heroes, those around me sometimes doubted me. Was I sure? they asked. Was I cut out for it? I wasn't the world's most outgoing person - I was shy and nerdy. It was a hard job. Wasn't I more suited for a job in administration, or I.T., or academia? I remember one melancholy trip to the pub with an old school friend who kept saying, 'Two years, mate. I give it two years before you're worn down, and you quit.'

This is the story of those two years. It's the story of the oath, and my quest, and the journey that it took me on.

Part One – Bridg Over Troubled Water[2]

1 - Morning Sickness

The lady behind the reception desk looked over her wide glasses at me. She had a kindly face and greying hair, and a postcard stuck to the wall behind her proclaimed: 'You can't scare me – I have children.'

'Are you here for an appointment?' she asked, smiling politely.

'Er, no,' I said, gesturing vaguely towards my feet, attempting to indicate that I wasn't carrying a cat box, and didn't have a hamster concealed anywhere about my person. 'I'm Alan Reece, I'm the new vet.'

'Ah,' the lady said. She clearly didn't believe that the youth standing before her should be trusted with a razor blade, let alone a scalpel. Then the smile returned.

'Of course, you're expected! Come through, come through!'

She indicated a door beside the reception desk. Sue, one of the senior vets, was waiting there to greet me. She was a tall, glamorous South African with an easy grin and a dirty laugh, and one of the two partners at Beech House Veterinary Hospital. She and David, the other partner, had interviewed me several weeks before, and had somehow come to the conclusion that I would be a valuable addition to their team. It was July, 1999, and it was my first ever working day as a vet.

'There he is,' she said, a smile on her face, 'our new recruit! How are you doing? Excited?'

'Yes, very!' I said, hoping my terror wasn't showing on my face.

'Don't worry.' Sue winked, as she led me towards the prep room. 'It gets better after a few months, I promise!'

A few *months*?

Ah well, I thought. At least the morning would be easy - all

---

[2] Yes, I know I missed the 'e'. More on this later.

health and safety forms and induction stuff. It would give me a chance to settle in before I was actually expected to do anything.

'I'll show you around quickly,' Sue said over her shoulder. 'You're consulting in ten minutes.'

At that moment the grey-haired lady on reception called across to us.

'Sue, I've got Mrs Keyes on the phone about Jackson.'

Sue made a face. 'Oh, not again.'

'She says it's out again. She wants to bring him in.'

Sue rolled her eyes and looked apologetically at me. 'Rectal prolapse. Can't seem to keep the bugger in. I'd better take this. Kate!'

A young woman with short brown hair popped her head round the corner from the prep room.

'Got to take this call, could you show our new recruit round? He's on morning consults.'

'Sure,' said Kate, and smiled at me as Sue disappeared. She screwed up her face. 'You're... Alan, right?'

I smiled the frozen grin of someone desperately trying to appear relaxed. 'Yes, Alan, Alan Reece. Er, pleased to meet you.'

I held out my hand, almost immediately feeling stupid for doing so. Kate looked at it, grinned, and shook it with exaggerated formality.

'Delighted to meet you, sir. Are you a little nervous, by any chance?'

I decided this was my chance to shine. University was behind me. No one here knew me. It was time to make a good impression, to appear relaxed, and calm. I had passed my exams, and I was a veterinary surgeon. A confident veterinary surgeon.

'I'm pissing myself,' I said.

Kate laughed, and looked me up and down. She shrugged. 'I think you're going to be okay, Alan.' She smiled again, and suddenly the day didn't seem quite so bad. 'C'mon,' she said as she walked through to the prep room.

The first thing I noticed - because he was hard to miss - was a huge, muscle-bound vet wearing a scrub top and shorts towering over a cat on one of the prep room tables. He didn't so much look well-built as carefully constructed to intimidate the enemy. Despite occupying roughly twice as much space as I did, he appeared a similar age to me.

'Cameron, meet Alan,' Kate said.

I held out my hand to him. Cameron shook his head, and waved one of the cat's testicles at me.

'Can't do that, mate, I'm sterile.' He grinned. 'Just like this poor guy, now.' He nodded at the cat on the table. Kate giggled. 'But it's grand to meet you, Alan.'

'He does the hand-shakey thing a lot,' Kate said. 'I think it's a nervous twitch.'

'It's that or faint, I think,' I said. Kate and Cameron laughed.

'Best to stick with the handshake then, I reckon,' Cameron said, and turned his attention back to his surgery.

'That's Ellie,' Kate said, pointing to the young girl in charge of Cameron's cat's anaesthetic, 'and over there we have Liz and Tracy, in charge of the inpatients today.'

I nodded and smiled at them, and they reciprocated. Beech House may not have been in the most culturally diverse area of the UK, but it was friendly enough.

'And in theatre?' I asked, nodding through the prep room window to a serious-looking thin man with thin wire-framed spectacles. He was concentrating very hard on some kind of complicated surgery, but exactly what surgery was impossible to determine as the animal was entirely smothered with green surgical drapes.

'That's James,' Kate said, rather shortly. She and Cameron looked at each other. At the mention of his name, the thin-faced man looked up, nodded perfunctorily at me, then returned his attention to the operation. A slightly awkward silence crept across the prep room, but it was mercifully almost immediately broken when David strolled cheerfully through the door.

David was a short, plump vet with greying hair and an extravagant bushy moustache, and he carried upon his face the world-weary look that comes with many years of dealing with the public.

'Just thought I'd say hi,' he said, smiling and shaking my hand. 'Settling in all right?'

'Er... it's a bit early for me to say,' I said, and he laughed.

'It's *always* too early to say,' he replied. 'Best of luck with it all.'

'Come on,' said Kate, 'let's find you a consulting top that fits.'

A few minutes later, now successfully dressed the part, I found myself standing in front of a computer screen in one of Beech House's consulting rooms, trying to look for all the world like I knew what I was doing.

2 - **Baptism by Fur**

The pen was working, my stethoscope was still around my neck[3], and the British Small Animal Veterinary Association drug reference guide was still in my drawer, exactly as they all had been the last seven times I had checked them. I stared at the computer screen, checking the afternoon's appointments again while I wondered how (and, perhaps more importantly, why) I had manoeuvred myself into a position of responsibility. Obviously, it wouldn't last. I would soon be discovered for the fraud I was, but until that happened I had to at least look like a professional.

The computer screen blinked and changed slightly. A client had arrived, and was, presumably, at this moment settling into a seat, unaware that the vet they were about to see was a complete idiot. I hovered my mouse cursor over the appointment, hoping for some clues before I called the person in.

Reason for appointment - ?unknown

Unknown? Brilliant. So it could be anything from rabies to pizzle rot... wait, no, isn't it only sheep that get that? Got to concentrate!

I looked at the breed. A border terrier. My brain, jammed full of encyclopaedic veterinary information from my finals, started automatically splurging out a list of the common diseases of that particular breed: primary lens luxation, glaucoma, epileptiform cramping, patellar luxation[4] and... something else?

Wasn't there another one? It's got to be one of those, hasn't it? The consult says 'unknown'. Oh, God, it's 'unknown', and *I'm*

[3] Yes, that's right – around my neck. Wearing a stethoscope in this way seems to have acquired an aura of arrogance or inappropriate coolness. 'Oh, look at him, wearing his stethoscope around his neck! Too poncy to put it in his pocket, is he?'. If you feel this way, then I apologise, but I also suggest trying to carry a stethoscope in your pocket. After twenty minutes of walking like a man with a slipped disc and a semi-erection, your perspective may have changed.

[4] Two diseases of the eye, one of the brain, and one of the hindlimbs, respectively.

the one who's supposed to know it!

Taking a deep breath, I opened my door and stepped out into the waiting room. A kindly-looking middle-aged lady with a friendly-looking scruffy terrier looked at me.

'Er... Rory,' I said, smiling. Well, I may actually have been grimacing, but I hoped it looked like smiling.

The woman looked down at the dog. 'That's you!' Rory wagged his tail, and the woman stood and started walking towards me. Rory followed, limping slightly on his front left leg.

Front leg? That didn't fit with anything! Even I knew that a patella was usually found in the back leg, and eyes and brains were even further afield.

I ushered the lady into my consult room, said hello to Rory, and lifted him up onto my table. Rory had been lame for a few days, the woman explained. She thought it was probably just a muscle sprain, but she wanted it checked out. I smiled, tickled Rory's ear, and began to examine the leg. Rory wagged his tail, and lifted his paw, helpfully indicating where it hurt.

Right, Alan, concentrate. No dislocations. That's a start. Can't feel any crepitus, except...wait, is that crepitus? There's a click, but not really a crunch, or a grind. Does that count? How are you supposed to know? God, I'm useless, useless!

I pulled myself together. Crepitus – a crackling sensation when a joint is moved or a leg is manipulated – can mean a break in the leg, or arthritis, or a number of other things, but the tiny click I felt when I flexed Rory's wrist was probably just a tendon shifting. Rory himself didn't seem concerned by the pop. He was sitting patiently, looking at his owner, wondering why this strange man had been shaking his paw for such a long time.

I felt around the bones of the leg – up the phalanges, the metacarpals, the radius and ulna, the humerus, the scapula – no swelling or pain on palpation. Probably not a bone tumour or bone cyst. Too old for panosteitis, or metaphyseal osteopathy[5], my mental encyclopaedia informed me. I extended Rory's shoulder.

[5] Growth disorders of young dogs

After a while, he looked at me, and politely pulled his leg back. Was that pain? Or was that normal for Rory? I tried the same on his right leg. Rory looked at me again, and pulled his leg back. He looked back at his owner. I think, if he had been human, he would have rolled his eyes.

'It's been a few days,' the owner repeated. 'He hasn't really got any worse, just not better,' she added.

'Yes,' I see,' I said. My mental encyclopaedia had suddenly become unhelpfully quiet. Mild lameness in the left fore... it didn't really fit with anything. Rory was barely even lame in the consulting room. It couldn't just be... surely it wouldn't be as simple as...

'I think it's just a muscle strain,' I heard myself saying. 'Let's get him on some painkillers for a few days and see how we go, shall we?' I smiled. His owner smiled. Rory wagged his tail and licked my ear as I lifted him down.

I tapped away at the computer, and disappeared into the pharmacy where I grabbed Sue and hurriedly explained the symptoms, and my plan. She agreed, and soon Rory and his owner were on their way.

I had done it. I had done a consult. I had survived. The client and the animal had both survived; it seemed like a success to me. The peculiar thing was that it hadn't felt peculiar. Once I got into the consult, it hadn't been all that bad. I did actually know a little about the job. The owner had believed me. Rory had even licked me! Maybe, just maybe, the boy voted 'most likely to write off the practice car in the first three months of being a vet' in the final year could actually do his job. Could my friend in the pub have been wrong? Could I make it through these two years after all?

I took through another consult – a vaccination. Another – a cat bite abscess. Another. Another. The afternoon passed. I lived. Afterwards, I stepped out into the pharmacy. Sue, who had been consulting with me, was talking to Kate. Sue looked up.

'He's not bad, is he?' she said, nodding and smiling in my direction. Kate looked at me, smiled, and nodded too. 'He'll do,' she said.

I managed not to faint, but instead smiled awkwardly back and mumbled, 'Thank you,' in surprise. In the many darker moments of self-doubt and self-loathing to come, I thought back to that unexpected and much-needed compliment, and took hope from it. [6]

My career had begun. Nothing had died. I hadn't died. Could it really be as easy as that?

Of course, beginner's luck doesn't just apply to card games.

---

[6] I didn't realise it at the time, but I suspect that Sue was impressed with my timekeeping as much as anything else. My consultations had all taken only the ten minutes they were allocated. It might seem like a lesser skill, but trust me – if you want to avoid getting garrotted by your colleagues at the end of an extremely busy surgery, try to make sure that they don't have to see three times as many clients as you do because you spend forty minutes vaccinating a cat when there's five people waiting.

3 - A Conveniently Situated Toilet

Beech House was on the outskirts of Bridgford, a small town in Somerset, about thirty miles north-east of Bristol – and yes, I spelled it correctly. Despite being pronounced 'bridge-ford', the inhabitants had conspired many years ago to make their town awkward to spell, and to forever mark out anyone who had the temerity to attempt to insert an 'e' anywhere into their beloved town's name as 'not from round 'ere'. Bridgford had been around a long time – it was an ancient port and market town, and Edward II (with an 'e', you may note) met his extremely unpleasant end in a nearby castle. Grimpen Water, the small village where Edward Jenner started his pioneering work in vaccination, and where the practice owned a small branch surgery, was just a few miles down the road.

Historic it may have been, but beautiful it was not. Bridgford was... well, let me tell you how Cameron described it when he gave me a lift from the practice that evening to take me to my new accommodation and my practice car.

'Bridgford,' he explained, cheerfully, 'is a conveniently situated toilet. Horrible place. Half the time it stinks from the fumes that the bloody chemical works give off, and the rest of the time it rains. It's close to the motorway, though, and the Cotswolds, which are lovely. You've just got to... well, put up with it, I suppose.'

'Ah, right,' I said, remembering the advert in the *Veterinary Record*, which had started: **Exciting Opportunity at 5-Vet Mixed Practice in Stunning, Picturesque South West**.

'You wouldn't call it picturesque, then?' I said, looking out of the window at the litter-strewn street as we drove past the station. 'Or stunning?'

Cameron raised an eyebrow. 'Well,' he mused, 'the smell from the factory can certainly make your eyes water, if that's what you mean.'

He flashed me a lopsided grin. 'So, how was your first day at work, then? That was me, a year ago. Brings back memories watching someone else go through it.'

'Actually,' I said, 'it wasn't too bad. I was so terrified last night, but everyone has been lovely. You, Sue, Kate, David.'

Cameron nodded, 'Yeah, well, we're all pretty laid back. The job's stressful enough, y'know?'

'I haven't seen so much of James,' I added. 'He spent most of the day in theatre.'

Cameron rolled his eyes. 'Yes, that's about normal. Enjoys his surgery, does James.'

'So I gathered,' I said. 'Kate didn't really say much about him.'

'Well, it probably wouldn't have been anything good, to be fair,' Cameron said. 'They broke up about three weeks ago. Not been great for the atmosphere at the practice, but they're being professional about it, at least at work.'

'Oh, right,' I said, suddenly feeling as if I was intruding. My split with my own girlfriend, a few months before finals, was still pretty fresh. Maybe James found it easier to throw himself into work.

'If you're thinking he's throwing himself into his work, you're wrong,' Cameron said. 'He's always been like that.'

I laughed, and looked out of the window as the streets of Bridgford crawled past. We were driving past a tiny, grimy pub, so covered in Union Jacks - painted on the door, posted in the window, quarter-sized ones hanging from a long plastic line running from end-to-end of the building - that I briefly wondered if I had forgotten if it there had been a royal wedding, birth or death. Then I noticed the name of the pub: *The Union Jack*. The small portion of window space that wasn't taken up with a British Flag instead displayed a small chalkboard upon which was written:

Today's Specials
Tanya
Louise
Denise

I blinked.

'Your local,' Cameron said with a smile.

'Brilliant,' I said. 'Um, any good?'

'Fucked if I know,' Cameron grinned. 'I've never dared set foot in the place.'

The car turned off the main road, twisted around some narrow streets and emerged into a small cul de sac.

'Here we are,' Cameron said. He stopped the car outside an extremely small semi-detached house. A supermarket trolley and an old fridge quietly rusted in the overgrown square metre of front lawn.

Cameron saw me looking at them. 'I think you get them as part of the package,' he said. 'Now get some rest, and we'll do it all again tomorrow.'

I clambered out of the car and retrieved my bag from the back seat. Cameron rolled down his window, leaned out, and said, 'enjoy Bridgford.'

He winked, and drove off into the night. I walked up the broken concrete path to my front door, and ventured inside.

The house wasn't large; houselet may be a more accurate term, because the general design was as if someone had constructed one wide, long house, then built a wall down the middle, bisecting it, and then several walls along its length, chopping it into eight little houselets like slices of a sausage. I dropped my bag on the floor in the lounge and decided to explore. It did not take long. There was just about enough room to turn around in the kitchen, so long as you weren't carrying anything. The lounge was the largest room, because it consisted of the entire lower floor of the houselet apart from the teeny kitchen. This, unfortunately, left nowhere else for the stairs to go, so they towered over the sofa, inconspicuous as an elephant. Upstairs had one bedroom, a bathroom, and a cupboard that had been mistakenly labelled as a second bedroom.

The bath was slightly larger than the sink.[7]

---

[7] Despite its small volume I soon discovered that the bath was still too much for the boiler to cope with. Many of my early memories of that house consist of sitting shivering in the bathroom, waiting for the kettle to boil in the bedroom so that I could pour another load in the bath and hope it would then be full enough to cover my legs.

I carried my bag up to my room, flopped onto the bed, and dreamed away my first night in Bridgford.

Over the next few weeks, I discovered that Cameron's description of the town largely fitted my experience of it. It was as if someone had managed to extract the greyest, most depressing areas from a larger city, trimmed away all the nice bits, and then dropped it in the middle of an area of outstanding natural beauty. I may be being unnecessarily harsh on Bridgford, linked as it is in my mind with the confused jumble of experiences of my first few years in practice. The best I can bring myself to say about the place is – it was in a lovely area.

Cameron was right about the chemical works, too. The nose is an amazing organ. The olfactory centre is right at the front of the brain, part of the limbic system – our emotional centre. Smells can bring back memories from years ago, make you experience feelings long forgotten. To this day, when I smell industrial chemicals and burning plastic, I think of Bridgford, and its missing bloody 'e'.

4 - Learning to Drive

The next morning I managed to navigate my way back to Beech House without any major mishaps. I left the practice car in the car park and headed into the practice.

'Good morning, Alan,' Kate said as I struggled into my consulting top. 'Enjoying Bridgford?'

'Well,' I mused, 'It's not exactly Darrowby, but it'll do.'

Kate nodded. 'I think it's twinned with Royston Vasey.'

A League of Gentleman joke! Was it possible that Kate could be into the same geeky things as I was? I started to think of a suitable response; the answer that would casually indicate that I knew what she meant without appearing uncoolly enthusiastic to meet a fellow nerd.

'Um,' I said.

'Better get your skates on today,' she said. 'You're consulting with David. He's very o...'

'Very what?' said David, appearing from the prep room, glasses and hair askew after his own battle with his consulting top. 'Were you about to say old?'

'No, no, of course not,' Kate said, innocently.

David rolled his eyes and looked at me. He was the practice principle; the main owner of the business and my employer. He was my first ever boss, and I was semi-terrified of him. He had agreed to hire me, so he must have seen some potential, though I was at a loss to explain what that was.

Kate headed towards the prep room, mouthing 'Good luck!' at me. David straightened his glasses, attempted vainly to flatten his wandering hair, and raised an eyebrow at me.

'Right,' he said. 'What do you think it means to be a vet?'

Well, this was an interesting way to start the morning. Couldn't it have been a Star Wars question?

'Erm,' I said. 'Well. I think really it's about helping...'

My voice tailed off as David starting shaking his head sadly.

'Okay,' I tried. I thought about the Quest, and my solemn oath. 'It's about... er... doing the best for the anim--'

'Compromise,' David said. 'Being a vet is about compromise.'

'Compromise?'

'Let me give you an example,' he said. He looked at the waiting list. 'Right, there's a client coming in this morning with a dog with diarrhoea. Say you look at it and decide it's got gastroenteritis. The client wants antibiotics because she knows that clears diarrhoea up. What do you do?'

'Well,' I said, deciding it was time to show off my knowledge. 'The vast majority of enteritis isn't related to an infection; not a bacterial infection, anyway. So, I'd recommend feeding a bland diet for a few days. It's better than starving because the enterocytes--'

David nodded quickly. 'Brilliant. Textbook answer. You know what happens then?'

'Er...'

'The client comes back the next day to see me and tells me that their dog is no better. She wants antibiotics. I give them to her. Her dog gets better, and she's very pleased with me. She also tells me that the vet she saw yesterday didn't know what he was talking about. I'd rather that didn't happen. The dog is going to get antibiotics anyway. If we cut out the middle-man then I won't have quite so much work to do, and clients will like you better.'

'But--'

'I know what they teach you at university, Alan,' David said, not unkindly. 'The *science*. Now it's time to learn the *art* of veterinary medicine.'

*

There was a saying at university - a nugget of wisdom, filtered down from those intrepid souls that had passed before us: taking your final exams is like taking your driving test, but starting work as a vet is like learning to drive.

At Beech House, David introduced me to the steepest learning curve of my life. I swiftly discovered that nothing my lecturers had taught me really prepared me for the shock of general practice. The principle problem was this: at university, I was taught by specialists in their field - surgeons, medics, anaesthesiologists, pathologists, radiologists, anatomists, and so on. In my early years of vet school, most of the tutors weren't vets at all. In my later years, they were often the sort of vets who, in their biographies (printed, as they were, at the side of academic papers or articles in the Veterinary Record), usually had a sentence that read something like '...after a short period in general practice, they returned to university to study...', which couldn't help but make me wonder how much they had enjoyed their 'short period in general practice'.

The upshot of all this high-level expertise in my training was that I left university with a head packed full of the symptoms and treatment of rare and exotic-sounding diseases such as Key-Gaskell syndrome, myasthenia gravis, tetralogy of Fallot, and leishmaniasis[8], but with no training at all on what I was actually supposed to do when I was faced with a cat fight abscess, or a sprained leg, or a dog that's vomiting a bit but not a lot, or any one of the dozens of different common conditions you're faced with multiple times a day in general practice.

It meant that, for me, every new consult was accompanied by a tiny sinking feeling as I mentally flicked through my notes, still jammed in my head from final exams, came up blank, and had to start again, working from 'first principles' (basic knowledge of anatomy, physiology, pharmacology and pathology) to come up with the best plan. Or (and honestly rather more often) looking back over the notes and doing whatever the last vet did until I had a bit more time to think about it.

David had been in the business long enough to realise that consulting was, to some extent, a performance. He knew as well as I did that antibiotics didn't cure diarrhoea in most instances, but he didn't believe they did any harm, and he knew the dog was probably going to get better whatever treatment was given. The client just needed the confidence to think their dog was going to

[8] As well as all you could ever wish to know about the various patterns of ventilation in a chicken shed. Seriously, there's fifteen of them, all designed to attempt to get fresh air to the chicken; a problem that would be more easily solved, I felt, by allowing the chicken to go outside.

get better. He had been trying to tell me, as gently as he could, that all my high-minded ideas of best practice and best medicine weren't going to survive contact with the clients.

The problem, of course, was that David was wrong about something. Antibiotics can cause harm - any drug can, if you're unlucky - and overusing them could mean that, very soon, we wouldn't have any antibiotics left to use. I wanted to do the right thing for the clients, but how could I square that with the fact that it wasn't always the right thing to do for the animals? I needed to find a way to practice the medicine I wanted to and keep the clients on my side. This wasn't quite how I had imagined the Quest going. It didn't seem like the sort of thing the Legionnaires of Moros would have done.

So, I kept consulting, trying to find my own way - my own artistic style of veterinary medicine. Almost before I noticed, that first week passed. Every little compromise - every time I avoided a blood sample because owner couldn't afford it, and instead treated for the most likely condition, and every time I gave in and gave steroids for itchy skin because 'the last vet had done it' - pricked at my conscience. This wasn't the logical job I had been expecting.

Over that first week, however, consulting became a little easier; I started seeing the same clients and animals back for a second time, realising that I hadn't made any horrific mistakes and, despite the frequent compromises, they had actually got better. The receptionists even began to get a few requests from people who wanted to come back specifically to see me again. This was completely baffling to me, but probably had a lot to do with the best piece of advice I was ever given during my time at vet school: people don't care what you know, they only want to know that you care. The basic sentiment behind this – that people want to know that you see their animal as a member of the family, and not just another case – seemed to come naturally to me, and a lot of clients responded to it.[9] I was worried, though. These compromises didn't

---

[9] In the interests of fairness, however, I will point out (in a footnote, of course) that there were also a minority of clients who politely asked if

feel right. It wouldn't have been good enough for the Legions of Moros. Was it good enough for me?

Maybe, given time, I would find a way to do things right. For now, I was just trying to survive. Only the month before, I had passed my driving test. Now I was learning what it was like on the roads. Eventually, those various dreaded boxes began to get ticked – first consult, tick. First anal gland squeezing, tick. First intravenous injection, tick. First bitch spay, tick. At the end of my second week, there was one very large tick waiting for me[10] - my first ever night on call.

---

there was anyone else working on the day they were due to come back. You can't win 'em all.

[10] And I don't mean one of the kind of whoppers you often find attached to hedgehogs.

5 - Nights in fright, sat in[11]

On call work (or Out Of Hours, as it's often called nowadays – not a phrase I'm keen on, as the acronym is OOH, which makes me think of Dick Emery rather than the dark misery of being on call) is a terror for new graduates. As students, like scouts sitting around a campfire telling ghost stories, we'd sometimes whisper in hushed and nervous tones about what it would be like on the first night that the buck would stop with us.[12]

'What if it's a bitch caesarean? Before you've even done a spay?'

'Bitch? Never mind bitch, what if the first one is a cow caesarean?'

'Or a uterine prolapse?'

'At my training practice, a vet there said that he once got called by the police to a traffic accident with a horse lorry!'

'How about glaucoma? Would you treat it? Refer it?'

'What if your first call is a GDV?!'[13]

With these fears in mind, it may be understating the case to say that it was with some trepidation that I watched my colleagues drive off into the night while I stood in the car park, the practice mobile phone in my pocket. Beech House was a Veterinary Hospital, and although that meant a number of things, the most important one to me at that moment was that we had twenty-four-hour nursing cover; a nurse was on duty all night in

---

[11] This is obviously an amusing pun on the Moody Blues song 'Nights in White Satin' - but if you have to explain 'em...

[12] Possibly literally, if the right kind of wildlife came in.

[13] GDV - Gastric dilatation/volvulus - was the trump card, the crappy first ever call-out to beat all crappy first ever call-outs. Also known as bloat, this dreadful condition occurs in larger dogs when the stomach spins around on its axis, preventing any food from getting into it, and (more critically) any gas escaping. The poor dog blows up like an agonized balloon, and the condition requires immediate treatment (almost always major surgery) or it won't live through the night.

the practice to take the phone calls and check the inpatients over, which was an immense weight off my mind. For a start, the nurse of my first night on call was Kate, and we already seemed to get on pretty well. I had the feeling that she would look after me. Some of my university friends didn't have such luxuries – when my mobile rang, it would be Kate telling me about the phone call she just received. For them, when it rang they would be talking directly to the client.

Thank heaven for small mercies, I thought. All I had to worry about was actually getting the animal better. On my own. In the day, I had been able to escape my consult room and interrogate Sue, David or Cameron about whether I was using the right drug, at the right dose, or if the animal needed to be admitted. No longer. If I saw something complicated then I could try and get in touch with Sue or David, but there was no official 'second on call' rota, and there were no guarantees.[14]

I took a deep breath. I checked the mobile was working. It was. It had been twenty seconds ago, and it still was now. There was no point standing around sighing in a car park – in fact, Kate had given me quite specific instructions on that front ('Just bugger off and relax, will you?') – so it was time to head home.

That first night I discovered something about myself – I was really, really not good at being on duty. When I was a student, I'd known vets come out for a drink, laughing and sociable, while they were doing OOH work. The only clues that they were still working would be that they'd be drinking Diet Cokes and surreptitiously checking their mobiles every half hour or so. A few would go out to restaurants, or to the gym, or rock climbing. It turned out that I wasn't one of those vets. The only thing I wanted to do when I got back to my little practice house was sit by the phone and wait for it to ring, stewing and worrying.

This was, it should be clarified, in no way a productive kind

---

[14] In retrospect, Sue and David would have been very aware that it was my first ever night on call, and would have, I suspect, absolutely been around if I needed them.

of stewing. I wouldn't read my notes, or research things that I might see. No, I just sat there, waiting. I put the TV on, but didn't watch it.

The phone rang. Oh. My. God.

I rushed to the phone and picked it up. 'Hello, sweetie. I just thought I'd check to see--'

My mum, checking to see if I was okay. What if she was blocking an emergency call? What if I was getting a call right this second and I was sitting here chin-wagging with my mother. 'I'm fine, mum, but I'm on call, I can't talk!' I interrupted, urgently. 'Please don't think I'm being rude,' I added as I rudely clunked the phone back into the receiver and stared at the TV, legs jiggling nervously. They seemed to want to pace, so I let them. It didn't help, but it was a change, so I let them do their stuff while I got on with the important business of worrying.

The phone could ring right now, I thought, helpfully. Right this second. It could be absolutely anything and it could ring now. Or now. Or now. Or in five seconds. Any time at all. God, it could be anything!

I sat down again, and looked at the phone. Or now. Or right now!

I was so convinced that, in my mind, I actually began to hear the phone ring, my brain reminding me of what it sounded like so that when it happened I would not mistake it for, say, a blackbird.

Thank you, brain, I thought, bitterly. That's useful. Very relaxing. I looked at my watch. I had been on call twenty-five minutes, including the fifteen minute drive home.

I thought about some dinner, but didn't feel hungry. I looked at the phone again. Or now! Or now!

Oh, this was stupid. I should stop worrying. It wasn't about to ring any time soon.

The phone rang.

In flat contradiction to all those things Einstein said about the speed limit of the universe, the receiver was at my ear before the photons that bounced off it had ventured more than a millimetre.

'Hello?' I said.

'Alan, I need you to come in.'

I strained as I listened, trying unsuccessfully to divine the problem from the tone of Kate's voice.

'Er...what is it?'

'I've got an injured peahen; it needs looking at,' Kate said.

'A what?'

It was about this time that I discovered that no matter how much revision you do, no matter how much you know about Cushing's syndrome or the internal structure of a nephron, none of it helps you look any less stupid when you've never even heard of the animal that you're supposed to be treating. Somehow I had made it through five years of veterinary training without it ever occurring to me that a peacock was thusly named because it was the male of the species.

As Kate politely explained this to me, I was no longer a veterinary surgeon. I was a geeky lad from Manchester who was out of his depth. It's fair to say that a call to an injured peahen was not in the top ten list of calls that I was expecting. Given that I hadn't even been aware of the existence of such an animal until thirty seconds previously, it was doubtful it would have made it into the top million.

However, I also discovered something else at that moment – sitting around waiting for the phone to ring is *almost always* worse than the thing you eventually get called in to see. The tension evaporated from me like spirit from a surgical wound, and it was a far more relaxed young man who drove to the surgery, extracted the surprised peahen - a small, fat, brown bird - from its concerned owner, anaesthetised it, stitched up its canine-caused injury, and watched it recover in one of the cat cages.

'Job well done,' I said, as I helped Kate to clean up the prep room. She raised an eyebrow.

'I suppose so,' she said with a grin, 'when you finally worked out what species you were dealing with.'

'Well, we don't have a lot of peacocks in Manchester,' I said, defensively.

'None roaming the estate, then?'

'No. Squirrels and cats mainly.'

Kate picked up the surgical kit from the sink where I had placed it and moved it to the correct one, then patiently took the spray from my hand as I started to clean the table.

'That one's for the animals,' she said. She picked up a seemingly identical spray bottle. '*This* one is for the table.'

'Oh, right. Er, sorry.'

Kate smiled. 'You don't have to help clean up, you know. None of the other buggers would.'

For some reason this cheered me up immensely. I wondered if she meant any vet in particular. Would James have stayed to help?

'Well,' I said, 'it seemed rude. You've got all this--'

Kate smiled. 'Alan, it's fine. Plus,' she added, picking up the reel of nylon and moving it to the correct place, 'you *really* aren't helping. Go home and get some sleep.'

'Oh,' I said. 'Right, okay. Well, you know where I am if you need me.'

Kate nodded and smiled and pointed to the white board where I had prominently displayed my home and mobile numbers.

'Okay,' I said, and headed for the exit.

'Alan,' Kate said as I reached the prep room door. I turned. 'Good start to the week,' she said. 'You're doing well.' She winked.

I danced back to my car.

I didn't get any more calls on that first night. The peahen made a full recovery. I was still a work in progress. The next thing I would have to face was the part I had been dreading - the hardest part of the job.

6 - The Hardest Part of the Job

The first patient that I ever saw die was at the start my second week in practice: Josie, a big, young and beautiful black Labrador retriever with wide brown eyes, a face that was always smiling, and a tail that was always wagging. Josie's owners were worried about her because she'd started vomiting at the weekend, and by Monday morning, when Cameron admitted her to the hospital, she was vomiting so badly that she couldn't keep water down - never an encouraging clinical sign. It was my 'ops' day - a morning where I wasn't consulting, but working behind the scenes on the operations and procedures that were booked in - and so it was my job to take the blood sample and place her on a drip. Josie licked my nose as I took the blood. A few minutes later, as we were bandaging the catheter in, she was sick again. I got on with my day.

Just before the start of evening surgery, I went to see how she was getting on: not well. She'd vomited several more times, and was now lying on her sternum, groaning. I lifted her lip, and was alarmed at the pallor of her gums. I went and grabbed Cameron, and asked him to look at his patient. Cameron examined her, checked her temperature, and frowned.

'Hm. You're right. Not going well. I think we're going to need to operate in the morning, find out what's going on in there. The x-ray wasn't all that helpful, but something's clearly not right in there.'

He ran his hand over his stubbly chin, obviously concerned. He was right; the x-ray hadn't revealed any foreign bodies, obvious tumours, or gas build-up. I looked at Josie. Her tail thumped against the inside of the kennel as my eyes caught hers, and I asked the question that so many owners have asked me since.

'She's not going to die, though, is she?'

Cameron shrugged. 'Wouldn't have thought so. She's strong. Not tonight, at any rate.' He left. I stayed with Josie for a little while, tickling her ears, still worried. I looked at her. It came to me very clearly that Cameron was right. She couldn't die tonight. She was too big, too vibrant an animal for that to happen to her overnight. Tickling her warm ears, with her grunting in pleasure, it was hard to imagine her dying at all.

I didn't have to imagine it. By the end of evening surgery, Josie's abdomen was so painful that if you even touched it, she vomited. Her colour was now deathly pale, tinged with red around the edges. She was in abdominal crisis - severe toxic changes were occurring somewhere in her peritoneal cavity - and Cameron had swiftly changed his mind; he knew we'd have to operate then and there.

We never made it that far. As we were prepping for surgery, Josie stopped breathing, and never started again despite all our efforts. Half an hour later I was standing in theatre with her dazed owner - a beautiful dark haired young woman with a large silver cross around her neck. She had her hand on her pet, who was already growing cold, and I was explaining to her about the pancreatic cancer.

'I just... I can't believe it,' she was saying. 'It doesn't make any sense.'

It didn't to me, either. I had somehow made it through my veterinary training without ever really believing that death happened like that. It seems that the human brain has something of a blank spot to do with death; unless you absolutely and finally hammer it home, it never really sinks in, which is why it's so important for people who have lost loved ones to know that the body has been found, to finally know that there is no more hope. That evening, it sunk in for me. Death, final and irrevocable, happens. It happens all the time.

Thinking back to that evening now, all these years later, it seems almost impossibly naive that I thought the Labrador couldn't die so swiftly. I can still clearly remember that thought, impertinent and against all logic, that she was too big to just... stop.

My error was made clear to me that night. As a veterinary surgeon, I was going to have to become used to dealing with, and frequently *in*, death. Another thing I would have to conquer if I was going to make it through these two years.

I had a lot to learn. I was lucky: I had some great veterinary surgeons to learn from.

7 - Colleagues

Before I arrived at Bristol Vet School, I had naively assumed that all the students would be there for the same reasons as me – a love of animals and science, coupled with a vague feeling of needing to do something 'good' (which is about as middle-class a reason as you can get for doing anything; replace 'science' with 'God' and I would have ended up as a vicar). Once there, I realised there were as many different reasons for aspiring to the career as there were students; some did it because it's what their parents did (though how on earth that failed to put them off, I have no idea), some had grown up on farms, or stables, or bred champions at CRUFTS. Some were impelled by a far more powerful urge than I was that the world needed to be made a better place for animals, and some... some didn't care about creatures at all. I was surprised and saddened that a select few people on my course were there simply because it was the hardest course to get onto; they were proving something to themselves – and everyone else, for that matter. So many different reasons, and so many different people.

I had met many qualified vets during my training, of course, many of whom I admired, and some of whom I didn't, but at Beech House I worked with other veterinary surgeons on a more or less equal footing for the first time. I was just taking my first steps as a vet, and if I was going to make it at least through those first two years I needed to discover what sort of vet I was going to be. A legionary of Moros was trained from the cradle in combat techniques and morally righteous decision making. I'd had five years of vet school with a one-day optional course in ethics. I was going to need to pick something up from the people I was working with if I was going to get anywhere near starting my Quest.

David had worked in a number of other practices, and he told me in this interview that he had seen 'things' happen in some of them. These 'things' made him swear to start his own practice, if only to make sure they wouldn't happen again if he had anything to do about it. He never told me what the legendary 'things' were, but over the coming months I would begin to understand exactly what he meant. Beech House was a veterinary hospital (as opposed to a veterinary practice) because David wanted things done for the best, both for the clients and for the animals.

He was an older vet in every sense. He had a paternalistic style with the clients - 'Here's what's definitely going on, here's what we're going to do to fix it' - in contrast to the informed decision making that many of the younger vets favoured, and a great deal of the clients responded to it. In his consult room, he was a charming and persuasive man, a good vet, and a great salesman. As well as his astute business skills and moral compass, David loved wildlife; consequently he spent a lot of time out of the practice, working at the local wildlife sanctuary, and writing a veterinary book on the care of wild animals. He took it upon himself to start to deconstruct my foolish notions of a perfect world, and to show me that keeping clients happy wasn't necessarily a sin; they paid our wages, after all. His veterinary style didn't suit me at all, but I could still learn a lot from him.

I was closer to Sue, the vet who had worked with David for a while and who had bought a share of Beech House from him a few years before. Sue was an impossibly glamorous, larger-than-life South African, who lived an enchanted, celebrity lifestyle – at least, that's what I always imagined Sue doing when she wasn't at the practice. She was the first person I ever heard of to get a bread maker; that's the sort of incredible exoticism we're dealing with here. Her father worked in some shadowy, vague but clearly high-up position in the British Government. I always imagined him as something like 'M', the mysterious figure who sends James Bond to wrestle megalomaniacs in undersea bases. Sue was friendly, helpful, with a fun sense of humour and a bright personality, and I enjoyed working with her (and trading terrible jokes with her) a great deal. She was caring with owners, and willing to try anything to help an animal in need. She was, in short, a great vet.

Cameron was large, cheerful, and - most annoyingly - effortlessly handsome. Even returning from a calving, waterproofs covered in God-knew-what, he looked as if he had just stepped from the pages of the Freeman's catalogue. He received a lot of calls from horse owners, who made sure that they put their make-up on before he arrived. I eventually got so tired of young female clients asking me if he was married that I took to telling them that we were a gay couple, much to Cameron's amusement.

I liked Cameron a great deal, largely because it would have taken a lot of effort not to like him; he wore an aura of reassurance that made me feel that however bad things got, it was all going to be okay.[15] For all this charm, however, Cameron was not designed for small animal work. A green consulting top always bulged under the strain of his frame, and he tended to loom in the consulting room, however much he smiled. A hamster, in Cameron's hands, looked like a tiny speck, an inconvenience that he could swat at a moment's notice. Although he was, like many big men, a deeply gentle and caring person, he tended to frighten the old dears. He also lacked some of the PR skills that are essential in a small animal vet. Once, after checking the temperature of an award-winning Bichon Frise, he wiped the thermometer on the surprised animal's back in front of the horrified owner, forgetting, temporarily, that he was not dealing with a cow.

And then there was James.

I first encountered James outside of his operating theatre on the Wednesday of my first week. It was our first evening consulting together, and I felt we hadn't really been properly introduced, so I approached him with a smile.

'Hi, we haven't really met. I'm Alan, the new vet.'

James looked up from the *Journal of Small Animal Practice*, nodded once, and returned his attention to the article he was reading on external fixation of feline humeral fractures. He didn't actually speak to me for another week, and that was to inform me that my choice of premedication for my dog that I was about to remove a lump from was reckless and borderline dangerous for the

---

[15] This inner glow of Cameron's must have also projected in some way to his body temperature, because he was the kind of man who wore shorts every day of the year, irrespective of weather conditions.

anaesthetic.

It's incredible to think that he was only a few years more qualified than I was. James was a hotshot – he oozed confidence from every pore of his body, and that was every bit as pleasant to experience as it sounds. He was cocky and going places, places that I almost certainly wasn't, and right from the start I liked him about as much as he liked me, which, let's be honest, wasn't very much.

To James, I was a stammering, weedy buffoon, always doubting myself (and with good reason). To me, James was a toweringly arrogant and unsupportive vet, and a spectacularly good surgeon. It seems a shame to confirm the stereotype that the best surgeons are the Lord Flashhearts of the medical world, but there does seem to be something about the God's Gift attitude which means that the people you least want to share a long car journey with are also the people you most want to crack open your chest when you've got a serious problem with your heart[16].

James was more interested in the techniques he could try rather than the creature upon which he was trying them. In my second week at Beech House he performed a bilateral total ear canal ablation on a middle-aged spaniel – he removed both the dog's ears external and middle ear canals, leaving nothing but the ear flaps remaining. Performed on one side, this surgery is very painful, as the surgeon has to delve into the side of the head and remove the ear as it emerges from the skull. Performed on both sides at once, it is excruciating. James filled the animal with morphine to control the pain. It didn't survive the night.

James was upset that his procedure had been unsuccessful.

In my darker moments in those first few weeks, I imagined myself in the place of that poor, deafened animal in those last few hours, and I counted myself glad that I'm no Lord Flashheart myself[17]. Whatever kind of vet James was, it was exactly the sort of

---

[16] I have, of course, since met many excellent surgeons who didn't have the personality of an F1 driver, but first impressions count for a lot.

[17] That's not to say I think the procedure itself is unhelpful – it relieves pain and the results can be amazing for dogs with end-stage ear disease...

vet that I didn't want to be.

My colleagues in Bridgford had a lot to teach me. However, I was about to realise that there are some lessons you can only learn on your own.

---

but it's a procedure that, in my opinion, should be carried out at a referral practice, by an experienced surgeon, and not something to 'have a go' at.

8 - Mistakes

Oscar Wilde once said, 'Experience is simply the name we give to our mistakes.' I was not an experienced vet, and I was in no position to argue with the man.[18]

It was my second week in Bridgford. In that time I had slowly been working away at banishing the Imposter Syndrome and starting to see some cases back that had actually got better under (or at least despite) my medical care. I had even developed a strange, alien notion in my head that I might possibly even be (whisper it) not actually that bad a vet after all. The clients seemed to like me. I had a nice way with the animals and my university notes were finally connecting with the things I saw day by day in my consult room, and I was beginning to think that I might actually make it through these two years after all. Maybe I could even make a career of this.

Pride. We all know what that comes before.

It was a busy evening surgery; beyond busy, in fact. Its sheer mass seemed to slow down time itself, so that I could no longer imagine ever having any other existence than seeing one sick animal after another, constantly returning to an ever-growing waiting room to call the next name from the increasingly mutinous crowds beyond. The appointments had been fully booked three days previously, and had only grown fuller since. I was consulting on my own. Normally the only surgeries we ever worked solo at Beech House were the comparatively quieter afternoon ones, but that night James had an exciting orthopaedic case booked in a slot at a local MRI scanner, and he was damned if he was going to miss the excitement for something as humdrum as working an evening surgery.

'Going to get my dog MRI scanned tonight; that's all right, isn't it?' he'd said to me that morning. 'Not too busy, is it?' They

---

[18] He'd been dead for quite a while, for one thing.

were the first words he had ever spoken to me.

'Erm...' I'd said, nervously, looking at the full-to-bursting consult list.

'You'll be fine,' he said, not looking up from his case notes. 'Nothing to it. I'll probably be back before the end, help bail you out.'

I nodded and smiled, and tried to ignore the looming list of consults for the rest of the day.

'Sure,' I agreed. 'It'll be fine.'

It was now five past six in the evening. I was twenty-five minutes behind, the waiting room was reaching capacity, and I was about ready to get down on my knees and beg for something as simple as a vaccination. Earlier on in this miserable evening, I'd been presented with a Chinese Water Dragon. Unlike the peahen, this one I *had* heard of, but reptile medicine was not my forte; consequently it took me at least five minutes to figure out that the cause of its 'lethargy' was that it had been dead for several hours. This had been one of my easy consultations. Three clients had stepped into the surgery without appointments, needing to be seen that night regardless. They had said at reception that they were happy to wait, but the expressions that greeted me every time I called someone else in suggested otherwise.

As I glanced at my computer screen, cleaning my table ready for the next onslaught, and wondering if it was possible for a person's head to actually crack under pressure, Kate opened the back door to my consulting room. The expression on her face - worried, sad and apologetic – was a revelation to me, because I didn't think it was possible for my heart to sink any lower than it already was. She was worried about me, which meant that I must have looked stressed as hell.

'Horrible evening,' she said, half-smiling.

'Getting there,' I said, cheerfully, wanting to forget our usual banter and for her to just tell me what it was and get it over with. Reading my expression, Kate frowned.

'Um... I've got Mrs Fitzroy on the phone.' I think my heart was actually below floor level at this point. Mrs Fitzroy was a breeder of Cavalier King Charles spaniels. I was starting to develop my own views on breeding pedigree animals[19] but Mrs Fitzroy brought an awful lot of business to the practice, and she was, if only in her own mind, a VERY IMPORTANT CLIENT.

'Riiight,' I said, less cheerfully.

'She wants a home visit,' Kate said, slowly, as if she was wondering the same thing I had about vets under pressure. 'There's a problem with one of her puppies.'

I looked at the waiting list, and wanted to scream. 'I just can't at the moment, Kate, I've got five... six people waiting now. If she can bring it in, I'll see it right away, but I can't leave now.'

Kate nodded. We both knew the likely response from the demanding Mrs Fitzroy, but it was worth a try. I called another consultation through. A mercifully simple bilateral otitis in a cocker spaniel. As I was out in the pharmacy putting a label on the ear ointment, Kate approached again. Her worried expression had not improved.

'She says she can't leave the mum, she's whelping. She can't leave her alone. She wants a visit, right now.'

Another glance at the computer screen. Even though I whizzed through the ear infection in record time, another two consults had been added to the list. I didn't have enough time to go to the toilet, let alone on a home visit.

If I was older or debatably wiser, I might have recommended that Mrs Fitzroy brought the whole gang to the practice: mum and puppies both. It does the mum no harm; in some cases, it even helps with the whelping - but I didn't have that experience. This was my first mistake of the evening.

My heart was racing now. 'What's wrong with the puppy?' I asked.

'She won't tell me,' Kate said.

I cradled my head in my hands for a moment, and took a deep breath. 'Okay, well, tell her I'll get there as soon as I possibly can, but it won't be for an hour or so yet.' Mistake number two. I

---

[19] About which more later.

should have phoned her right then to discuss the situation, assessing whether it was serious enough to call David or Sue and see if they might have been able to go.

I called through another consult. A West Highland white terrier with allergic skin disease. The owner didn't understand why the skin allergy hadn't been cured with the previous treatment, and wanted a long chat about where to go next. Another deep breath.

Halfway through this chat, there was a knock on the door. Kate peered in. She looked about as miserable as I felt.

'Alan, I've got Mrs Fitzroy on the phone again. She insists on speaking to a vet.'

I apologised to my client, who was already fuming after the long wait, and scurried out into the prep room, picking up the phone. I'd only spoken to Mrs Fitzroy once before. She was normally a client that would only see David.

'Who is this?' she demanded as soon as I started to speak.

'It's Alan,' I replied, 'the... uh... duty vet for tonight.'

'I need a home visit immediately.'

'I'm afraid that's not possible right at the moment,' I said, as politely as I could. 'If there's any way you could make it to the practice, I'd be very happy to see you straight away.'

'No,' Mrs Fitzroy said, slowly, 'there is no way.' I was obviously not the first junior vet that she had dealt with. 'One of my puppies is in severe difficulty and needs to be put to sleep.'

'Exactly what is the difficulty, Mrs Fitzroy?'

'His guts are out. All over the place. There's a hole in his belly.'

The likely problem was that the mum (or possibly Mrs Fitzroy) had bitten (or cut) the umbilical cord off too close to the abdominal muscle, allowing the intestinal loops to herniate through the hole.

'I simply can't leave the mother,' Mrs Fitzroy said, 'but I can't leave him like this. Is there anything that can be done?'

I pictured the puppy, gasping, on its side, bowel loops exposed. 'Er...' I said. I was trying to think: was this treatable? Could they survive?

'They can't survive this, can they?' Mrs Fitzroy said. 'I've had several, they've never made it. It needs putting to sleep.'

Mrs Fitzroy evidently knew more than I did in this case. 'No,' I agreed, reassuringly. 'They can't survive. If you get someone to bring him in, we'll put--'

'No need,' said Mrs Fitzroy. 'I'll take care of it.' I didn't know what she meant. Except... except that was a lie I told myself. I knew exactly what she meant. I wanted to beg her to find someone, anyone, to bring the puppy in, to let me see it, to just give me some bloody time to think! Instead, I hesitated. The phone was silent for a moment. I still didn't say anything. My mouth was paralysed.

'Thank you for your help,' Mrs Fitzroy said, almost politely. The phone went dead. I stared at it for a moment, a cold feeling in my stomach. Then I returned to my consulting room, to talk about skin disease.

Thirty minutes later, things weren't looking so bad. The cold feeling hadn't gone, but the waiting room was clearing. There was only one person left to see. My hand was on the door to the waiting room when Kate entered again. She looked pale.

'David's on the phone,' she said. 'He wants to speak to you.'

My heart plumbing abyssal depths, I headed out to the pharmacy. On the phone, David, his voice cool with anger, explained that he'd been out of mobile range, but he'd had a missed called from Mrs Fitzroy – presumably she'd tried to contact him in between calls to the practice. Finally phoning her back, David learned the fate of the puppy. He quietly explained to me that the condition was not necessarily fatal. Prompt surgical replacement of the intestines can be successful. The pups don't always survive; shock and general anaesthetics take a heavy toll on a newborn. But it is treatable.

'Do you know what she did to the puppy?' David asked. I didn't want to know, but David told me anyway.

'She drowned it,' David said. The three words burned into my heart, ready to stay with me for the rest of my life. Mrs Fitzroy filled up a bucket of cold water, and held the puppy under the surface. I imagined the scene as if I was present myself; tiny legs kicking, bubbles bursting from its newborn lips. I've seen it many times since, late on sleepless nights.

If I had possessed a simple piece of knowledge about the condition, I might have saved the puppy's life. If I'd been less passive and meek on the phone, I might have saved its life. If I hadn't allowed myself to panic, I might have saved its life. None of it mattered now, because the puppy was dead.

David finally calmed down as he began to understand the pressure I had been under that night. He was annoyed with James, he was annoyed with himself, but he was, more than anything, annoyed with me.

So was I. Annoyed, upset, and... cold. I felt like I was evil; like I just wanted to escape myself and get away to some other, untainted soul.

This was how it felt to cause a death in error.

At seven-thirty, an hour after the surgery was supposed to finish, the last client left the surgery. Jane, the receptionist, locked the door behind him and fell against it dramatically, blowing her cheeks out.

'Bloody hell,' she said. I tried to smile, and walked back into my room. I hung my stethoscope on the wall, pressed my head against the cool wall, closed my eyes, and wished desperately to be someone, anyone, else. Anything to get away from the rotting, terrible feeling inside.

I couldn't do it. I never could. Anyone could hand out vaccinations and ear ointment when they needed to. Tonight had been my first real test, and I had failed spectacularly. David was angry, and the pup was dead. Because of me. Two years? I had barely lasted two weeks before I had screwed up enough for something to die. So much for making the world better one animal at a time. I couldn't do it. Better to admit that now.

I pressed my knuckles into my eyelids and massaged my aching eyes. My head felt better but the new dark creature in my gut still writhed and snarled and told me exactly what kind of a person I was. I flicked the light switch and stood in the dark, thinking of the puppy's last moments.

'Alan?'

I opened my eyes. Kate was looking into my consulting room. 'Are you okay?' she said. I tried to come up with a banal answer but here I was, in the dark. Was I crying? I wasn't even sure. Either way, the answer to Kate's question was obvious.

Other people might have tried to talk it through, to try to reassure me or at least cheer me up, but the thing in my gut couldn't be silenced with words or logic. Kate stepped into my room, opened her arms, and held me until I felt like I was human again. The worst night of my career so far was also the night that I fell in love.

9 - Deep in to that darkness, peering...

'We just feel, your dad and I... well, we just wonder if you're doing the right thing, Alan.'

My mother dropped this bombshell on me whilst I was morosely pushing some beans around my plate in the Bridgford Little Chef restaurant[20] , and the 'thing' that she was talking about was the thing that I had devoted the last ten-plus years towards achieving: being a veterinary surgeon.

I looked up. Dad was looking out of the window, studiously studying a family of holidaymakers in the midst of some titanic argument, as if he would rather be out there than in here. Mum was gazing concernedly at me over her cup of tea. They had travelled down to spend the weekend with me and to 'see how it was going', but they couldn't really have picked a worse time to do it. Finding me in a state of depression that morning - the morning after the puppy died - they immediately whisked me out for a breakfast in the hope that it would help matters.

'Mum,' I said, poking my fork into the fried egg and watching the yolk slowly ooze from the ruptured centre, 'it's not that bad, I just...'

Just what? I hadn't told them exactly what had happened. I didn't want to talk about it. I didn't want to think about it, ever again. 'I'm just tired,' I finished.

'They're working you too hard, aren't they?' Mum said, indignantly.

Dad snorted, though I wasn't sure what that was supposed to mean. 'No, mum, I'm just... well, it's been a long week, that's all.'

'You've been crying, haven't you?'

I couldn't get much past my mum; she had been a teacher for too long to fail to spot a child that had been crying, even a twenty-five year-old one. I returned my fork to the beans and tried not to

---

[20] Actually at the Bridgford motorway service station rather than in Bridgford itself; it was the closest place that we'd found where we actually wanted to eat.

think about anything.

'Alan, listen,' Mum said, in a soft tone of voice that suggested I probably wasn't going to enjoy what she said next, 'when you said you wanted to be a vet, your dad and I were thrilled, weren't we, Oliver?'

Dad looked briefly at me and smiled, then looked back out of the window. He looked embarrassed, but he also looked worried, which got me worried. How bad did I look this morning?

'It's just,' my mum continued, 'that we were a little worried that you might not be... er...'

Cut out for it? I thought. Any good at all? Safe to treat animals without letting people drown them?

'Well, we just thought it might not necessarily suit you, that's all. It's very hard work.'

'Bloody hard work,' my dad muttered.

'Mum, Dad,' I said, finally giving up with the Olympic English Breakfast Meal, 'it's really not as bad as it looks. It was just a bit of a bad night, that's all. I'm a bit tired.'

Mum and Dad exchanged an infuriatingly meaningful look. 'We just want you to be sure, Alan,' Mum said. 'We just want you to be sure that you're doing the right thing. There's no shame in admitting it now.'

Wasn't there? What about the Quest?

The 'Quest' - how idiotic that seemed now. My stupid, simplistic idea of making the world better seemed a very long way away from Bridgford, with its peahens, its water dragons and its puppies. In these last two weeks, had I actually done anything good at all? If someone else was in my place, would they have caused less harm than me?

I tried to think of the good things about Bridgford that I had seen since I moved here, but I could only think of one. Kate had helped me feel like I wasn't the worst person on the face of the planet the night before. Then she had put on her coat, smiled, and left, telling me that things would get better soon. Her words got me through the night.

What did I have to get me through the next two years?

*

In the middle of the next week, David said that it would be good for 'practice morale' if we all went to the local pub that night and 'blew the froth off a few'.

'Everybody in?' he said, looking pointedly at me as he announced it in the prep room at our mid-morning coffee break.

'Um,' I said, 'I'm not really sure that I'm in the--'

'Great,' he said. 'Seven-thirty, Bridgford Arms. See you all then!'

He swept out. Sue, half-way through digging out a rock-solid canine tooth from a greyhound's lower jaw, smiled up at me. 'Great, should be fun. Just don't buy David too many drinks.'

Becky, the trainee nurse helping Sue with her anaesthetic, flushed red. 'Oh, God, no,' she said.

'Why not?' I asked.

Kate looked back from the sink where she was scrubbing up; James had roped her in as a 'spare pair of hands' for his hip replacement surgery that he was performing that morning.

'Our fearless leader has an unfortunate habit when he's got a few inside him,' she said.

'Swearing?' I guessed. 'Gambling?' Heads were being shaken. 'Er, long-distance angry telephone calling?'

'Try stripping,' Kate said.

'Stripping?'

Kate, Sue and Becky all nodded sadly. 'Not really sure why,' Kate said. 'He's been banned from the Bridgford Arms twice, but he looks after the owner's Labrador, so he always manages to get back in. Usually we manage to stop him before he goes... um... too far.'

'Bloody hell,' I said.

Kate opened her mouth to reply but an angry shout of 'Kate!' from the op theatre signalled that James was growing impatient. Kate rolled her eyes, and backed through the doors to theatre, slowly mouthing 'help me!' as she disappeared from view.

'Seriously, Alan,' Sue said, 'you should come. I think we could all do with letting our hair down a little.'

I made it through the day without anything else dying because of me, but the new thing that lived in my gut wouldn't let me relax. At half-past seven I entered the Bridgford Arms - an old, cramped traditional pub that proudly sold real ales and pork scratchings, and absolutely didn't serve food. Cameron was already there, looking perfectly at home towering over the bar. His huge hand made the pint he was holding look more like a half.

'Alan!' he said. 'Over here! What's yours?'

'Oh, er, pint of lager, please,' I said.

'Pint of insipid horse piss,' Cameron said to the barman, who nodded and poured me out a glass of Fosters.

Cameron handed me the glass as I looked around the pub. Sue, David, and James were deep in discussion about something at a table by the window, while Kate, Becky and Laura, the practice manager, were sitting at another table nearby. Becky saw me looking and smiled, elbowing Kate in the ribs. Kate turned red but didn't look up.

'Everything all right, Alan?' Cameron said as I turned back to him.

'It's.... yeah, it's... fine, really.'

Cameron rolled his eyes. 'Okay. Well, look. I know you're not all right, because I know what happened.' He smiled at me. 'You've been down all week. Can't say I blame you, but I'm here to tell you that it wasn't your fault.'

'Cameron, that's very nice of you,' I said, 'but it really--'

'We make mistakes,' Cameron said. 'It's hard to admit it, but we do. Everyone does. The difference for us is that sometimes, when we make mistakes, things die.'

I winced. 'But--'

'You're going to make more, too, so you need to get used to it. It won't be often, but it will happen. Trust me,' he said, looking into his ale. 'It'll happen.'

'I know, but--'

'Okay,' Cameron said, swigging his ale, 'a few things to keep in mind. Firstly, Mrs Fitzroy is a bitch of the highest order. You didn't drown that puppy. She did.'

He plonked his pint on the bar for emphasis. 'Second,' he said, 'James should never have left you alone that night, and he knows it. David's mad as hell with him. James says he feels awful about it, but don't expect an apology from him.'

I looked over at James, Sue and David. James glanced over at me, expressionless, then returned to the conversation.

'Thirdly - and most importantly - you're not a bad vet, Alan. Sometimes things conspire against us. Sometimes we make mistakes. But you're not bad. Not as good as me, obviously. But not bad.'

'Well of course not,' I smiled. Cameron's infectious good humour was managing to work its magic. 'I'm only human after all.'

Cameron grinned and nodded. 'Quite right. That's the spirit. Right, let's get drunk.'

I followed him over to the table with Kate, Becky and Laura.

'Bit better?' said Kate as we approached.

'He'll be okay,' Cameron said. I nodded and smiled. Right then and there, I believed it. Kate smiled too. 'Good,' she said. 'Now let's concentrate on making sure David keeps his clothes on all night.' I sat down next to her, and she smiled again. Suddenly the world didn't look quite so bad.

Several pints of insipid horse piss later, I was standing at the bar waiting for service and watching David sing '*Waterloo*' shirtless and red-faced beside the fruit machine. I noticed James stand up from his table and walk slowly and deliberately towards me. He had been drinking as much as the rest of us, but appeared outwardly as sober as he did during one of his heroic orthopaedic operations. He had a serious and slightly worried expression on his face. My God, I thought, Cameron was wrong. He's actually going to apologise to me.

His eyes met mine as he approached the bar.

'Alan,' he said, perfunctorily.

'Hello, James,' I said, as amiably as I could manage. 'Want a drink?'

James shook his head and frowned a little, indicating his still half-full glass. It is actually physically painful for him to say sorry, I thought.

He opened his mouth to speak. He frowned and closed it again. Then he leaned in very close to me, and said in a voice that was just over a whisper:

'You stay the fuck away from Kate.'

He leaned back and fixed me with his penetrating eyes. Then he turned his back to me and I gazed at him open-mouthed, while Cameron tackled David to the ground to prevent him from taking off his trousers.

10 - The Wages of Sin

The next week was one of the more miserable of my life. By night, I was haunted by dreams of the puppy; sometimes it felt like I was the one being held down, unable to breathe, while James's face peered down at me through the rippling water, mouthing the words 'Stay the fuck away from Kate.' At Beech House, I avoided both Kate and James as much as possible. Occasionally, Kate would try to talk to me - offering to help with an operation, or come out with me on a house visit - but somehow James always found a way to be hovering in the background, glowering at me through those damned thin-wire glasses of his, and I would find some excuse to work with someone else. I had expected the first few weeks as a vet to be tough, but I hadn't expected love to come in and complicate the whole scenario. It was a dark, confusing week at Beech House for me.

There was, at least, one tiny bright spot on the horizon. Even though the job wasn't proving as emotionally rewarding as I had hoped, there were, at least, other rewards to full time work. At the end of the week, I was holding one of them in my hand. It felt as rare and fantastic to me as one of Willy Wonka's golden tickets. I'd seen them before of course; my parents, used to their magical nature, had left them lying around the house from time to time before they were filed. I remembered being fascinated by them as a kid; a small slip of paper, covered in squiggly black ink as if a thousand spiders had been ceremonially squished onto the thin paper in order to prevent unwanted peeping at the contents. It hadn't really struck me before that I might ever have one of my own, but now, here it was. My first pay slip.

Earlier in the week, sick of sitting around at home thinking about puppies, orthopaedic surgeons and veterinary nurses, and aware of the glimmering riches that awaited me at the end of the month, I had driven to Bridgford's local electrical goods store, where I gazed avariciously at a huge television until an attendant, noting my gaze and politely ignoring my drool, introduced me to the concept of 'Hire Purchase', and that same afternoon we were driving back to my house with the television in the boot.

I was so proud. A man provides for his family. At the moment, the family consisted of me, and the thing that I was providing today was a massive telly. Literally massive; this was before the days of plasma screens and LCDs, and so the 32-inch screen tube television weighed forty kilos[21]. A wise man would have left the TV in the boot and asked for help from his neighbours. I was neither wise nor patient and so I lifted the monster out of the back of my car, screamed in pain, and dropped it on the floor. The front panel that covered the various input sockets snapped off but otherwise the damage was minimal, and so I proceeded to drag the thing up the small path to my house like a murderer disposing of a small, square, dense body - or perhaps more accurately, like an idiot attempting to move a very heavy television set on his own[22].

The TV now looked wonderful in my living room, but it had been frighteningly expensive. I had student loans and numerous other debts to pay, but none of that mattered because the fabled pay slip had been delivered to my in-tray this morning, and now here I stood with it in my hand.

I tore it open and read the figure at the top of the page. I frowned a little. I read the figure at the bottom of the page.

'Hmm,' I said.

The one thing that everyone knows about vets, of course, is that they, along with the Royal Mint, have a licence to print money. It had been at the back of my mind during vet school that the pay was pretty good. It certainly wasn't why I had joined the profession - if it was, I might have looked into it a little more carefully - but I always thought things would be very nice, pay-wise. Seeing practice as a veterinary student, I'd had a few vets tell me, 'Well, you know,

[21] Which is nearly ninety pounds, to those of you who haven't come over to the far, far less confusing metric side of the fence.

[22] It may have been heavy, but it still works perfectly - unlike three LCD TVs I have bought since then. It wasn't that long ago that we were making things that were actually built to last, you see.

the pay isn't *quite* as good as you might think...' I had nodded, and smiled, and secretly thought, 'Greedy bastards, how much more do they want?'

I stood and looked at the figure at the bottom of the pay slip. I mentally subtracted the student loans repayment, and the first instalment of my now-looking-rather-extravagant TV hire-purchase. I added the total to my current bank balance. My face went a little pale.

The preceding week, I had worked (including on-call work, which certainly felt like work to me) around about a hundred hours. I looked again at the pay slip. Before tax, I had earned roughly three pounds fifty an hour.

Hm. I wasn't very experienced in such matters, but that didn't sound like an awful lot. I drove home, where my huge telly stared accusingly at me, evidence of my near-Liberace levels of excess.

Now, I'm not telling this part of my story for sympathy - I was an idiot in just assuming that I would be absolutely loaded the moment I became a vet. All that I needed to do was mentally readjust quite how much money I had, and I was fine. Having had to make this surprise mental realignment on receiving my first pay slip, though, I found that I still frequently encountered people who, the moment they learned of my profession, got a little glint in their eye and smiled at me knowingly[23]. I understood the perception: you go to the vets, you're in there for ten minutes, she tells you to pop these drops down your dog's ear, and you have to pay fifty pounds for the privilege. What may not occur to you is that of that fifty pounds, the vet earns about fifty pence. The rest pays for the receptionist's and nurse's salaries, the rental of the premises, the ear drops that you bought, the electricity bill, and so on. Vet salaries are lower (quite a lot lower, in some cases) than the average salaries of doctors, dentists, teachers, police officers, architects and many other professions[24].

---

[23] The kind of glint that suggested the drinks were on me for the rest of the night.

I was content with my pay. Once I was over the shock of not being able to live like Tony Stark, I thought it was fair, and I definitely *earned* what I got. I was far from destitute, although it was a little while before I allowed myself to visit that electrical store again.

That weekend, I stared at the enormous screen in my otherwise quiet house, utterly failing to keep images of puppies, veterinary nurses and orthopaedic surgeons from my mind, and it suddenly hit me how lonely I felt. The rich social life that I had enjoyed at university had vanished quicker than free beer at a student party, and here I was, wavering from my Quest, doubting and miserable. I was afraid to talk to my parents any more in case they talked me in to doing the thing I secretly knew I wanted to do: give it all up and go home, defeated. I needed someone safe to talk to.

Suddenly, I realised what the house was missing. Why hadn't I thought of it before? I was a vet, after all. I needed a pet.

I'm sure I must have had worse ideas in that first month in practice, but none of them spring to mind at the time of writing.

---

[24] It's tangential to my point, but shamefully (especially considering we're an increasingly female-oriented profession) there is still a 10-20% gap between male and female vet's pay.

11 - Satan's Right Paw

Now, this may be read with horror by readers who are regular inhabitants of the internet, where a single picture of a cat looking halfway cute can spread across the world in less time than it takes to meow, but I was more of a dog person in general. I liked cats, don't get me wrong, but I was with Charles Darwin on this[25]– Who could not love dogs, when they're such good sports?

Nevertheless, logically, a pet cat made more sense – I was working long hours and on call a lot. I was worried that I might not have the time to give to a dog. Also, I had met more than a few friendly felines in my short career, so I was fairly confident that I'd find the right pet for me. The following week, foolishly as it turns out, expressed my desire for a companion to Laura, the youngest and most enthusiastic nurse at the practice. She immediately decided that her new mission in life was to fix me up with a pet - and I had already realised that there were very few things on the planet more determined than a veterinary nurse on a mission. That same night, a cardboard box was dropped at the door of Beech House in the small hours of the night. Inside the box was a small, very thin, black cat, with a tiny splash of white on her chest. Inside the cat were seven kittens, although they weren't inside her for long.

I arrived at work the next morning to general excitement - Laura grabbed me before the door had time to close behind me and hurried me through to the cat ward. The poor, thin cat – not even a year old herself, by the looks of her – had kittened overnight, and was now huddled at the back of a cage, staring nervously out at us.

'Here you go, Alan! Kittens! Just what you were looking for! Somebody is trying to tell you something!'

I peered into the cage as the tiny, impossibly cute little creatures pushed their way onto their mother's teats, suckling. The thin cat's eyes met mine.

---

[25] And, as it happens, quite a few other things.

'I think we'll find homes for the kittens very quickly,' I said, smiling at the thin cat. 'I'm going to take the mum.'

The thin cat blinked. A shiver of ice passed down my spine, and for some reason a fragment of Poe's famous poem 'The Raven' drifted through my mind.

'...and his eyes have all the seeming of a demon's that is dreaming...'

'Er...' I said, suddenly nervous. I wondered exactly what it was that somebody was trying to tell me.

'Brilliant!' Laura said, rushing off to the front desk to announce the decision to the world. 'Alan's going to take the mum!'

I smiled again, opened the cage door, and reached my hand very slowly and calmly forwards to tickle the thin cat's chin. The cat lowered its ears, narrowed its eyes, and hissed menacingly at me.

My new pet was starting as she meant to go on.

Around this time, my parents had been planning to have a weekend break somewhere in a city in Europe. They were still trying to decide where to go (though, having watched *The Third Man* at an impressionable age, I gave them some strong advice) when the small furry ball of wrath entered my life. My mother claimed that she was too worried about me to go 'gallivanting across Europe', so the holiday was cancelled, but the aborted vacation at least gave my new companion her name – Vienna[26].

Vienna spent several more weeks in the practice, until the kittens were weaned. Obviously, no more kittens were wanted, so I decided that it was my responsibility to spay Vienna. I was still finding my feet with surgery, but the operation went very smoothly[27].

A day later, I placed Vienna (not without protest) into a cat box,

---

[26] Shamefully, I had totally forgotten that Rigsby's cat in *Rising Damp* also shared this sobriquet – and this obviously would have been a far better reason for the name; consequently, I have pretended this was the real reason ever since.

[27] Or, from Vienna's point of view, not so much an operation than an act of mutilation that could never, ever be forgiven.

put her in my car, and nervously drove her home, with her singing further protest songs the whole of the short trip. In the living room, I opened the cat box, whereupon she shot out, hurtled up the stairs, and managed to find somewhere in the tiny house to hide.

Vienna was... complicated. I've encountered several cats like her in my career since; semi-feral is the term I've heard used most often to describe them - although Cameron, popping round a few days after she arrived to admire the size of my telly, put it rather more bluntly

'Bastard psychopath bloody cat!' he muttered as she raked her claws bloodily down his unprotected shin because... well, because Vienna. Owning her wasn't really like having a pet, it was like having a lodger that I rarely saw, but that I knew was just bound to cause trouble the moment they entered the room. She would tolerate being tickled for a very short period of time, if it would get her what she wanted (i.e. food) but if my tickling hand outstayed its welcome for a fraction of a second, out would come the claws and teeth, and I would be cursing, running for the tap to clean yet another cat scratch, whilst Vienna rocketed back to her favourite hiding place.

Every so often, for reasons known only to herself, Vienna would jump on my lap while I was watching the telly or reading. She would be purring heavily – Vienna is the only cat I have ever known that managed to make a purr sound like a threat – and would push her face into mine, roughly and repeatedly, while I sat, rigid and terrified, feeling very much like I was a piece of territory that was being marked. It would often go on for long enough that I would sometimes dare to lift my hand to stroke her, and then Vienna would do her stuff and I would be running for the sink again. Looking down at my hands as I type, I can count more scars given to me by Vienna than from all the other cat scratches and dog bites I've received put together.

This strong and consistent negative reinforcement would probably have put me off cats forever if I didn't repeatedly meet lovely felines at the surgery. Every time I saw a black cat in my waiting room, I'd secretly wonder if the owner would notice should I do a switcheroo with my own little psycho. Perhaps unsurprisingly, once I started letting her out, Vienna was a hit with the local wildlife. Hit as in hitman. Once, early in the morning on a summer's day, I opened my front door to find a perfectly dissected pair of rabbit's eyes gazing up at me reproachfully from the doorstep, beside a single shard of bone.

Another problem was that, although she understood what a litter tray was for, she never had much truck with them herself. She'd use it most the time if she wasn't outdoors, but she also had an unerring ability to track down the most expensive piece of electrical equipment in the house, and then pee on it. I lost a number of speakers, a PC and a radio to Vienna. She was, in short, the living embodiment of the maxim that no good deed goes unpunished. As Ultravox once said – ahhh, Vienna.

Despite her Hannibal Lecter personality, Vienna did actually seem happy. She could be impossibly cute from a distance, and watching her sleeping on the lawn, or stalking through the bushes in search of more small creatures to torture, did give me a certain uneasy sense of satisfaction. Okay, so the plan to help with the loneliness hadn't really worked - except that living with Vienna certainly made living alone seem less depressing – but I had rescued her, and she was content. At least while I was washing blood down the sink once again, and swearing under my breath, I wasn't dwelling on the Kate and James situation, which I was doing my best to avoid. I was about to discover that cowards can't dodge bullets forever.

12 - An Unexpected Party

It was a typical night on call for me, in that I was thoroughly miserable. I was, as ever, sitting beside the telephone, watching the TV with the sound muted (just to make one hundred percent sure that I would hear the phone when it rang). Every few minutes I would check my mobile phone, to ensure it still had a signal. It always did, so I would return to staring at the silent images on the screen again. Nights on call always passed this way until the horrible and blessed relief of actually getting called in, or until I finally trudged upstairs to bed at around midnight. Tonight was going to be a little different.

I was reaching for my phone for the tenth time of the evening when there was a knock at the door. This confused me a great deal. I was expecting to be interrupted, but not by a knock on the door. Could someone have found out that I was a vet on call and brought a sick animal to my house?

The knock at the door came again, accompanied by a muffled 'Come on Alan, I'm not standing out here all night!'

A woman. Kate?

I jumped to my feet and hurried to the door, to find Sue standing on my doorstep. She beamed at me as the door swung open.

'Get your glad rags on,' she said. 'We're going out.'

'Going... but... I'm on call, Sue.'

She nodded. 'Yep, yes, I know that, Alan, I write the rota. But we're going to the party at Laura's house. You need to get out more.'

'I knew about the party, Sue, I just... when I'm on call I don't like to...'

She nodded again. 'Yes, yes, we've all been there. It's balls. You need to get over it. You're coming out. I think you need it. Go and get changed. Besides,' she added, as she pushed her way inside, 'I need a lift there, and you were closest. Don't tell me I walked here for nothing.'

I ran upstairs, changed my shirt for a near-identical one, and before I had really worked out what was going on, found myself driving to Laura's house with Sue in the passenger seat.

'Left here. You really need to relax more,' Sue was saying.

'You know, telling me that really doesn't help me to relax,' I said.

Sue laughed. 'Fair comment. But you're doing okay, Alan. I know you've had a bumpy start, but you're getting there, trust me. You're not going to get much further if you don't take it a little easier, though.'

'Again, not really helping,' I said. Sue winked and made a zipping motion across her lips.

'Oh, balls, it was that left,' she said a moment later.

Eventually, we pulled up to Laura's house. It was a houselet, just like mine, which struck me as a less-than-ideal place to hold a party. In my house, I was strongly suspicious that there wasn't room to swing a cat, though it would have taken a braver person than me to test this theory with Vienna. Laura had just moved into her houselet, moving away from her parents, and she was determined to have a housewarming party regardless. Most of the practice, and more of her friends, had been invited. I had politely declined. Parties were not my favourite places at the best of times, bringing my social awkwardness to the fore. I wondered if anyone really enjoyed going to parties except for the people that held them, but Sue seemed pretty keen.

'Come on,' she said, jumping out of the car. I opened the door to follow her, then: 'Shit!'

Sue looked at me, quizzically.

'Shit shit shit. My mobile! I forgot it! I can't believe I forgot it!'

Sue rolled her eyes in an 'is that it?' gesture. 'We'll phone through to the practice from Laura's, let Becky know you're here. Don't *worry* so much, Alan! Now come on, you're cutting in to my drinking time.'

I reluctantly followed Sue down the path. Not only was I on call, and not only was this a party, but the whole practice had been invited. That meant Kate might be there, and the thought of that filled me with such a mixture of emotions that I didn't know if I was excited or terrified at the prospect. At least James was unlikely to turn up; Laura had invited him out of politeness, but he had said that parties really weren't 'his thing'. I had managed to feel smug about his joyless attitude when he said it even though I felt exactly the same way.

Laura's house was full in the way that only a house party can produce - the small entryway, which was just about big enough to allow people to turn left to the kitchen or right to the lounge, somehow contained around fifteen people. Sue lifted the bottles of wine over her head and pushed her way into the throng, shouting 'Coming through! Veterinary emergency!' I followed in her wake, nodding and smiling at people as best I could as I stepped on toes and received elbows in the ribs. The lounge was slightly less densely packed; more like a sardine tin than the neutron star of the entryway. Laura stood in the middle of the room, bouncing around as much as possible while *'The Size of a Cow'* blared out from speakers in the corners of the room. She saw us enter through the sea of faces.

'Sue! Alan! Hey, you came, great!'

She pushed her way towards us and gave us a cramped hug.

'I didn't bring anything, I'm afraid,' I said as she squeezed against me. 'Didn't think I'd be coming. Um, could I just use your phone? I'm on call and, y'know.'

Laura nodded and smiled, distracted by more new arrivals behind me.

'Oh, sure, just over there,' she said, waving her arm vaguely at a section of crowd.

'Right, thanks,' I said, and began wading through the human sea to the area she had indicated. I found a sofa concealed in the throng, and a small table beside on, with a telephone sitting on top of it.

'Ah, 'scuse me,' I said to the person in front of it.

'Oh, hi Alan,' Kate said, turning to me. She pushed her dark hair away from her brown eyes, smiling at me, and I immediately forgot about the phone.

'Alan?' she asked. I had forgotten to breathe as well.

'Kate,' I said, attempting to sound casual. 'How are you doing? How are things?'

Kate raised an eyebrow.

'Oh, now you want to know?' she said. 'I got the impression you've been avoiding me at work.'

'Avoiding? No, no, just, y'know, concentrating on the job. Trying not to kill anything, that sort of thing.'

I winced. Why would I make a joke about a subject like that? Nevertheless, Kate smiled a little.

'Heh, okay. I just thought...'

'Thought what?'

Kate paused and waved her empty can of lager at me. 'Are you going to get me a drink or not?'

A can of lager each later, and everything suddenly seemed right with the world. Kate was laughing at my jokes (although that may have been because she hadn't heard them very well), I had learned a little about her childhood growing up in Devon and, best of all, we hadn't mentioned James at all. I was currently trying to think of a way of explaining why I had become a vet without mentioning anything about alien mercenaries, the mention of which tended to make people switch off almost immediately, when Kate took my hand.

'Wanna dance?' she said, a mischievous glint in her eyes. Something about that glint told me that dancing would almost certainly lead to more things. My heart was singing with excitement - in fact, it felt like it was ringing with excitement.

'Absolutely!' I said.

Kate frowned. 'What's the ringing?'

I blinked. She could hear that too? Wasn't it my heart?

We both paused and strained to listen over '*Tubthumping*'.

'Shit!' I said, suddenly remembering. 'The phone! I'm on call! I never told Becky!'

I grabbed the phone. It was, indeed, Becky, who had called Laura's house in desperation after trying my home and my mobile.

'Alan, you need to come in right away, I've got an RTA cat coming in.'

'Okay, okay, I'm sorry, I meant to ring, I'll be right there.'

'Fire brigade stuff?' Kate asked as I put the phone down.

'I've got to go and be a hero,' I said, looking into the middle distance. 'It's a tough job.'

She grinned. 'Idiot. Go on. Don't be too long.' She opened another can.

The cat never turned up. When, three hours later, the owners eventually answered their mobile phone, they apologised and explained that they had been confused in the panic and phoned the wrong practice. Their cat was currently recuperating in one of the cages of our rivals, nursing a fractured pelvis and several nasty grazes. It would take six weeks or so, but it was going to be okay.

It was now two o'clock in the morning. I hadn't dared leave the practice in case the cat had suddenly arrived in dire need of emergency treatment. There didn't seem a lot of point heading back to Laura's and so I drove home, my heart still singing. Screw James. Tomorrow I was going to pick things up with Kate where I had left off. I was going to get that dance.

I arrived at the practice the following day trying to keep the smile off my face. Even the jam-packed morning surgery, filled with *'No better'*, *'unknown'* and *'worse'* cases couldn't impact my mood. These were simply little trials to get past until eleven o'clock, when Kate got in.

I grinned cheerfully at Cameron in the dispensary. He smiled back, and then frowned. 'You're in a cheerful mood, considering,' he said.

'Well, I...' I paused. 'Considering what?'

Cameron nodded. 'Ah, well, that explains it. Kate and James.'

'What about them?'

'James turned up to Laura's party last night. They spent some time playing tonsil tennis while they were dancing. Looks like they're back together.'

13 - Surgical Spirit

I couldn't have picked a worse time to fall in love than my first month in practice. Love is an amplifier; the peaks become mountains, the troughs abyssal. The job was already a rollercoaster for my emotions. With my feelings for Kate added to the mix, it was like riding a rollercoaster on a ship caught in a tsunami. The Quest felt a very long way away; it was all I could do to just try to get through the day. Mercifully, Kate was off sick for the rest of the day and then on holiday for the rest of the week, returning to Devon to spend a long weekend with her family.

I wasn't so lucky with James. When I trudged up the stairs to the staff room for a coffee break after the first onslaught of morning surgery, he was sitting reading a surgical journal in the otherwise empty room. As I entered, his normal dour expression cracked into a wide grin - the one he had specially reserved for enjoying other people's misery.

'Good morning, Alan!' he said, cheerfully. I ignored him and walked over to the kettle. 'It's just boiled,' James said. I resisted the temptation to pour it onto his head, and made myself a strong cup of coffee. The rest of the morning surgery didn't look too bad, but I really wasn't in the best place mentally for meeting the general public. I certainly wasn't in the mood for James.

'Having a nice day, mate?' he asked, winking at me.

'Why don't you just go and poo yourself, you bloody shit, James,' I said. James blinked, simultaneously stunned and confused by the infantile insult. It was the best I could manage on the amount of sleep I'd had. I squared my shoulders, gathered my dignity, and got on with the rest of the day. It was time to stop worrying about romance. It was time to get back to the Quest. It was time to concentrate on the job.

*

I always felt (and in fact was often told) that being a vet would be a very rewarding job – what could create a better feeling of well-being in oneself than saving lives? The problem is that it doesn't really work like that. The animals that I helped to restore to health – even after a tough battle – were the ones I didn't see very often afterwards. At their vaccine, months later, I might dimly remember sweating and worrying about the case, and feel pleased to have a healthy, bright animal in front of me, but it was a delayed and rather unsatisfactory form of satisfaction.

The animals I really got to know were the ones I saw again and again – the ones that were very ill. The animals that frequently ended up dying. These were the cases that came back to me, that haunted me, and that kept me awake at night. It was easy to dwell upon my failures and ignore my successes, because my successes took a little while to show themselves as such[28].

One aspect of the job that *was* immediately rewarding, however, was surgery[29]. Ops days were equally more laid-back and more stressful than consulting. Working an ops day meant that I didn't have to talk to members of the public, and, as I'm sure anyone who has a job that involves heavy interaction with Joe or Jane Public can confirm, this automatically makes the day less worrisome. I enjoyed my ops days because it gave me a chance to work more closely with the nurses. Consulting can be a lonely occupation – seeing client after client, only rushing out intermittently for the sweet nepenthe of a cup of tea or to grab a colleague and ask their opinion. When I was operating, I was part of a team. We could talk, I could tell terrible jokes that I had made up the night before, the nurses could groan. It was an altogether more sociable activity, and we got to cuddle animals too. I felt that when I was operating, I was a person again.

It helped that Kate was away. The rest of the nurses were great fun to work with. As welcoming and friendly as Sue, Cameron and David were, I still felt like an imposter in their ranks.

[28] This is why your vet really, really appreciates those thank you cards. The wine and chocolates don't go amiss either.

[29] Surgery as in surgical procedures instead of, say, morning surgery, which means consulting. Confusing, isn't it?

Working with the nurses, who were generally younger and (in my mind, at least) less imposing, I felt amongst friends again. James was always quick to criticise the nurses; he felt they were lazy, incompetent, and (crucially) unhappy with his occasionally prolonged surgical procedures. He seemed to hold them in a general sort of contempt for reasons that weren't entirely clear to me (a feeling that was largely reciprocated) and I was starting to realise that whatever kind of vet James was, it was the exact opposite of the kind of vet that I wanted to be.

My two favourite nurses (when I wasn't thinking about Kate) were Becky and Nicki. I had worked with Becky on every ops day so far (all three of them) I greatly appreciated that she felt relaxed enough in my company to call me a moron when I admitted that I had no idea what I was doing. They were both excellent nurses, and, like all veterinary nurses everywhere, they were grossly underpaid[30] and largely unappreciated.

The stressful bits of the ops day were, of course, the ops themselves. Before I graduated, I had performed five cat castrates, two dog castrates, and half of a bitch spay (another student did the other half, in case you're worrying). This actually made me relatively experienced as far as new graduates go; it wasn't unheard of for a vet student to qualify without a single surgical procedure under their belt. On my first ops day, I was faced with a list of operations that contained more than twice as many surgical procedures as I had hitherto performed. The stress was reduced by the knowledge that Sue, currently consulting but joining me on ops at eleven, could spay a cat faster than it took me to put on my surgical gloves (i.e. in about ten minutes), but it was still a daunting prospect.

---

[30] Not a particular failing of David or Sue's – in fact, they paid their nurses relatively well. But relatively well, for a veterinary nurse, is still piss-poor; unqualified they earn the minimum wage, and qualified they're lucky to earn as much as a car park attendant, despite being highly trained, professional and caring. Don't misunderstand me – I've worked with my fair share of bad nurses, but every single one of them deserved more than they were actually getting paid.

The surgical procedures on a typical Beech House ops day were roughly half neutering and half 'other': x-rays, tumour removals, medical work-ups, or whatever dynamic surgical procedure James had read about in the *Journal of Small Animal Practice* the week before. As a new graduate, the majority of my time in those early ops days was learning how to remove various animals' capacity to make other animals, and so, if you're game, it's worth taking a moment out from the narrative to discuss the fine art of animal neutering. If not, feel free to skip the next chapter; you won't miss any of the story.

14 - Calling a Spayed a Spayed[31]

Neutering is the generic term for the removal of an animal's reproductive ability. In males, it's castration (removing the testicles). For females, it's spaying. You might think that is rather too obvious to spell out, but trust me: it isn't.[32]

Castration is a relatively simple (if eye-watering, for male readers) procedure in both dogs and cats – relatively low risk exercises in ligation (tying off blood vessels) and suturing. There are a few variations in the actual technique, based largely on personal preference, but for my first few weeks, they were good operations to sharpen my surgical teeth on (if you'll forgive the slightly disturbing mental image that metaphor creates). It gets a little more complicated with rabbits, guinea pigs and the small furry brigade (rats, gerbils and hamsters, the last of which legitimises the common typo 'small fury', because they're vicious little sods) but, other than a simple stitch up, castration is amongst the easiest surgical procedure a vet is likely to undertake.

Spaying... spaying is a different matter. The medical term is *ovariohysterectomy* – the surgical removal of both the uterus and the ovaries[33],[34] - and it is much more involved surgery than castration.

---

[31] As opposed to the not-infrequently heard description in the consult room, 'He's been spayded'.

[32] For the curious - more on this in chapter seventeen.

[33] As opposed to the human *hysterectomy* – removal of just the uterus (*hystera* being the Greek word for uterus, and the same root word from which we derive the word hysteria – which probably tells you all you need to know about the male attitude towards women throughout history).

[34] Our domestic pets don't suffer from hormone deficiency problems in the same way that humans do, on account of having a different reproductive cycle: the oestrus cycle, as opposed to the human (and other primate) menstrual cycle. This explains both why female dogs and cats don't go through a menopause as they age, and also why humans don't come on heat. This is also why you never see un-neutered male humans roaming from their homes, searching for other women to mate with. Oh,

The ovaries are inside the animal (just behind to the kidneys, to be precise) and so harder to get to. Ligation is trickier, because the blood vessels supplying the ovaries and the uterus are similarly harder to get into a position where you can tie your knot.

Just for fun in the UK, veterinary surgeons have decided to add their own little twist to make life more complicated: we have decided to make the flank approach to the uterus our approach of choice for speying cats. The flank approach means what it sounds like – making an incision in the side of the cat's abdomen, rather than the midline approach that we choose for every other abdominal surgery we ever do. I'm still not sure of the reasoning behind this; I've heard the arguments for it - it's quicker, that you get fewer post-operative reactions, or that if the wound develops a hernia[35] it tends to be a less serious problem in the flank than the midline – but I'm not convinced by any of them. I suspect that a well-practised surgeon would be equally speedy with either technique; I've seen my fair share of post-operative reactions with flank cat spays, and if you're faced with a hernia then you need to surgically repair it, whichever hole the internal organs happen to have popped out of. I can just about see the argument that it's a useful technique for animals that are lactating - because the wound is further away from the teats, the mother is less likely to reject the kittens when they come to suckle, and milk is less likely to leak into your wound and cause an infection (because if there's one thing that bacteria love, it's a bit of milk) – except that in lactating dogs we still operate midline[36] and don't seem to have any of those problems.

The main issue with the flank cat spay is that if you make

wait...

[35] Abdominal contents (fat, intestines, or anything else) working their way through the muscle incision.

[36] Except in one practice that I was visiting during an interview and was astonished to see the vet had performed a caesarean in a large Rottweiler via a flank incision. I didn't take the job.

your incision even slightly in the wrong place it is an absolute *bugger* to find that bloody uterus. In those early months of my career, I spent many, many hours peering into a cat's abdomen, fruitlessly searching for its reproductive organs like Smeagol forlornly searching for his lost ring, only to discover that I had, yet again, failed to poke my scalpel through the peritoneum (a thin membrane coating the abdominal organs, which shrink-wraps them away from hapless surgeons that fail to make their cut deep enough), or that my incision was too high, or too low, or (on one occasion) so far back that I had managed to enter the poor cat's abdomen through the muscles of its hind leg; this last individual seemed fine when she woke up, but I made sure she had extra pain-relief at home. I began to wonder why it is we persisted in our approach, and came to the conclusion that it had become tradition rather than anything else - a surprising (and depressing) number of medical decisions are made on the basis of tradition rather than evidence.

The last, and by no means at all the least of the 'routine' neutering procedures is the bitch spay. Ahh, bitch spay, my old nemesis. The bitch spay is the same procedure as a cat spay, in that you're performing an ovariohysterectomy, but it's much, much harder. Everything is bigger, more difficult to get to, and more likely to bleed. Spaying fat, deep-chested dogs would be the most difficult surgical procedure I would encounter in my first months. There's a feeling that only surgeons know – a warm, prickly, feeling, experienced during an operation that isn't going very well; the surgeon's sweats, we'll call it: a terrible feeling that you want to escape, you don't know what you're doing, and that you want to be anywhere in the world but standing in a hot, humid operating theatre wondering what the hell you are going to do to sort this mess out. I came to associate bitch spays with the surgeon's sweats.

Here's how I saw it: a bitch spay is a no-win procedure. You're starting with a completely healthy animal who, given the choice, would rather not have you ferreting about in its abdomen, and you're performing major abdominal surgery upon it. The blood vessels of the ovaries, those difficult-to-get-to ones up by the kidneys, are no small potatoes. If you don't ligate them properly, the dog could bleed to death. Now, it's worth pointing out that in all my years as a vet, I have never once seen or even heard of a bitch spay bleeding to death either during the procedure or afterwards (although I have seen a handful need to be re-operated on to re-tie oozing blood vessels) but the knowledge that it was at least theoretically possible was very much on my mind as I learned my surgical skills. When you add abdominal fat, which obscures your vision and makes everything – including your gloves, instruments and suture material - as greasy and slippery as a bacon sandwich, into the mix, then you have a recipe for a young veterinary surgeon such as myself turning the air blue as he attempts to complete a procedure that he wishes he had never started, in the full blush of the surgeon sweats.[37] I discovered to my surprise that during a long, hot and unpleasant surgical procedure is the time that I seem most likely to be afflicted with an 'earworm' – the internet term for a song repeatedly playing unasked-for inside your head. There were many times at Beech House where I stood with my hands placed inside a still-living animal, surgical gloves covered with a slippery sheen of fat, feeling hot, stressed, sweaty and miserable, with 'Memories are made of this' inexplicably blaring at full volume within my skull.

Much as I had started to do with consultations that I might have to see the next morning in the aftermath of the nightmare puppy surgery, I started to check the ops board the day before my ops day. A board that featured a bitch spay larger that fifteen kilos, or older than a couple of years (and so likely to be fatter) would mean a restless and worried night's sleep for me. I grew to loathe them. However, I decided that the best way to deal with my 'thing' about bitch spays was to confront it full on, and do as many as possible, rather than try to avoid them (which is what I desperately wanted to do). In my third week as a vet, my worst nightmare – the one that had deprived me of so many hours of sleep worrying

---

[37] Actually, it wasn't when I swore when I was operating that the nurses got worried – it was when I went quiet.

about it- came true. During the spay of a particularly chubby Doberman, one of my ligatures slipped off an ovarian stump, and the dog's abdomen began to fill rapidly with blood. I panicked, and called for Sue, who very calmly scrubbed in with me, helped me find the stump, made me ligate it again, smiled, and walked back out whilst I got on with the rest of the spay. This was a surgical epiphany for me, because I realised that all that worry and fear over what would happen if one of my stumps wasn't ligated properly had been for nothing, because all that *actually* happened was that the operation took about ten minutes longer than it otherwise would have done. That's all. Everyone, at some point in their career, has a bleeding stump from a bitch spay, and everyone goes through that same realisation – what was all the worry about?

So, the days passed, and the stresses of surgery began to recede. Neutering, taking bloods, hitting veins, placing catheters (intravenous and urethral[38]), placing ET-tubes and the scores of other practical things that I had lain awake at night wondering whether I would actually be able to do became easier and easier - as things tend to do when you're doing them all day, every day. What I hadn't realised is that, in veterinary medicine, as with every other aspect of life, it's not generally the things you worry about that end up becoming a problem. It's the things that jump out upon you unexpectedly, like a phone call at three in the morning, that really cause you trouble.

---

[38] A lot of people call IV catheters 'cannulas' instead to avoid the confusion between the two, but they'll always be catheters to me.

15 - White Night

The phone rang. I squinted myopically at my watch. Three in the morning. It was never going to be good news at three in the morning. I sat up, trembling, confused, until my sleep-jangled jigsaw brain reassembled itself and I remembered who I was, which was a good job because by this time I'd already picked up the phone on instinct. I was becoming, if not exactly relaxed, then less terrified at the prospect of being called out. Half the time, I wasn't dealing with an emergency, but with a worried owner that needed reassurance. When things did go badly, then I could (in veterinary parlance) extract the pet from the owner, and take it out the back, where I had my nurse, anaesthetic machines and textbooks waiting for me.

The calls where that sanctuary couldn't be found, of course, were large animal calls. Beech House was one of those rare and dying breeds: a mixed practice. Although we did predominantly small animal work, David still had a few farmers and horse owners that had followed him to his new practice, and at the time he hadn't been able to afford to turn the business away. The problem with this arrangement was that those clients were very much 'David' clients, and never wanted to see anyone else. This led to the worst of both worlds for us junior vets – never doing routine large animal work in the day, so not getting to know the farmers or their animals, but every so often getting a call in the middle of the night for the fire brigade stuff.

'He-hello?' I said to the phone, blearily.

'Alan, it's Becky. I'm really sorry.'

Really sorry. She hadn't even got to the call-out, and she was sorry. Not great news.

'Oh?' Nervously.

'It's Mr White at King's Barton. He's got a ewe in trouble lambing.'

Of course he had. Sigh. 'I'll be right there.'

Adrenaline purging the sleep from my body, I pulled on my clothes and headed out into the pouring rain (what other weather could it be?) to my car.

In other aspects of my job, I was starting to feel less like a new graduate, but when I got a call from a farmer, all the old doubts came flying back. Farmers had usually grown up surrounded by animals; they had almost certainly seen more lambings than I had seen sheep. There was no 'extracting from the owner' with a farm call – everything I did, I did it being watched by someone who has seen it all dozens of times before.

This was (and you've no idea how old it makes me feel to say this) years before the days of Satnavs and smart phones. Mobile phones had progressed from their legendarily brick-like 80s' origins, but they were still basically only used for phoning people and playing snake.[39] This meant that finding a farm in the middle of the night meant exactly that – finding it. One of the skills I learned as a young vet was driving with an ordnance survey map pressed against the steering wheel, a skill now sadly lost to posterity in these technological times. Twenty-three minutes after I received the call, my battered old Nissan Sunny[40] was pulling into a bumpy, pitted farm lane, with what I hoped fervently was the bumpy, pitted farmhouse of King's Barton farm at the end of it.

I parked in the small yard at the bottom of the lane, relieved to see lights on in a nearby barn, and what appeared to be a torch beam heading in my direction. I stepped out of the car. My shoe immediately sank into five inches of mud, soaking it, my foot and my sock. The same thing happened with my other foot as I trudged towards the boot of my car, where I pulled on my wellingtons. My feet were already soaked, making the wellies pointless, but it seemed like the right thing to do. I picked up my waterproof top and shrugged it on as the rain bucketed down, realising too late in the dim light from the boot that the top was inside out, and so all the blood, mud and other fluids that I had failed to scrub off properly from my last large animal visit were

---

[39] And I can remember when it was all fields, too.

[40] Somewhat more battered since I had taken possession of it, to be fair.

now pressed against my shirt. Ah well, at least the top looked clean this way around.

'Vetin'ry?'

I turned to see a tall, wiry, weather-beaten man shining a torch dubiously in my direction. It's a difficult thing to shine a torch dubiously, but he was obviously an old hand at it.

'Mr White?' I said, stepping forward and extending my hand. 'Alan Reece, from Beech House.'

Mr White looked me up and down, very slowly, then grunted in a heavily accented affirmative. 'Yarp.' There was a pause as he looked me up and down again. 'David not around then, is 'e?'

One of the many disadvantages of only being a large animal vet by night was that the first time you encountered many farmers was in a crisis situation. First impressions can count for a lot, and I was always painfully aware, unlike Cameron, that I didn't immediately come across as a rugged manly type. I could almost see Mr White mentally calculating whether he'd actually have been better off if (horror of horrors) a female vet had turned up.[41]

'What can I do for you, Mr White?' I asked, possibly deepening my voice a little for effect. In an effort to pre-empt any judgements on my manliness, I squeezed his extended hand with mine as firmly as I could.

Mr White winced and extricated his hand from mine. 'Got a ewe in the shed,' he said. 'Lamb were stuck, stuck tight, so I took hold of the front 'alf, of 'ee and pulled.' He demonstrated a pulling action.

'And what happened?'

'Well, I sort of pulled the front 'alf... off, really.' He further demonstrated this rather unpleasant image in mime.

'Ah... um... is the lamb dead?' I asked.

Mr White paused, poker-faced, possibly to consider if this was the stupidest question he had ever been asked. He blinked.

'Well,' he deadpanned, 'I reckon 'tis.'

---

[41] Farmers in rural Somerset are not generally noted for their progressive attitude towards sexual equality.

While Mr White considered if it was too late to call another vet, I decided to grab my large animal box from the boot, and march decisively toward the shed. Mr White followed. Of course the lamb was dead. It was dead before he had started, because that was the only way you could accidentally pull one in half. This would be patently obvious to anyone with half a brain. What Mr White was, very patiently, trying to explain to me was that the lamb had died inside its mother, and now in attempting to get it out Mr White had left the dead back half still inside it's mother's womb. This was potentially very bad indeed, and what was left of the lamb needed to come out as soon as possible.

The ewe was lying on her side in the barn, held by one of Mr White's sons. After a quick application of gloves and lubricant, I felt inside the womb, and my fears were confirmed. The pelvis and the back legs of the lamb remained inside. They were dry in the way that only dead tissue inside a womb can be, large, and no amount of lubrication was going to get them out of the ewe without further work.

I looked up at White as professionally as I could with my arm inside a sheep; difficult but not impossible to manage.[42]

'Caesarean?' he said, dolefully. He wasn't an uncaring man, but a caesarean would probably cost him more than the ewe was worth; especially with a dead lamb.

'No,' I said, hopefully. I'd never performed a caesarean on a sheep before, but it looked like I wasn't going to start tonight. 'No, I think we should be able to manage with an embryotomy.'

Mr White nodded sadly. It was better news than he feared, but it was still a difficult and depressing job. In many ways a caesarean is easier to perform.

'Roight,' he said. 'Better get on wi' it, then.'

Embryotomy: *the dismemberment of a foetus in the uterus or vagina to facilitate delivery that is impossible by natural means*. Difficult and depressing. It's depressing because what should be a naturally joyful experience – birth, and the arrival of a lamb – has now

[42] As a vet, at least. It's much harder to pull off as, say, a banker.

turned into the in-utero dissection of a corpse to save the mother's life. It's difficult because I would be trying to perform my dissection through a tube just wide enough to fit my arm through, and I needed to do it without damaging the ewe herself.

There are worse situations in which an embryotomy must be performed, though. Cows, for instance – everything is bigger, and an order of magnitude harder to deal with, with calves. The most depressing embryotomies are those where the calf or lamb is absolutely locked in the pelvic canal, but still alive - very rare, but it does happen. I was getting off relatively lightly here.

I pushed the thought that this had been a lamb from my mind, and started concentrating upon the task. The problem – and the reason for Mr White's nasty experience with his attempted lambing – was that the lamb's hips were simply too big to fit through her mother's. I needed to reduce the size of the lamb's pelvis.

Exiting the sheep, I opened the large animal box, and found my embryotomy wire. It was still in the packet I had bought it in a few months previously from a farm shop. I took it out of the packet. Mr White gazed at its pristine, metallic surface, and looked at me, but politely didn't ask the obvious question. He would have been right, though – I hadn't done one before. I put it back in the box; I wouldn't need it for a moment. Instead, I took a scalpel blade, and realised I didn't have a blade guard – it's very easy to forget things when you're packing a large animal box in the light of a stress-free day; things that you would sell your spleen for faced with an emergency in the middle of the night. Holding the blade very, very carefully in my palm, I slipped my hand back into the ewe's womb. I located the lamb's tail, and incised through the dry skin down to the pelvis. Step one done.

Removing my hand from the sheep once more, I dropped the blade carefully into the lid of my large animal box, which I then opened to retrieve my embryotomy wire. Needles, syringes, and the scalpel blade promptly fell out of the lid, which I had failed to close correctly, and scattered over the floor of the barn. Mr White's poker face didn't crack, but he may have rolled his eyes, just a little. I quickly crammed everything back into the box, covering it all with lubricant, blood and tissue fluid, thus rendering most of it unsterile and thus entirely unusable, and unrolled the wire. Embryotomy wire is a length of abrasive stainless steel, so that when you run it across a bony surface, it saws through it - slowly. I pushed one end of the wire back into the womb, feeling a moment's sympathy for the ewe as she struggled against the unwanted intrusion, but only a moment's. I needed to concentrate. It was an incredibly fiddly job, trying to find the incision that I had just made, and slot the wire into it one handed – much trickier than I had expected. This wasn't the sort of thing that was easy to practise. Mr White watched me struggle and grunt for several minutes.

'Everythin' all right?' he asked, presumably because he noticed my lips moving. From his point of view, I was either silently praying or swearing, and neither must have seemed like a very good sign.

'Fine, fine,' I replied, cheerfully as I could, once again failing to get the wire in the right position. 'Bollocks,' I said out loud, and Mr White nodded.

'Ar,' he said, seemingly reassured by the profanity. I probably sounded more like a normal vet at that point.

I needed to get the wire placed correctly; if it was at the wrong angle, I would end up simply removing the leg without reducing the size of the pelvis, and all the work would have been for nothing. Several minutes and swear words later, my hand emerged. The wire was now in position over the bone of the lamb's pelvis. I picked up the wire guard – a piece of plastic to protect the ewe from the abrasive surface of the wire – and slid it into place on the two ends of wire that emerged from the ewe's vulva. Piece of cake, I thought. Now comes the tricky bit.

I quickly attached the handles to the ends of the wire, and started to move them back and forth, pulling back, and slowly, ever so slowly, starting to saw through the pelvis. Five minutes of effort followed, back and forth, back and forth with the wire. I paused, red-faced, and reached my hand inside to check the rewards of my labours. I could feel the tiniest groove scored into the pelvis bone under the wire. I gritted my teeth, thanked the stars that it wasn't a calf, and took hold of the handles again.

Twenty minutes later, I was retrieving the last leg of the successfully bisected hindquarters from the ewe. My arms were numb, and I was covered in sweat, but I felt elated. I discovered two things about large animal calls that evening: firstly, there's nothing quite so terrifying as getting called out to a farm in the middle of the night, and secondly, there's nothing quite like the sense of achievement when a farm call goes well. The second doesn't quite make up for the first, but it's close.

Mr White's face had almost cracked into something resembling a smile as the ewe stood up after the surgery, and took in a mouthful of hay. He nodded at me, once. It may have been the finest compliment I have received in my veterinary career. I cleaned myself up, accepted his offered cup of tea gratefully, shook his hand, and headed back to bed, where my alarm woke me ninety-seven minutes later for my next day's work.

16 - Seen and Not Heard

The weeks passed. Kate returned from her trip home, and we settled into an awkward working relationship. We always got on well, but enough time had passed since the party that it seemed okay for neither of us to mention it, so neither of us did. No one at the practice really knew whether Kate and James were back together or not; certainly their antagonism at work didn't seem to have eased at all, and James's smugness with me swiftly sunk into the background of his usual surly arrogance. Kate and I talked and joked like normal in the day, and I tried not to think about her very much at night.

For myself - I was back on my Quest: making the world better, one animal at a time. I had lost it for a while - to be expected in the first few weeks of the job, I thought - but I was getting back on track now. I had a plan - a simple one. Take each and every consultation as an opportunity to do the best thing for the animal, and for the owner. A simple plan.

Of course, no plan survives contact with the enemy.

*

My morning started in what was becoming the traditional way: eyeing up the consultations from the dispensary computer, seeing which ones might be interesting, while I sipped my muddy coffee. The list was busy, but not quite full, and seemed manageable. I would be having an easier morning than Cameron, regardless; Kate had told me that he had been called out to one of the practice's rare calvings in the middle of the night, and having worked my fair share of days after very little sleep (most recently after the embryotomy at White's farm), Cameron had my sympathies.

I slurped my drink, waiting in vain for it to blow some of the cobwebs from my mind, and saw that the first consult had arrived: a second vaccination. Nice and easy on the brain, and a good way to start the day. As I began to head to my consulting room,

Cameron bounded into the pharmacy.

'Morning Alan!' he said, grinning brightly.

I peered at him over the coffee. He looked annoyingly chirpy.

'I thought you had a calving last night?' I said wearily.

'I did!' he said, even more brightly. 'Great fun, leg back, nothing too complicated. Calf and mum are fine. Why can't we get more like that, eh?'

Sue emerged from the doorway behind him, clutching her own mug of coffee, and narrowed her eyes at him. 'Frustrating, isn't he?' she said to me.

'Somehow,' I said, 'I feel more tired just looking at him.'

Cameron grinned broadly. 'Frustrating? Inspirational, I think you mean.' Sue muttered something that she would never say in front of a client, and disappeared into the peace of the prep room.

'Come on, Alan,' Cameron said as he struggled into his consulting top. 'You and me against the world, eh? Who've we got this morning?' He glanced at the consulting list on the monitor. He paused. He raised an eyebrow.

'You... uh... you've got that cat second vac, haven't you?'

Suspicion suddenly crept over me. 'I was about to do it... why?'

'Oh, no reason.' Cameron smiled enigmatically. 'None at all. Have fun.'

I entered my own room, grabbed a stethoscope, then stepped out to the waiting room to call in my client.

This early in the morning, there were only a few people in the waiting room: the first couple of consultations, and a few people waiting for their animals to be admitted for surgery. Only one person had a cat box, a young woman, sitting with a small boy[43], so I looked at her, patented veterinary smile on my face, and called the cat's name.

The young boy looked at me, caught my gaze, and shouted

---

[43] I'm not good at estimating ages with kids; puppies and kittens, fine, but not kids, so I'll leave that up to your imagination; all I can say is that he was less than half my size.

out, 'You sound gay!'

I'd had a number of unusual responses in waiting rooms, but this was a new one. I lost control of my jaw for a moment, but the smile remained on my face. My mouth lolled open as if I had been sedated. The child grinned. So did a number of other people in the waiting room, which had suddenly grown remarkably quiet.

The truth is, the little git had struck something of a nerve with his opening salvo. I have not been blessed with the deepest voice in the civilised world, something I started to realise due to the number of times I had spoken to clients on the phone, and then subsequently met them in the practice only to have them tell me that they had talked to 'a very nice lady vet who recommended we came in to be seen'.

The young woman uttered not one word of remonstration to my new arch-nemesis, but instead picked up the cat box and headed towards my consulting room. As I closed the door behind them I could see the receptionists leaping to my defence by doubling up with laughter at the front desk.

The waiting room episode set the tone for the rest of the consultation. A second vaccination is simple enough - just a quick check and a jab - but the child from *The Omen* had already chosen the next torment he would visit upon me.

'Hello,' I said, cheerfully, opening the door of the cat box. 'Here for a second vaccination, are we?'

'Here for a second vaccination, are we?' repeated the child, in an exaggerated high-pitched tone that would have put Dick Emery to shame.

Manfully ignoring this, I extracted the cat from the box,

whilst the young woman watched. The cat began to purr, and I decided that it was quite the nicest person in the room.

'I'll just give him a quick check over,' I said.

'I'll just give him a quick check over,' Satan's spawn repeated squeakily. I looked at the mother. She looked back at me. I gritted my teeth, and thought longingly about the needles in my cupboard, weighing up whether it was worth doing some prison time. I completed my clinical exam, then said 'I'll just pop and get his vaccine then,' and hurried out of the door before the irritating echo could reach me.

In the prep from, Cameron and Kate stood pretending they were looking for drugs, rather than listening intently to my consult. Kate's shoulders were shaking with suppressed giggles. Cameron wasn't even bothering to suppress his.

'Everything all right, dear?' Cameron said, finally getting his revenge for the all times I had told people we were a couple.

'I,' I said calmly, 'am going to kill you.'

Cameron guffawed. 'I did the first vaccine. Charming little kid, isn't he?'

I drew up the vaccination, and headed back into the breach. By now, the demonspawn had found my sharps bin, and was doing his level best to pour the contents into his eyeball, whilst his mother watched. Hesitating only a moment, I took the bin from the child. This induced a full-blown tantrum in the creature from hell, including some impressive floor-diving, screaming and kicking. The kid obviously had a future in premier league football. I vaccinated the cat, and managed to complete the consult without strangling anyone to death, or bursting into tears.

The woman picked up the cat basket, ushered her little terror out of the door, then paused. For a moment I was foolish enough to believe that I was about to receive an apology. She turned, looked at me, and said in a conspiratorial tone, 'He's Asperger's.'

Brilliant. Not only had I been bullied by a child for my entire consultation, I was also a complete bastard for wishing various sharp unpleasant things to happen to the kid, because he was disabled, rather than, say, an undisciplined little turd. I shrugged and smiled.

'It's fine,' I said, feeling very British.

I finished my coffee, and then told Kate and Cameron that if they wanted me, I would be in the x-ray room, repeatedly radiographing my testicles until they couldn't produce a sperm if their lives depended upon it.

17 - The Mutt's Nuts

Autumn turned to winter in Bridgford, and the plastic-sulphur smell that hung over the town like an eggy fart in a cheap suit slowly dissipated as the air grew cooler. About this time, Beech House decided to perform a consumer survey; Sue and David sent out hundreds of questionnaires to clients, asking about all aspects of the surgery. Could the client park easily? Was their phone call handled well by reception? Were our prices too expensive? And, crucially (from my point of view), what did they feel about the vet that handled their case?

I awaited the results from this survey with trepidation. What did the clients think of me? Hopefully they had more confidence in me than I did in myself. Was I reassuring, or bumbling? Compassionate, or cold? I tried to be honest and true to myself when I was talking to clients, so I started to see the survey as some kind of judgement upon my own personality. It was a nervous time.

The results, when they came, were surprising. Of the several hundred surveys that were sent out, Beech House received around fifty or sixty replies. Most of them were quite non-specific, and the majority were satisfied with the practice. It was rare that any of the staff members were mentioned by name; rare, that is, except for me. I was singled out half a dozen times by clients - in a good way. The public seemed to respond well to me. Those that mentioned me said that I obviously cared about their animals, and that they liked how I spoke to the pets too, and not just them. I had always felt a little self-conscious about doing this prior to the survey, but I had wanted to try to put the animals at ease too.

It felt like a reward for the stresses and strains of those first few months. David and Sue were extremely pleased with the survey, and especially pleased with me. I was working with James in the evening after the vets' meeting in which Sue had talked us through the results of the survey. It was a quiet surgery, for a change, and James, who fared rather less well when it came to clients' opinions of him, was in a foul mood. He grumbled that the survey was a waste of time, and that people didn't know what was good for them. He muttered that the public were idiots, and needed to listen when someone better educated than them was talking. I, rather smugly and condescendingly, and still flying high from my glowing review from the men and women in the street, disagreed. People were fundamentally good, I argued. Treat them with respect and honesty, and that's what you will receive in return.

'Fuck that,' James said, glancing at the waiting room list, where a client had just appeared. 'Your turn.'

I walked into my consult room, and clicked on the client. Ah, that one. The 'see out' post-castration. We didn't usually see the routine neutering cases out ourselves in the evening; normally, one of the nurses would discuss post-operative care. In this case, however, I had some things I needed to discuss with the owner. When I came to anaesthetise it, I had noticed that Staffordshire bull terrier had a nearly bald muzzle, with similar patches of alopecia over its paws and flanks. The skin revealed by the fur loss was thickened and inflamed. Suspicious, and after trying and failing to contact the owner, I had performed a skin scrape. Sure enough, under the microscope I spied dozens of tiny cigar-shaped creatures, their eight legs wriggling in surprise under the heat of the microscope bulb. Demodex mites.

When you see what you think of as a 'mangy' dog in the street, or on the TV, it's a fair bet it's suffering from demodicosis ('mange' itself means 'mite infestation, and demodicosis means the mites involved are demodex). It can be an extremely serious condition, but the staffy was relatively mildly affected, and I fully expected the treatment (a medicated shampoo) to cure the problem.

I called the client in. She was, not to put too fine a point on it and even with my newfound love of humanity after the survey, dog-rough. Comprehensively tattooed, pierced, and with a shaved head and grungy clothes, she stomped into my consulting room with an air of anger and suspicion, and stared at me malevolently. I explained about the mites, and about the shampoo I finished speaking. The woman glared at me in silence. Then she said:

'Fuckin' mites? Where the fuck would he get fuckin' mites from?'

I explained, carefully, that demodex mites were ubiquitous; they were always present in small numbers on canine skin. Sometimes, they crept through a crack in the immune system and managed to get a foothold.

The woman considered this for a moment.

'Fuck off. I'm not paying for any fuckin' shampoo, either. Fuckin' robber. Linin' your fuckin' pockets.'

This wasn't getting us very far. The case was mild, and we weren't the normal vets for the client - the dog had been castrated under a charity scheme. I hoped that I could demonstrate that I wasn't interested in money for myself, but just in getting the dog better, so I strongly recommend she took him to her own vets for further treatment. The woman said nothing, but glared at me sullenly. I hoped this meant that she might consider it.

Well, that was the tricky bit of the consultation over. Now I just had to talk through the post-operative care of a castration. I explained that her dog should have a light meal tonight, such as chicken and rice, as he might feel a little sick after his anaesthetic. She frowned. 'How the fuck am I supposed to cook fuckin' rice without a cooker, eh?'

Moving on, I explained where the wound was, and how although her dog's scrotum would look a bit peculiar now it was empty, it would all shrink down over the next few months.

The woman went quiet, and stayed that way for quite some time. I cleared my throat. She had started to look very angry.

'You what?' she growled.

'Erm... I'm just saying, it will all shrink down, and look very normal in a few months.'

The woman's mouth was a thin line of rage. Her cheeks were turning scarlet.

'Are you telling me,' she said, slowly, 'that you've cut his bollocks off?'

It was my turn to be quiet for a moment. Recovering myself, I asked nervously, 'Well, he was in today to be castrated, wasn't he?'

The woman nodded. 'Yeah, but I didn't think you'd cut his balls off as well!'

Now, at this point, I wasn't really sure what else to say. My gaze moved to the consent form for her dog, which she had signed right under the words 'General Anaesthetic Dog Castrate'. The owner was now in a state of some consternation, huffing and swearing, and muttering, 'I don't believe it.' I decided to go for the scientific approach.

'Erm... can I ask you what you think castration is?'

'It's the snip, innit? His tubes. Don't fuckin' believe it!'

'Um... no, I think you're thinking of a vasectomy. Castration is... well, removing the testicles.' Distressingly, I caught myself gesturing to my own crotch, as if this would somehow help to illustrate the procedure. Thankfully, the owner distracted me before I got too much further into that particular mime.

'Well, that's great!' she bawled. 'He's gonna attack all the other dogs now, isn't he?'

Not really following the logic at this point, I resorted to saying, 'What?'

'He's gonna be jealous, isn't he? Lookin' at himself, and then seeing them with their balls hanging out, he's gonna kick right off, innee?'

It slowly dawned on me that the owner genuinely believed her dog was going to have such a self-image problem that he was going to take out his anger and frustration on other dogs. I wondered if this sort of thing ever happened to James Herriot.

'I... um... dogs don't really think that way, to be honest.'

'Are you saying my dog is stupid?'

This is the point where my last, faint hope for humankind waved its little white flag and surrendered. Several minutes, and lots of swearing (more on her part than mine) finally convinced my owner that her poor puppy was not going to develop some kind of castrato-complex, and that castrated dogs tended, on average, to be less aggressive than entire ones. It took a long time, and a lot of nodding, and listening, and compromising, but somehow, I managed to survive the rest of the consultation without getting thumped. The woman left my room, slammed the door, and stomped off to reception to complain about the fifteen pounds that the charity was charging her for us to castrate her dog.

I left the room. James was standing in the prep room, smiling at me.

I hated it when he was right.

18 - Royal College

At the end of that evening surgery, I found Sue waiting for me in the prep room with an envelope in her hand. At first I assumed it was another survey result, but then I noticed the serious expression on her face, and the words 'Royal College of Veterinary Surgeons' printed in red along the top of the envelope.

'This arrived for you,' Sue said quietly, as she handed me the envelope. 'I thought I should give it to you personally.'

'What is it?' I asked, looking at the envelope nervously.

'Open it,' Sue suggested. That felt the last thing I wanted to do, but I peeled open the envelope and pulled out the sheets inside. My heart sank as I unfurled the first page. I was no expert in such matters, but I didn't think that any letter which started with the words:

'Pursuant to a resolution'

was going to be good news. I scanned the rest of the first page.

'... response to the complainants Mr and Mrs Jackson in respect to their dog Khan... an allegation of serious professional misconduct... please further clinical notes and any other documentation you have regarding this case... decision upon whether the disciplinary committee of the Royal College will investigate this allegation further...'

I looked up at Sue, who smiled sympathetically, if sadly.

'Disciplinary?' she asked.

I nodded slowly, too numb to talk.

'I've seen one before,' she said. I noticed that she didn't say that she had received one herself. 'It's... well, try not to panic. It's not the end of the world.'

Maybe not for Sue, but I could feel the world collapsing around me. This was it. My career was over. I was going to be exposed for the fraud that I was. Three months. I thought I might have lasted a little longer than that.

Sue led me up to the coffee room and made me a strong brew. Sitting opposite me, she read through the letter.

Misconduct,' she murmured as she read it. 'Balls.'

As a vet, you could be disciplined for two reasons. Negligence was the less serious of the two, and if the complaint was upheld it meant that you had failed to act in a way that a reasonably competent veterinary surgeon could have been expected to act - you had missed an obvious diagnosis, or given poor advice, to the detriment of the client's pet. Professional misconduct was far more serious - an upheld complaint of this nature would mean that you actively mislead the client for your own personal gain, or behaved in a way unbecoming of a veterinary surgeon.

'Want to talk me through the case, Alan?' Sue said as I stared at my coffee cooling on the table. 'Alan? Do you remember the case?'

Of course I remembered it. A few weeks ago, the Jacksons, a friendly young couple, had brought Khan in to see me. Khan was a two-year old Dogue de Bordeaux - a large breed of dog that looks as if someone has pumped a mastiff full of sausages. They are generally friendly, the classic gentle giants, and Khan in particular was very friendly indeed. He kept trying to turn around and lick my face while I was palpating his abdomen, and after I had finished my consultation he rolled on his back. There was no way he was leaving my room without having his tummy tickled. I obliged, but I didn't give him a treat, because the reason the Jacksons had brought Khan in was because he had a stomach upset. He had vomited a few times the day before, and was now suffering with diarrhoea.

Clinically, Khan appeared normal, if thin. His heart sounded fine, his gums were an encouraging pink colour, and his temperature was normal. His abdomen felt a little bit squidgy when I palpated it - and it was very easy to palpate because, unlike a lot of his breed, Khan was quite a slim dog. Squidgy bowels usually meant some degree of inflammation, but I couldn't feel anything that made me worry about a foreign body. It looked like we were dealing with gastroenteritis, so I told the owner to put Khan onto bland food[44] and gave him some probiotics and stool-binders. I reassured the worried owners that I didn't think we had anything too concerning happening with Khan at the moment, but I advised them that we had a twenty-four hour emergency service, and if they were at all worried about anything, or if Khan seemed to be getting worse, to give us a ring. It was part of my standard talk that I had developed over the previous weeks. They thanked me, Khan licked my hand, and walked out of my room with his tail wagging. I got on with my next consultation.

The next morning, Kate rushed to me as soon as I had entered the practice.

'Cameron's in theatre,' she said, her face pale. 'He needs help, can you come?'

I hurried through the practice into the operating theatre. Cameron was sweating in his surgical scrubs, gloved hands deep inside a large dog's abdomen. He had exteriorised most of the dog's small intestine, which for its whole length was a horrible purplish-black colour.

'He's stopped breathing!' Cameron said as I rushed to the dog's head. My blood ran cold. Khan.

As I watched, Khan gasped, and his whole chest contracted, his neck flexing. Cheyne-stokes breathing. An abnormal respiratory pattern that, in a veterinary context, usually meant that death was near. Khan's brainstem was beginning to die. His pulseoximeter wasn't registering a heartbeat, and I couldn't hear one with my stethoscope.

Kate arrived with the crash box, and I injected a millilitre of adrenaline into Khan's drip line. Nothing happened. I started chest compressions, while Kate breathed for Khan using the anaesthetic circuit. None of it mattered. Khan had died almost as soon as I had stepped into the theatre, and nothing we did could bring him

---

[44] Chicken, rice, scrambled egg, that sort of thing. Very easy to digest and not a lot left to come out of the back end. A good way of giving the gastrointestinal system a bit of a rest without actually starving the dog. If you starve for diarrhoea, you will get less of the unpleasant stuff coming out, but it actually tends to delay recovery because the only way the topmost gut cells get nutrition is by food passing over them.

back. I looked down at the mass of purple intestines.

'Shit,' Cameron said.

'What... what happened?' I asked, stunned at the sudden change the morning had taken.

'He came in last night... you saw him in the morning, didn't you?'

I nodded, shaken.

'He'd been fine all day, but had vomited a little about seven. I checked his abdomen, still wasn't worried, decided to admit him and x-ray him in the morning if he still wasn't right. I put him on a drip but I thought it was a bit of overkill, he seemed fine.'

'The owners wanted to take him home,' Kate added,' but we thought it might be safest just to keep an eye on him.'

'Not that I thought...' Cameron looked at Khan and sighed. He shook his head. 'He started vomiting again about five o'clock this morning. Then his temperature started shooting up, and his abdomen started swelling. His colour turned awful. He went into shock.'

The signs of abdominal crisis. Somewhere around five am, something very serious had happened in Khan's abdomen.

'I didn't know what was going on,' Cameron continued. 'He had looked fine all night! Then... I just didn't have any time! God, I wish I'd taken that bloody x-ray! We got him straight to theatre, opened him up, to find... this.'

I had never seen anything like it. The whole length of Khan's small intestine was dying, as if the blood supply had suddenly been pinched off.

'Mesenteric torsion?' I wondered out loud. Mesenteric torsion is a vanishingly rare condition where the whole intestines swing around on their axis, closing off the blood supply to them. It is invariably, and almost immediately, fatal. No one is really sure what causes it.

Cameron nodded. 'Maybe. Or a blood clot, or a horrible infection, or God bloody knows what.' He sighed deeply. 'I'd better get on the phone to the owners.'

Kate squeezed his hand. 'You didn't do anything wrong, you

know. How could you have known?'

Cameron gritted his teeth. 'Should have taken that bloody x-ray,' he muttered again, although we all knew it wouldn't have made any difference. Whatever happened to Khan, it happened at five am. An x-ray before then probably wouldn't have shown anything at all other than some gas in the bowel.

'You didn't do anything wrong,' she repeated, and then looked at me. 'Neither of you.'

The Jacksons didn't agree.

*

Sue nodded as she listened to the story. She hadn't been directly involved in Khan's case, but very little happened in the practice that she wasn't aware of.

'Okay, well, Kate was right, of course,' she said. 'You didn't screw up.'

I shrugged. Sue frowned.

'Alan, if there's one thing vets are good at... well, most vets, anyway... it's blaming themselves for things. You, I have noticed, are particularly good at it. What else could you have done when you saw Khan?'

'Booked him in, taken that x-ray, run some bloods.'

Sue sighed. 'Okay, here's how to look at it. What would you do if you saw the exact same case as Khan tomorrow?'

I thought about it. 'Honestly... honestly I would do the same as I did the first time. There was nothing that made me think--'

'Exactly,' Sue said, draining her own coffee. 'Look, we'll sort this out. Go home, and write down everything you can remember about that consultation, absolutely everything. Then we'll work it into something we can send to the Royal College.' She smiled. 'Don't worry, Alan.'

Don't worry. It was like telling a dog not to lick its own genitals. The problem was, I could absolutely understand why the Jackson's felt as they did. They were worried about their dog, so they did the right thing - they brought it in to see a vet, and yet within twenty-four hours Khan was dead. How were they supposed to feel? Of course they would think I missed something. I would think it myself, but I genuinely couldn't think of anything else I could have done. That was the terrible truth of medicine that hadn't changed since the days of the first shamans and witch doctors: sometimes, despite your best efforts, and even when you haven't done anything wrong, your patients die. If it's a hard thing for vets to accept, then how must it be for the owners? They had lost their companion, and they were confused and in pain. I understood why they had complained.

There was another truth I was starting to understand about veterinary medicine: it didn't matter how good a vet you were. I had made a serious error a few months ago, and a puppy had died because of it. David's stern telling-off aside, I didn't get into any trouble for it at all. With Khan, I had done everything I should have done, and I was going to be taken to a disciplinary hearing because of it.

Depressed, miserable, and in something of a state of shock, I returned home and started to write down everything about the consultation. There wasn't very much more to tell than in my clinical notes. What kind of a profession was I in? How did this relate to my Quest? The Jackson's would say I was a terrible vet. Maybe I was. Maybe there was something I was missing.

Maybe it was time to admit that I just wasn't cut out for the job.

I finished my write up of the consult. Then I opened up a new word document. My CV. It was time to see if there was anything else I could do with my degree than continue in general practice.

'Two years, mate. I give it two years before you're worn down and you quit.'

The words stung, because it looked as if they were going to be right. I had tried to complete the Quest, but it was an impossible task. I needed a way out.

19 - Season of Goodwill

The leaves fell from the trees. As autumn began to turn into winter, I felt as if a black cloud followed me wherever I went - and it wasn't the smog from the chemical factory. The wheels of RCVS justice turned slowly - I still hadn't heard anything after my response to the complaint against me. Cameron felt awful that he hadn't received any complaint at all; it was squarely levelled at me. I understood, though. I had been the first person the Jacksons had met at the practice, and I was the person they felt betrayed by. It was just one of those things.

I didn't feel that I could take any more of 'those things', though. I had sent off a my CV to a number of different places, including a clinical pathology position at one of the larger veterinary laboratories. I wasn't entirely sure I was ready to spend the rest of my life looking down a microscope, but veterinary pathology had the tremendous advantage that the tissues you were looking at were already dead. It appealed because it seemed to offer all the interesting puzzles of medicine, without any of the messiness of general practice. It would take a lot of retraining, but I had always enjoyed the process of learning. I would still need to be a member of the RCVS, however, so the outcome of disciplinary action was still vital. I had an interview at the laboratory in the new year. My days as a veterinary general practitioner were numbered.

David and Sue knew nothing about my intentions: I hadn't told anyone at the practice. It seemed best to wait until I had had the interview, at least, but as the annual practice Christmas do rolled around, I felt something of a fraud for going. I loved the people, though, (well, most of the people) and I was aware that it might be one of the last chances I would have to see Kate socially, never mind if James was there or not.

The party was at a pub in a nearby village; one of the few that David hadn't yet been banned from. It was a smallish pub, and David had managed to hire the whole place out for the evening – which worryingly gave him (in his own mind, at least) free rein to expose as much flesh as he could get away with. The theme for the evening, decided by Sue, was gangsters and molls, and so when Cameron picked me up on a chilly December evening, he found me dressed in a suit, with a trilby, a pencilled-on moustache, and carrying a small plastic Tommy gun.

'Nice,' he said, grinning. 'Good effort.'

Cameron didn't have the right sort of build for suits, and he appeared painful squeezed into his, but this gave him the appearance of a Mafia thug, so it did fit the theme. At least he hadn't gone for 'Moll' - I had a horrible feeling that David might have done.

'Speech ready?' he asked, nonchalantly, as we headed to his car.

'Er... speech?' I said.

'Oh, didn't we tell you? Newbie does a speech at the Christmas do, always does.'

'What? When?'

'Right before the meal. Don't worry, you've got half an hour or so. Gives you some time to get some drinks inside you.'

A speech? Bloody hell. I settled down into my seat, and began to do the thing I did best. Worry. It wasn't the speaking itself that terrified me - strangely, I had always rather enjoyed public speaking. Shy as I could be in social situations, I found speeches similar to consulting - it was all a performance. At university, when we had to present cases to other students, I discovered that everybody was usually bracing themselves to find them boring or embarrassing. It was such a surprise for them when I threw in a few half-decent jokes that the sheer relief got them laughing. No, it wasn't the speaking itself, it was the content. What was I going to say to these people - my friends - when I was planning to leave the practice at the earliest possible opportunity?

We arrived at the pub - a small but cosy and quaint village inn, all oak beams and horse brass, with a great roaring fire - and Cameron (who was abandoning his car at the pub and getting a taxi home) and I headed straight for the bar. Most of the practice was there already, including Kate, who was also dressed as a gangster rather than a moll. Dressed in a sharp suit, with a scar and moustache pencilled onto her face, she still managed to look amazing. Cameron dragged me towards her, and she smiled as we approached.

'Hullo, you two,' she said. 'You're both looking ravishing, of course.'

Cameron shrugged. 'Of course,' he said. 'Shame you didn't go for moll. Criminal to hide legs like yours.'

Kate raised an eyebrow. 'Yes, well, I am a criminal, remember?' She brandished her small plastic pistol.

'Don't mind him,' I said. 'He's just the muscle. I'm the brains of the operation.'

'God help us,' Kate said with a smile. 'Did Cameron tell you about the speech?'

'He did,' I said, solemnly.

'Let me guess,' she said. 'You're pissing yourself?'

I laughed, suddenly wondering why on earth I would want to do anything at all that would take me further away from Kate. Suddenly, there was a loud clanking of glasses as David, mercifully still fully-dressed, clambered up onto a table, and smiled benignly down at us all.

'Well,' he said. 'I suppose it's time for me to declare the Beech House practice party officially open!' Cheers from the assembled crowd. 'It's been another good year,' he continued, 'some comings, some goings, as ever. Life carries us all in different directions. We're only travelling together for a short while. My advice,' he lifted his glass and winked directly at me as he did so, 'is to enjoy the journey.'

'Get on with it!' Cameron called from my side.'

'I consider myself lucky to work with such wonderful friends and colleagues,' David said. 'I know it can be challenging at times. I want to thank you all from the bottom of my heart--'

'And the heart of his bottom!' Cameron called. The room laughed, but David carried on regardless.

'From the bottom of my heart,' he repeated, 'for all your hard work this year. I couldn't do it without you. Any of you. Thank you.'

People clapped and cheered, until eventually David raised his hands. 'And now, it's time for a few words from our newest member of the team. Alan, come up here, son.'

I walked nervously up to the table as David clambered down. 'Thanks, Dad,' I said, as I turned and faced my colleagues. James, sitting next to Sue, shook his head, slowly, but everyone else in the room laughed.

'I'll keep it short,' I said, 'largely because I need the toilet.' This was true, but mostly I wanted to make sure that I didn't start crying in front of everyone. Especially not Kate.

'I'll bring you a bucket, you carry on,' Cameron shouted from the back, but he was quickly shushed. I thought about telling my 'I read two books when I was a child' alien mercenary story, but although it was mostly a joke it felt a little too close to home, and the fact that I was about to leave the profession felt as though it cast the anecdote in a somewhat different light.

'You've all been so welcoming,' I said, 'and made a very difficult six months so much easier, each and every one of you.' Cheers and clapping from around the room, except from James. 'I was so terrified when I walked through that door for the first time. I couldn't have asked for a better group of people to help me through it.' Smiles from the crowd. This was going terribly well. 'I've learned so much in such a short time, but I still have...' I tailed off. I was going to say 'Still have so much to learn', but that wasn't true anymore, was it?

'I can't thank you all enough for all you've done. It's been a... well, I've had some difficult moments.' I paused. 'Becoming a vet was my dream from when I was a boy, and I wanted to say that... that...' What did I want to say? I paused.

'I guess I wanted to say that... er... it's been quite a ride. And thank you. Thank you all. And...' My gaze fell upon Cameron, who was making frantic cutting gestures across this throat. 'And... er... thank you.'

James rolled his eyes. Everyone else clapped politely. I walked back to my table, and hoped that I hadn't made too much of a prat of myself.

A few drinks later, I was sitting at my table, wondering if I had drunk enough to dance to the cheesy eighties music that had started playing. Not quite, I decided, taking another swig.

'Alan?'

I turned. Kate had taken the seat beside me.

'Oh, hey, Kate,' I said, as nonchalantly as I could manage, while my heart did the peculiar things that it always did when Kate was nearby.

'Nice speech,' she said, with a grin.

'Well,' I said, defensively, 'I didn't really get much warning, to be honest.'

Kate nodded, and said 'Hm.' A serious expression crossed her face. 'Alan, are you leaving us?'

'I... er... what?'

'Your speech. Sounded more like you were at a wake than a Christmas party. Are you thinking of moving on?'

I sighed. 'I had wondered... I mean, it's been difficult recently. The job, the disciplinary...' I stopped, because I was pretty sure the next words out of my mouth were going to be 'You and James.' I didn't want to mention the interview.

Kate leaned towards me, took my hand, and gave it a gentle squeeze. 'Alan,' she said, 'I don't want you to go.'

I looked at her. My brain was fizzing with something that wasn't alcohol, and I had suddenly forgotten how to speak.

'But...' I managed. 'James...?'

Kate rolled her eyes. 'That man,' she said, slowly and deliberately, 'is a cock.'

There was a cry of 'Kate, come on!' from the door. Laura was standing there, waving her arm and pointedly tapping her watch.

'Listen, Alan, I've got to go, but... I think we need to talk. Can I come round to yours tomorrow night?'

My brain belatedly started working. 'Er, sure, yes, I'll cook you something. You... uh... you don't mind being savaged by Vienna, do you?'

Kate grinned. 'It'll be worth it,' she said. She squeezed my hand again. This time, I squeezed back. Then she jumped up, and headed for the door.

20 - That Empire Strikes Back Moment

'Looks lovely,' Kate said. 'Really, really lovely. What... er... what is it?'

'Well, the recipe book calls it a 'vegetable jalousie'. It said it was really easy to make, but that it looked impressive.' I looked at the mulch of vegetables and pastry on the backing tray. 'So it was half right.'

Kate smiled and sipped her wine. 'Well, so long as it tastes alright, it doesn't really matter that it looks like... um...'

'A turd?' I suggested. Kate nodded in agreement.

'Yes. Like a turd. Come on then, dish it out!'

I plonked a splat of the jalousie onto Kate's plate. 'There's a little white wine in it, so, y'know, be careful not to have too much.' There was a lot more white wine in me. I'd helped myself to most of the rest of the bottle. It had helped with my nerves, but not with my cooking. 'If you're in the market for dinner that looks like poo, you're going to be blown away by my chocolate cake dessert,' I said.

Kate wrinkled her nose. 'Can't wait,' she said, as I dished up my own meal and sat down opposite her. She took a mouthful. 'Edible,' she said, chewing thoughtfully. 'Actually, pretty bloody tasty.' She put her fork down. 'Now then. Are you going to tell me what you were talking about last night? Are you leaving?'

I sighed. 'I have an interview. Beginning of January, at Veldin Labs. They're looking for a clinical pathology resident.'

'Pathology?'

I shrugged. 'I don't know. I mean, I don't seem to be a very good vet, do I?'

Kate grimaced. I didn't think it was the food.

'What are you talking about?' she said.

'I mean, well, the Jacksons... Khan. The puppy.' It felt hard to say it, even months later.

'Oh my God, Alan, these things happen to everyone! You think you're the only vet to ever make a mistake? To ever get a disciplinary letter?'

'No,' I said, seriously, 'I don't. But... well... it's important to me to get it right, you know. I mean, I... well, I made a promise to myself. I was going to make animals better.'

'You have! You do! You just dwell on the ones that you haven't. That's normal! you don't want to know what keeps me up at night. But you make a difference, even if it's just reassuring people.'

'It's not always reassuring people,' I said, thinking of Henry, the cat I had seen last week, that the owners just wanted to checked over because 'he wasn't quite right'. Within a few moments of the consultation, I had felt the large swelling in his abdomen. A tumour. An easy diagnosis. Sometimes, the easy ones were the hardest to make.

'You make a difference there, too,' Kate said. 'When the time comes, if you can make it less stressful for the animals, and the owners, that's important.' She paused and took a sip of her wine. 'Maybe it's the most important thing we do. Helping people to say goodbye.'

I hadn't really thought about it like that before. I had been thinking of euthanasia as a failure, an admission of defeat. Maybe that was stupid. Nothing and nobody lives forever. Maybe Kate was right. Maybe what I did at the end of an animal's life was more just as important as what I did before it.

'Pathology?' Kate was saying again. 'Will you definitely get it?'

'I don't know. They seemed very keen on the phone. I've been looking into it, it sounds very interesting, I think I could really enjoy it.

'Hmm,' Kate said. 'Sounds dead boring to me.' She grinned. It took me a few moments to realise that was supposed to be a joke.

'Ha ha,' I said, smiling.

'Listen, Alan,' she said, serious again. 'Don't go. You're a good vet. You know your stuff, you're good with the clients and... and you care. You really do care. Don't give it up.'

I sat and thought for a moment.

'Why is it important to you?' I said. 'I mean, why would you want me to stay?'

Kate sat back, suddenly looking shy. It was such a strange mood for her that it caught me by surprise. 'Don't you know?' she said quietly.

I felt my cheeks go red despite me desperately willing them not to. 'But,' I managed, 'the party... James...'

Kate hung her head. 'I know. That was stupid.' She whistled. 'Boy, was it stupid. But, I was drunk, and you were there, and I wanted to dance. I wanted... anyway, suddenly you weren't there anymore. James was. And it was kind of easy, and I just needed... it was just a dance, a kiss. Nothing more. He read it wrong, but I was just...'

'Just a kiss?' I said.

Kate stood up, and walked over to me.

'Just a kiss,' she said. 'Like this one.'

She bent down and kissed me.

'I think I might love you,' I said.

She grinned. 'I know.'

We never made it as far as dessert.

21 - Honesty is ALWAYS the best policy

I had agreed to working the morning of Boxing Day for Cameron so that he could get home to Oxford for a few days, which meant I was effectively stuck in Bridgford for Christmas. Suddenly, this didn't seem like such a bad thing, because Kate *was* working at Christmas; she was on call with James, and we decided that it might be nice to try to spend the day together, even if it was in the practice. It sounded like a pretty good Christmas to me.

Bridgford was surrounded by numerous picturesque little villages, like flowers growing around a cowpat, and Kate was renting the top-floor flat of a pretty house in one of them. I turned up there early - for some reason I still felt obliged to go home at night to check that Vienna was okay - in order to cook Kate breakfast and try to take her mind off being stuck in the practice all day on Christmas Day. The breakfast did its job, and a festively cheerful Kate phoned through to the practice to check what inpatients she would be dealing with: an elderly guinea pig with gut stasis, and a young cat with a bite abscess on its head. In short, nothing too serious, so in a concession to the season, Kate told Laura she could get on and enjoy her day, as we knew we'd be arriving at the practice shortly. A grateful Laura diverted the practice phone lines to Kate's mobile phone, and we headed on in to work.

Kate had grown up in Devon, and so she was well used to driving down (and, as is frequently necessary, reversing back up) narrow country lanes. She knew you had to go carefully, because at any moment, round an bend, you might meet a car coming the other way. Unfortunately for us, however carefully you drive yourself, it's all for nothing if the car approaching you is travelling at reckless moron speed.

While we were still about two miles from the practice, a small white Citroen suddenly leapt around the corner ahead of us. Kate reacted quickly, and brought her car to a halt. The driver of the other car either didn't notice, or didn't slam the brakes on quickly enough. It kept coming. Kate and I had a moment to look at each other in a 'Oh God they're really going to hit us!' kind of way before the car bounced off our bonnet, knocking us five feet backwards, and then proceeded to attempt to escape the situation by clambering up the hedgerow along the side of the road.

Doors were slammed; swear words and insurance details were exchanged with the young couple from the Citroen, and blame was acknowledged by no one. Infuriating as this was, what we were really concerned with was the fact that there was no one in the practice right now. Kate's Peugeot was badly dented and minus a headlight, but still drivable. However, the terminally-injured Citroen was blocking the roadway, and we were going to have to wait for her to get assistance. What if a call came in? What about the inpatients?

Kate quickly phoned James, who took in the situation with less than seasonal cheer. After lecturing Kate on how irresponsible she had been, he eventually agreed to go into the practice to check on the inpatients and make sure everything was all right. Twenty minutes later, having done just that, he phoned Kate to reassure her that all was well at work, and that the inpatients were fine. He was going home again, because there was 'nothing to do but cleaning work'.

We were, at that moment, sitting in the car, watching the recovery truck slowly extract the Citroen from the hedgerow. Kate, I noticed, was starting to develop the kind of jitter that I recognised well. She was an extremely conscientious nurse, and I could tell that she really wasn't going to be happy until she had checked on her patients herself. She was blaming herself for sending Laura home.

'It'll be fine,' I said,' they've all been checked, twice now. We'll be there soon.'

Kate nodded, but she was still unhappy, nervous, and twitchy. A few minutes after that, Kate's mobile rang again, with a phone number diverted from the practice's answering machine. Kate did something I had never seen anyone do before, which was to lean into her steering wheel and bite it hard out of sheer frustration.

'Mnnnnnngh!' she said. While I was deciding how best to approach this delicate situation without getting punched on the nose, she picked up her mobile phone and said politely: Beech House Veterinary Hospital emergency service, how may I help you?'

'Ah, hello,' I heard a nervous voice say on the other end of the line. 'It's Mrs Pierce.'

'Ah, Hello, Mrs Pierce,' Kate said, obviously desperately trying to work out who on Earth Mrs Pierce was.

'I'm just... I'm just phoning to see how little Bubbles is getting on.'

'Ah, Bubbles, yes...' Kate glanced over to me. I did my best to mime a guinea pig - no easy task, but something must have worked because comprehension dawned on Kate's face. 'Ahh, yes. He's fine, he's fine.'

'Oh, good, has he eaten something?' Mrs Pierce asked. Kate winced. James's description of the inpatients as 'fine' hadn't covered a lot of the fine details.

'Possibly a tiny amount,' Kate said, desperately bet-hedging.

'And has be pooed at all? David said that if he pooed today he should be able to come home.'

'Er... not quite yet,' Kate said. 'But he looks... well, fine.' We watched the Citroen finally get pulled free from the foliage. 'I'm just in the middle of something right now, Mrs Pierce, but if you want to come and visit him today, it shouldn't be a problem. Then we can ask the vet whether we should send him home or not. Could you ring me again in half an hour?'

'Okay,' said Mrs Pierce, sounding a little excited. 'I'll talk to you then.'

Kate dropped the phone onto her lap. Her face was pale.

'I lied,' she said. 'I lied to her.'

'Well, ' I said, 'Not really, I mean, Laura and James both checked.'

'That was half an hour ago. And about the eating.' She looked at me. 'We never lie to clients, not ever. That was crazy.'

She was clearly very upset, but I couldn't help feel she was overreacting to a little white lie. What harm could it do?

I was about to find out.

The Peugeot's steering seemed a little wonky, but ten minutes later, we were pulling into the car park in front of the practice.

'Well, at least we're finally ready for the next thing to go wrong,' I said, cheerfully. Kate gave me a look that made me grateful that it was all she did. We hurried through to the ward. Kate was anxious to check the inpatients herself before the owner of Rags, the cat with the fight wound, phoned up to check on him too.

Rags purred a hello and yowled in hunger. James's check-up had clearly been of a very cursory nature; it certainly hadn't included emptying Rag's litter tray or giving him any breakfast. I did so, while Kate checked Rags himself.

'Looking better,' she said examining the wound critically. 'Drying up nicely, eh boy? I think you'll be home for Christmas!'

Rags purred in response. 'At least that'll be one of us,' I said, filling up Rag's food bowl while Kate moved down the ward to check on Bubbles.

'Oh, I knew it! He hasn't eaten!' she said, looking into his cage. 'Why did I say he had? The plate of grass and dandelion leaves is untouched. We'd better syringe... feed....'

Her voice tailed off into silence as she opened the cage. I looked across at her. Her mouth had dropped open, and she was wrestling with the cage catch.

'Erm... everything okay?' I asked.

'Fuck fuck fuck,' Kate was saying as she flung the cage door open and reached inside.

'What, what is it?'

Kate looked across in horror. 'He's dead! Bubbles! He's bloody dead!'

I quickly slammed Rags's door. 'What? He just died?'

Kate extracted the small, sad body of a guinea pig from the cage. Its legs stuck out stiffly from its body.

'He's been dead for hours! Why the fuck didn't--'

Her phone began to ring. She picked it up in a daze, handing the dead guinea pig to me. I looked him over. Stiff as the proverbial; I could have knocked a nail in with him.

'Beech House Veterinary Hospital Emergency Service,' Kate said.

'Ah, hello dear,' said a familiar voice. 'It's Mrs Pierce here, I phoned earlier? I was hoping--'

'Mrs Pierce!' Kate blurted. 'I was just about to ring you.'

Mrs Pierce paused at the end of the line. 'Oh dear. Is everything all right? Is he... is he okay?'

Kate glanced at me, holding Mrs Pierce's deceased pet. She pressed her thumb over the microphone. 'What am I going to say?' she whispered urgently.

I thought quickly. 'Tell her... tell her he's taken a turn for the worse. That we think we might need to put him to sleep!' I said. Kate raised her eyebrows.

'More lies?'

'Got any better ideas?' I said.

Experience is not always a barrier to making a serious mistake.

Kate took a deep breath. 'He's... he taken a bit of a turn for the worse, I'm afraid, Mrs Pierce.'

'He's going to be okay, though, isn't he?' Mrs Pierce asked. Kate paused for just long enough for the question to answer itself.

'I don't think he is, Mrs Pierce.'

'Oh dear, oh dear. I don't want him to suffer, dear, please don't let him suffer.'

'I think it might be kinder to call it a day with Bubbles, Mrs Pierce. He really isn't looking very well right at the moment.' I looked down at my hands, and silently agreed with Kate.

'Do what you must, my dear,' Mrs Pierce said. 'I'd hate for him to be in pain.'

Kate sighed out of sheer relief. 'Of course, of course. We won't let him suffer.'

'I live just five minutes away, dear,' Mrs Pierce added. 'I'll be there as soon as I can, I'd like to be with him.'

The line went dead. Kate went white. We both looked at the small body in my hands. It was very stiff, and very cold, and very obviously hadn't died within the last five minutes.

'Oh shit!' Kate said. 'Shit shit shit! She's going to be here any minute! I bloody knew it! Why the bloody hell did I listen to you? Why did I lie? What are we going to do!'

'Come on,' I said, as I ran over and quickly set up an anaesthetic machine. We swiftly covered the table with ET tubes, masks, needles, the crash box, vials of adrenalin and other resuscitation equipment that would have made the makers of ER proud. We put Bubbles on the table, with his face in the mask. His legs stuck out like porcupine spines.

'It's no good,' Kate said, frantically. 'I'm just going to have to... I'll just have to tell her... God, I'll get struck off for this!'

'Screw it,' I said, defeated. 'I'm getting us a coffee.'

I walked into the kitchen, and the flipped the kettle on. My gaze fell upon the microwave in the corner of the room. I stopped. I thought. I looked out to the prep room, where I could see Bubbles's body on the table. I looked back at the microwave.

'No,' I muttered to myself. 'No no no.'

I found myself halfway to the prep room table. 'No no no,' I was still saying. Kate stood aghast.

'What are you doing?'

I picked up Bubbles and carried him back to the microwave.

'What are you...' Kate looked at me, too terrified to stop watching. I turned the dial to thirty seconds, opened the door, and placed Bubbles inside. Kate came and stood next to me at the microwave. I closed the door. I thought for a moment, then pressed 'DEFROST'. Then Kate and I looked at each other, and I pressed 'START'.

The doorbell rang.

A week later, Kate received a box of chocolates and a thank you card from Mrs Pierce. I learned a lesson that I should have known already: never, ever, under any circumstances, lie to your clients. If you think you had problems before, just wait and see what happens to you when you try to deceive the people who have placed their trust in you.

22 - Millennium Baby

Having a job where you work a lot of hours – particularly a lot of 'out of' hours – does mean that you tend to miss out on events that a lot of people take for granted. Some of you may remember the solar eclipse that passed over the south west of England in 1999 – in which case you remember it better than I did, because I spent the totality of the totality in theatre draining fluid from a cat's chest[45]. Many vets, and people with similar jobs, will be familiar with the routine of attempting to explain to families that you don't actually get much time off for Christmas, and that it's going to be hard to get home this year.

I was resigned to my likely fate of being on call as humanity transitioned from the second millennium since the birth of Christ into the third.[46] Sure enough, when the rota rolled around, my name was on the duty list for New Year's Eve, 1999.

Kate had some incredibly understanding friends who agreed to forego the usual festivities and actually come to up to Bridgford from Devon to spend it with us. I wasn't really in the mood, worrying as I was about the impending judgement from the Royal College, but Kate insisted it would take my mind off things. Quite what the attraction for her friends of spending time with a tense young vet on call and a tense young veterinary nurse worrying about her exams in January was, I don't know. It probably wasn't the opportunity to visit the 'toilet of the South West', as James liked to call it. I remain eternally grateful for their sacrifice, but as it turned out, I wouldn't be celebrating with them. In fact, I was going to see in the next thousand years with Becky, and a young Springer spaniel called Sprocket.

[45] The cat recovered nicely, so it was worth it in the end.

[46] Pedants: yes, technically, as there was no year '0', the millennium change didn't actually occur until New Year's Eve 2000... but as the whole dating system is rather arbitrary anyway (in that Christ definitely wasn't born when the calendar says he was), I think it's safe to say that it happened whenever everybody said it did – which was 1999.

At eleven p.m., as I sat around trying to look like I was enjoying myself whilst I watched the others drink, the phone rang. As ever when I was on call, I picked it up with the vertiginous mixed sense of panic about the call, and relief that the waiting was over.

'Am I coming in, Becks?'

'Afraid so, Alan. I've got a very agitated Springer for you.'

'I know how he feels.'

Except that I didn't. Fortunately, I've never felt anything remotely like how Sprocket felt that night. He had become restless around about an hour before his owners had phoned Becky. Initially, the owners had put it down to the fireworks that had already started bursting over Bridgford. After a while he had settled and gone back to sleep, only to wake up a few minutes later, very distressed, trembling all over and salivating profusely. Fortunately, one of them hadn't been drinking – it would have been a nightmare trying to get a taxi to the practice – and so Sprocket had been bundled into the car and was currently en route to Beech House.

As ever, I ran through the possibilities in my mind on the way to the practice. Top of the list was some form of epileptic seizure. Sprocket was a young dog and had had a number of trembling episodes before, albeit nothing like he was experiencing at the moment. Most seizures occur at rest, which is exactly what Sprocket had been doing prior to the current episode. A fit is not necessarily an emergency in itself, so long as it settles, but the owners were worried, and I didn't know for sure that was what was going on.

The hopes I had on my journey that Sprocket's trembling may have started to subside by the time he got to the practice were dashed as I pulled into the car park. Sprocket's owners – a young couple – had just arrived, and were leading their pet to the front of the practice. Even from a distance, I could see the froth around the poor dog's mouth, and the wide nervous eyes.

'We think he's getting worse,' the woman said to me as I rushed to the door, unlocking it and leading the family straight into my consulting room. Sprocket was indeed getting worse. The tremors were now so bad that he couldn't walk, and his eyes were starting to flick from side to side – nystagmus. A sign of abnormal brain activity. Sprocket was moments away from a full seizure.

'Diazepam,' I said to Becky as we lifted Sprocket onto my table. Becky, excellent nurse that she was, had already got some ready, just in case. I popped open the glass vial, using my tie to protect my fingers from the sharp edge[47], and drew up ten milligrams.

'What's happening? It's poison, isn't it?' the young man said. For some reason, owners frequently suspect poisoning whenever something acutely unexplained happens to their pet. I think, perhaps, it's easier to believe malicious neighbours than that something could have gone wrong internally to a valued pet with no obvious cause at all. That's not to say we never see cases of poisoning, but in my experience the suspicion of it far outweighs the incidence.

'Has he eaten anything unusual? Could he have got to anything outside? Do you use slug pellets?' I asked. Slug bait poisoning is the most common cause of toxicity-induced seizures in dogs.

'No, no,' the woman said. 'He's been with us all day, we didn't let him off the lead today because he was in the park and tends to run off.'

I clipped a small patch of fur over Sprocket's cephalic vein. 'Has he ever had anything like this before?'

Becky raised the vein as I poured surgical spirit over Sprocket's skin and attempted to hold his leg steady.

'Yes, yes,' the man said. 'About once a month. Only lasts for a few moments, though. We didn't think it was too much to worry about.'

I inserted the needle into Sprocket's leg and pulled back on the syringe, seeing the always-satisfying bloom of blood that

[47] I eventually stopped wearing ties after I lost too many of them to accidental dangling in anal gland fluid.

indicated I had hit the vein. I injected the diazepam. Almost immediately, Sprocket's trembling slowed... but it didn't stop. I waited. Thirty seconds later, Sprocket's tremors were as bad as ever. Thirty seconds after that, he was in a full-blown epileptiform seizure.

A brief digression on epilepsy: a seizure is, effectively, an electrical storm passing through the brain[48]. There's no co-ordinated activity, and no consciousness. The muscles fire off in a cacophony of randomness, like an orchestra trying to play after it's had all of its sheet music mischievously shuffled. The pathological process whereby this actually happens is not well understood, but any brain has within it the potential to seizure. Many things can set such a storm off: infections, liver disease, kidney disease, poisoning, diabetes, over-exercise, overheating, tumours and so on, but the most common reason we encounter in practice is *idiopathic[49]*. An animal that we call 'epileptic' is really an animal that has a lower threshold for, or is more prone to, epileptic seizures.

As mentioned before, a seizure usually isn't life threatening, and almost always abates within a few minutes.Almost. Sometimes, in process of coming out of a seizure, the patient can go into another one. And another one. And another. *Status epilepticus* is the medical condition of being caught in one, long, continuous seizure, and it rapidly becomes very serious   All that trembling and twitching of the muscles generates heat (which is why we shiver when we're cold) - and heat generated in such an uncontrolled manner quickly starts to overheat the body.

Not only that, the mere fact of the storm raging through the cerebrum starts, after a time, to injure the neurones. The heat and the electricity conspire to damage the brain so that when the animal that comes out of the seizure (if it ever does) is,

[48] And, of course, it's not exclusive to humans; any animal with a cerebral cortex can suffer from epilepsy.

[49] Medical terminology for 'we don't know what causes this'. A very useful word when you need to sound as if you know what you're talking about in a hurry.

unfortunately, not the animal that went into it.

This was my fear with Sprocket; he was starting to seizure even with intravenous diazepam. I needed to stop him fitting as soon as possible.

Explaining my worries to Sprocket's owners, I carried him out into the prep room while Becky got them to sign a consent form. We sent them home to try and enjoy their evening, while we got to work with Sprocket.

By the time I'd placed him on the prep room table, Sprocket had already been fitting for a couple of minutes. We placed an intravenous line and I took a blood sample to check Sprocket's blood glucose - normal. Sprocket wasn't diabetic, or fitting due to extreme exercise leading to glucose exhaustion. Coupled with his history, this suggested that Sprocket was a true idiopathic epileptic, and things were getting worse. My shoulder was soaked with saliva from where I had carried the young dog through to the prep room, and his trembling was now extreme, despite the extra ten milligrams of diazepam I had given Sprocket as soon we had the IV line in place in the prep room.

Our remaining option was one that would be familiar to IT technicians. We were going to anaesthetise Sprocket, and then very, very slowly wake him up, in the hope that the seizure wouldn't reappear; effectively, we were turning Sprocket off and on again. A hard reset[50].

In those days, the drug of choice for such emergencies was pentobarbitone solution, which causes a very deep and profound anaesthesia. It is, in fact, a very dilute version of the drug used in euthanasia, and so, naturally, you have to be pretty careful with the dose. It has been superseded nowadays by safer and more effective anaesthetics: one of the principle problems with pentobarbitone was that it was very effective at stopping the muscle tremors, but not wonderful at stopping that electrical storm. On New Year's

[50] And, writing this, it occurs to me there's a surprising number of medical conditions where we attempt to reboot from start: using immunosuppressive agents for autoimmune disease, or defibrillators in ventricular fibrillation, for instance.

Eve, 1999, though, it was all I had. I gave Sprocket his first dose - he'd been seizuring for seven or eight minutes now, due to the time it had taken me to place the catheter, check the bloods for other problems and see if another dose of diazepam had any effect.

The pentobarb worked very quickly. The muscle tremors began to subside almost immediately. Sprocket started to relax. I smiled at Becky. 'Well, that's a good start. Now we've got to wait and--'

'Alan,' Becky said, frowning. 'He's stopped breathing!'

I looked down at Sprocket's now-unconscious head, with the tongue protruding. The tongue had gone blue.

'Shit!' I said. My first thought was that we had induction apnoea - a temporary suspension of breathing due to the anaesthetic - but that didn't happen very often with pentobarb; at least, not at the dose we had given. Then I saw the puddle of drool around Sprocket's mouth. If there was that much coming out of the mouth... how much was left in the back of the throat?

The ABC of emergencies ran through my mind... Airway, Breathing, Circulation. What kind of an airway would you have with a mouth full of mucous?

Becky lifted Sprocket's head, and I opened his mouth. Thick, ropy saliva filled the whole back of his throat. Somehow he had been managing to breathe through it even while he was seizuring, but the moment I had anaesthetised him, he had relaxed, and the saliva had fallen back and blocked the throat. We tilted the table, to make the fluid run out of Sprocket's mouth, but nothing happened. Sprocket's tongue turned even bluer. The fluid was far too thick.

'Shit shit shit, ' I muttered. Becky remained silent. She was quite used to stressed vets. I asked her to lift Sprocket's head again. Holding the mouth open with one hand, I started to scoop out the slimy drool as quickly as I could.

'Come on, come on,' I muttered. It seemed like an endless task; for every handful I scooped out, another seemed to fill the throat. I wondered about giving Sprocket atropine - an anticholinergic drug that dries secretions (among other things) but I felt that it wouldn't get rid of the saliva that was already there, and that it would just waste time. I also wasn't sure how it would interact with the epilepsy, so I just kept scooping.

After what seemed like an age, the Sisyphean saliva-clearing finally rewarded me with a view of Sprocket's larynx. Becky passed me an endo-tracheal tube, and I managed to pass it into Sprocket's trachea. We lowered his head back to the table, and attached him to the anaesthetic circuit. Becky closed the valve on the circuit, and squeezed the bag, filling Spocket's lungs with oxygen.

Within a second, Sprocket's tongue was a healthy pink colour. I thought that it was the finest colour I had ever seen. Becky gave Sprocket another breath. And another. And then she didn't have to, because Sprocket was breathing by himself.

Somewhere during the crisis, we passed from one millennium to another. I may not have had the wildest party of 1999, but when, after six hours of being asleep, Sprocket woke up, looked at us groggily, and weakly wagged his tail, I thought that Becky and I could lay claim to having one of the happiest.

23 - Irresistible Farce

Kate closed the door and leaned against it, turning to me with a wicked smile.

'Well, we missed seeing in the next millennium last night. What are we going to do about that today?'

I had arrived back at her flat an hour or so before, just in time to say goodbye to her friends, who had to leave to spend the day with family.

'Well,' I said, 'We could head out for a greasy breakfast, maybe take a walk in the park?'

Kate rubbed her chin thoughtfully. 'Hm.' She advanced a step towards me. 'Or you could cook me breakfast, and we could spend the rest of the day in bed together.'

I had to admit this sounded like a better plan. Kate helped me out of my coat as I kissed her.

'Are we going to tell people at work?' I asked.

Kate shook her head. 'You know, I'm sick of my personal life being part of the practice bulletin. They can find out in their own time. Let's just enjoy ourselves for a while.'

It sounded perfect to me. I could still remember the expression on James's face when he had warned me off Kate. He hadn't looked as if he would take the news that we were sleeping together in good humour.

The first throes of a new relationship are exhilarating, crazy and timeless. They are also pretty exhausting, which may explain why I was dozing when the doorbell rang in the early afternoon.

'Whuh?' I said, raising my head. Kate, next to me, frowned, jumped up and peered out of the window. Her eyes went wide.

'Holy shit!' she said. 'It's James!'

I jumped up, suddenly wide awake, but I daren't look out of the window for fear of being spotted myself.

'James?' I said. 'What the hell does he want? Why would he be here?'

'I don't know,' Kate said, flustered. 'Why don't you go and ask him?'

The doorbell rang again.

'He knows I'm here,' she said. 'He's seen my car.'

'Don't answer it,' I said. 'Leave him down there.' Kate was getting out of bed and hurriedly pulling on the jeans and t-shirt that lay crumpled on the floor.

'He knows I'm in,' she said, muttering. 'My car's there. He'll think I'm avoiding him.'

'He's bloody right!' I said. 'Avoid him!'

Kate squeezed my hand. 'It's fine, I'll tell him I'm tired, got a hangover or something, I'll get rid of him.'

'But...' I said, but she was already closing the bedroom door behind her. I lay back, heart thumping around in my thorax, feeling like a rabbit caught in... well, in the wrong person's bed. From below I heard James's harsh, deep, Scottish vowels booming around the staircase leading up to Kate's flat, but I couldn't make out any words.

This is stupid, a voice inside me whispered dangerously. You've done nothing wrong. What are you afraid of? Get up, go out and tell him to piss off.

'Shut up!' I said aloud to the voice, almost worried that James might be able to hear it. James. James was what I was afraid of. He had terrified me that night in the pub, and if nothing else he had the ability to make mine and Kate's working lives total hell for as long as he wished. I got the feeling that James was a man who would wish it for quite a long time.

I suddenly felt very naked and exposed; this may, in part, have had something to do with the fact that I was actually naked. My own clothes, however, were in a heap in the living room and so there was nothing I could do about it at the moment. Not that it would matter, because any moment now, the front door would close behind James, and Kate would--

I heard the front door close. A second later, I heard James's voice again. It was getting closer. He was coming up the stairs! Why would he be coming up the stairs?

'--really wanted to talk to you,' James was saying as he reached the top of the landing and entered the flat. 'I mean, I hope it's convenient.'

'No problem,' Kate was saying as she marched him quickly past the bedroom door and into the kitchen. 'Cup of tea?'

Their voices faded into the background again as they entered the kitchen.

The kitchen. Adjoining the living room. The living room in which my clothes lay on the floor, inside-out and clearly not currently being worn by anyone.

Shit. Shit shit shit.

'Now's your chance,' the voice in my head began. 'Go out there and tell him what you think of--'

'And you can shut the bloody hell up as well,' I hissed, afraid that I actually might start listening to it if it kept that up.

James raised his voice. I made out the words '...still have feelings for you, Kate...'. Oh, this really wasn't going to end well, was it?

It occurred to me that I was only one door away from James discovering me cowering in Kate's bed. Because that's what I was doing, wasn't it? Cowering. Did I really want to be discovered cowering if James took it upon himself to fling open Kate's bedroom door?

I decided that I didn't.

I decided that if I was going to cower, I may as well do it in Kate's walk-in wardrobe instead. At least there would be less chance of discovery that way. I slipped out of the bed and clambered naked into the wardrobe, thinking as I did so that I really hadn't thought of myself as the sort of person who would have to hide from a jilted lover in a lady's wardrobe. Funny old thing, life.

I heard another door open from the direction of the kitchen. I heard James make a startled cry.

'What the hell--?' I heard him yell. 'Whose are these?'

Kate's reply was too quiet to hear but it apparently didn't do much to mollify a suddenly enraged orthopaedic surgeon. He must have found the clothes. Rapid footsteps sounded in the hall, closer and closer to the bedroom door. Suddenly, I heard the door fly open.

'Who's in here?' James yelled from the doorway. He paused. 'Alan?' he said, in a low voice that made my skin want to crawl off my body and find some safer place to hide. I heard him take a few steps into the room, and I listened to his breathing, ragged and rage-filled, for some of the longest seconds of my life.

What was I doing? This was pathetic. It was time to face my fear. I wasn't going to leave an angry James alone with Kate any longer. I took a slow, deep breath, and I slid open the wardrobe door, stepping out into the room in time to see James turning to face Kate as she yelled, 'What the hell do you think you're doing? Get out of my bedroom!'

'There's someone--' James said, slowly.

'There's no one! And it wouldn't be any business of yours if there was! Get out! OUT!' Kate dragged James out of the room and slammed the door behind him. I blinked. It was probably a good idea never to get on the wrong side of Kate. A few moments later I heard the front door slam, and soon afterwards Kate appeared at the doorway, flushed and panting.

'Wow,' I said. 'My hero.'

Kate sat down on the bed, flustered. 'I can't believe he came in here! The nerve of that bastard. Who does he think he is?'

I sat down next to her. She looked at me. 'And I can't believe you hid in the wardrobe! Who does that?' she grinned.

'Worked, didn't it?' I said, sheepishly. 'I was coming out, I wasn't going to leave you--'

'I know, I know,' Kate said, smiling. 'Well, seeing as how you've hidden in my wardrobe now, I'm pretty sure that means we're officially a couple now.'

I nodded. 'Yeah, that's one of the standard ways of telling, I think.'

'Well then,' Kate said, putting her arms around me. 'My first official act as girlfriend is to tell you that you're not going to that bloody interview, are you?'

I took a deep breath. 'I suppose not.'

'You're a good vet, Alan. Don't throw it all away because of a few mistakes. Those things are what make you better vets. I'm here to help you now.'

I smiled. 'You always were, Kate. Thank you. And I've learned that a vet isn't any use at all without a decent nurse.'

Kate thought about this, then winked. 'I'm not that decent, you know.'

We didn't make it out of the flat for the rest of the day.

There have been worse starts to a year. I had made it through the first six months as a veterinary surgeon. Kate had convinced me to stay at Beech House, and to stick with the job, wherever it lead me. She had convinced me, finally, that I was right for the job. Here's the question I would soon be asking, though: was the job right for me?

Part Two - Bridg too Far

1 - Animal Magic

It may seem trite and clichéd that a vet was set upon his career path by James Herriot; it certainly felt so to me when I said it during my interviews for the undergraduate BVSc degree course, but in my case it was literally true.

It didn't have to be this way. There's a number of different ways my life could have turned out. I am, as you may be gathering by this point, something of a geek[51] and it's entirely possible that I could have spent my working life cheerfully writing programs, debugging computers and drinking enormous amounts of carbonated beverages.

I am also fascinated by, and passionate about, science. I still remember my biology class where Mr Schofield showed us the way that muscles work – an intricate spiral of protein molecules forming and breaking millions of chains in fractions of a second, so perfectly aligned and controlled that I can sit here and press individual squares on a keyboard whilst words appear before me like magic (and the muscles are just the tip of the iceberg – what about the brain that is processing it?). Scripture has got a long way to go to beat any of that for me. I could have devoted my life to the peaceful study and petty political machinations of a university career.

So, what stopped me? Well, neither of the above would have involved animals[52], and I have always loved animals to a degree

---

[51] The definition of what a 'geek' is varies tremendously depending on who you ask. Two different definitions, for instance, could be 'someone who is passionately devoted to a particular (and probably eccentric) field of knowledge' or 'someone who has very strong opinions about who was the greatest captain of the Starship *Enterprise*, but who will happily spend several hours arguing about it'. Take your pick, because they both apply to me (and, if you're interested: Kirk, obviously).

[52] At least, not in a good way. I did look into studying neurophsyiolology – the study of how something as real and concrete as a person emerges from

that... well, let me tell you about something that happened to me, many years ago.

As a child, on the aforementioned expeditions across Germany and Switzerland, one of my great hobbies was attempting to catch grasshoppers. I found them absolutely fascinating, quite the most exotic creature I had ever encountered (I grew up in Manchester, where even rabbits were a rarity) and what's more, I found that if you crept through the grass *just like this*, with your hands held *just like this*, you stood a fair chance of grabbing one as it leaped away. I took to carrying a matchbox around with me, so I could pop my temporary prisoners in and run back to show my parents before magnanimously offering them freedom once again (the grasshoppers, not my parents; they were stuck with me). One day – I must have been about six or seven[53] - I'd grabbed a particularly impressive specimen and put him in my matchbox, swiftly sliding it closed in a well-practised manoeuvre. This time, something went wrong. My victim had sensibly decided that it didn't want to be placed in a cardboard coffin, and was attempting to jump out at the same time. The image of that sadly bisected grasshopper poking half-out of the matchbox is etched onto my brain. Its front legs twitched feebly as a tremendous wave of guilt and shock descended upon me. I had killed it. The poor thing was only out trying to live its life as best a grasshopper can, and I had caused its death for... for nothing.

I dropped the matchbox as if it was a hot coal and ran screaming and crying to my parents. Eventually they realised that, despite my reaction, I hadn't actually lost any limbs or been bitten on the foot by a cobra, and they slowly pieced the story together amidst blubbery sobs and penitent howls. My mum walked over to

a grey blancmange-like lump of neurones, but the quite horrible things that were done to octopuses as part of the degree course put me off for good.

[53] This is a complete guess; I'm dreadful at remembering what age things happened to me. Please mentally insert whatever age you feel makes me emerge from the anecdote in the best light.

the matchbox to assess the damage.

'Alan,' she called. I didn't want to look. How could she show me my cruel handiwork again? I stayed close by the reassuring presence of my dad.

'Alan,' she said again. I looked. She opened the matchbox. The intact grasshopper, freed from its uncomfortably wedged position between the cover and the tray, jumped happily away to freedom.

I couldn't believe it. Watching Lazarus rise from the dead could not have rivalled the joy of the miracle I saw on that day, and the fact that even now, sitting writing this, I can still almost taste the guilt and joy of that otherwise trivial experience probably tells you a lot about me.

Animals. It was always going to be something with animals. And so my Quest, marrying my two halves perfectly: to save the world, one animal at a time. What better way could there possibly be to do that than become a veterinary surgeon, someone for whom saving animal's lives was literally in the job description? Surely there could be no greater profession for me, or for my Quest.

In those bumpy first six months, I had been too busy worrying about whether I could do it at all to stop and think about whether it was actually the job that I thought it was. It was only after the millennium, when I got together with Kate and my life improved immeasurably, that I started to wonder just what it meant to be a veterinary surgeon.

2 - What's in a name?

One of my growing concerns was that being a veterinary surgeon wasn't necessarily grounded in science in the way I had hoped that it would be. I had grown up on stories of heroic scientists pouring over seismographs, oscilloscopes and spectrometers whilst they tackled alien invasions, giant insects and unspeakable horrors from other dimensions, I certainly considered myself a scientist too, and said as much to Sue one morning.

'Hm,' she had replied, thoughtfully. 'Well, I suppose there's an element of science to what we do.' An element! 'Listen,' she continued, 'at university, you learn the *science* of veterinary medicine, that's true. But here on the front lines,' she gestured to the consulting rooms, echoing David's words from months ago, 'that's where you learn the *art*.'

Sue was, as ever, right. I was quickly discovering that science goes out of the window when your job involves meeting other people. A small example: in five years at university, I never received lectures on how to call clients in from the waiting room - in fact, it hadn't even crossed my mind that there was something to learn about it. At Beech House, however, I found that every one of the vets had a different way of calling clients in. Each technique had its own advantages and disadvantages, and each revealed a little about that vet's approach to the job - their own artistry.

David, always paternalistic in his approach to clients, favoured the simple surname. He would head out into the waiting room, and call out 'Mitchell' (or whatever) to the expectant faces, whereupon the lucky chosen one would stand and smile, and be escorted into David's room. The technique was undeniably efficient, but (when I tried it at least) somewhat cold; it felt too much like reading the register at school. It fitted perfectly with David's approach to consultation, but it did little to put the client at ease, which was always my main aim. The 'register' technique could also come unstuck with the surnames of certain clients; it's hard to walk into a room filled with people and shout 'Fuchs' with a straight face[54]. Similar problems occurred with Cock, Uren and

Handaside-Dick.

James, when he couldn't find a nurse to send out to the waiting room to collect his client and thus save him the trouble, preferred the title-surname technique, or the 'modified register' approach, as I thought of it. He would walk out into the waiting room and call 'Mr Mitchell' to attract the attention of his current client. On the face of it, this seems a superior method; it feels more polite with a minimum of effort. However, trying it myself, I soon discovered why David had decided to ditch the title and go with the raw surname. The problem was that the client who had registered the animal may not be the person who was bringing the animal to the vets - a pet registered under 'Mr Mitchell' might well be brought in by Mrs Mitchell, or the couple's teenage daughter, or a friend of the family, and so on. There was no way of telling this from the computer list, which meant that you had to instead make a snap judgement of the person's title the moment that you laid eyes on them, which could be surprisingly difficult. It was embarrassing calling 'Mrs Mitchell' in front of fifteen strangers to have a middle-aged woman stand up, straighten her skirt and say, 'It's *Miss*, actually,' with a raised eyebrow, an annoyed expression, or (even worse) a suggestive purr. It was the very peak of embarrassment to call *'Mr* Mitchell' and have the same thing happen.

Cameron, chattier with the clients, but not totally informal, used the animal-plus-surname method: 'Tiddles Mitchell'. Again, on the face of it, this seems like a good solution, so I tried it myself for a time. However, I found that it often produced a strange response in clients. Some of them would look at me, frowning and mystified that I had described their animal in such an apparently bizarre way. Another common reaction was to start giggling, and look down at the pet, saying, 'See, Tiddles, he thinks you're one of the family!' Neither were disastrous problems, but experiencing such slightly confused looks thirty times a day began to get

---

[54] Well, it's hard for me; it always reminds me of an old Rowan Atkinson sketch... 'Mypric? Has anyone seen Mypric?'

wearing.

Sue's approach seemed like it would work best for me. It was the exact opposite of David's; she would stroll out and cheerfully call 'Tiddles'. It was, after all, the animal that was coming to see us. Clients liked it, and it fitted with the sort of style I was developing for myself. It wasn't without its problems, of course. Calling 'Honey' in a packed room, only to have a large hairy man glare at you while he picks up his cat box, can feel a little awkward. Nevertheless, this approach seemed to work best for me, the odd 'Peaches Fru Fru' notwithstanding, and I soon settled with it. Sue was right - these little touches were all part of the art of veterinary medicine, and had nothing to do with textbooks and blood samples. The waiting room was a stage, and I was a poor player strutting and fretting my hour upon it. A small taste of celebrity, and, I was soon to discover, not an especially welcome one.

3 - Z-List

Being a vet in a small town means (much like being a doctor, I suspect) that people start to recognise you: on the street, in restaurants, and in the supermarket. Particularly in the supermarket. To all intents and purposes, you become a very low grade celebrity. After a number of awkward trips to Tesco, I was starting to understand why celebrities hate it so much.

The most difficult part is that I stood out to clients more than they stood out to me. To them, I was the vet that they saw the other week, obviously. They knew my name, and what I did for a living. To me, suddenly accosted by a friendly smile in the frozen peas section, they were a vaguely familiar face that I was desperately trying to place.

I can remember so many awful encounters, nodding and smiling politely, searching my mental database in the hope that I would remember whether the owner I'm speaking to has a dog, or a cat, or a rabbit, asking appallingly generic questions in the hope that I'd get some clues: 'How are things?' or 'Everyone all right at home?'

Looming over every one of these cringeworthy conversations was the spectre of the possibility that I'd actually euthanised their pet, so that they no longer had a pet to inquire about. Eight months into the job, I had performed enough that they had, despite my attempts to resist it, started to blend together in my mind - so that even if I could remember that I had ended the life of a near-stranger's pet, I would be very hard pressed to remember exactly which animal it was.

The worst, though, was reserved for those clients that I *did* remember. There was one particular checkout lady in the local Tesco that fate frequently conspired to send me towards no matter how much I tried to avoid her. In the course of a fortnight, I had put three of this cheerful lady's hamsters to sleep, for unrelated reasons. By the third one, she had started to joke about whether we would reserve her a parking space, and if I would give a discount if she brought the next batch in together. Somehow, whenever I went to Tesco for my weekly shop, she always seemed to be the lady to check out my shopping. Every time she did, she'd smile at me, and cheerfully joke in a booming voice, 'I've not got any more hamsters for you to kill, yet, Alan!' or something equally inappropriate and mortifying when all I wanted to do was escape with my six-pack of toilet roll. One time I managed to pick a till with the blessed relief of a miserable-looking stranger working at the end of it, only for the shifts to change as I approached, and my jolly conspirator in hamster-murder to appear before me. Eventually I started driving fifteen miles to a different supermarket to avoid the social awkwardness of it all. I can only apologise to the Earth for the damage those extra miles did to our atmosphere.

The most awkward of all situations, the cringing crème de la crème, occurred after a euthanasia during one Friday evening surgery. I had put to sleep an elderly cat in kidney failure. The owner had been too distressed to attend, and so had sent her son, a broad-shouldered man in his early twenties, in her stead. The young man, though not uncaring, was very matter-of-fact about the situation. He stayed with the cat as I injected the anaesthetic (something that I always appreciated), thanked me, and took the now-deceased pet with him in its cat box, to be buried at home.

After work, I met Kate in the pub near the practice to unwind. I was just taking my first sip of lager when I heard a voice calling out across the packed drinking house.

'Hey, that's him! That's the one that killed my cat!'

I looked across and was horrified to see the young man from the consultation waving cheerfully at me across a room of frowning faces. On the table, next to his pint, was the cat box, still containing the dead cat. Inexplicably, on his way home from the vets, he had decided to take his ex-cat to the pub with him - maybe this was the Bridgford equivalent of a wake. As I tried to smile as politely as possible while my soul shrivelled, the man picked up the cat box and wiggled it for emphasis. All eyes in the pub were on the cat murderer. I slowly finished my pint, and we decided against eating.

Despite these minor setbacks, my life in the new millennium

was pretty good. Kate and I were going strong, and still managing to keep our relationship secret from the rest of the practice. James had his suspicions, but he didn't react any differently to either of us, in that he was just as surly and condescending as ever.

I still had a lot to learn about what it meant to be a veterinary surgeon, though. Some of those lessons were going to be a lot harder, and darker, than others.

4 - Dog #86324

I recall a drunken conversation, years ago, in a student bar at Bristol University. It's a conversation I'll be dragged into frequently in the future, but this is the first time. A trainee biochemist has discovered that I am learning to be a vet, and is now informing me at length how much money I am going to earn. 'Licence to print money,' he slurs, looking at my shoulder, 'it's a licence to print fucking money!'

Not quite understanding why he's getting angry, I try to say that I'm not so sure, that I don't think vets earn any more than teachers, but he brushes this aside with a wave of his hand.

'You, mate,' he says, finally focusing on me, and pointing a finger at my face, 'are going to make a killing.' He pauses for a moment, then concedes generously, 'A small killing.'

*

Eight months into my career at Beech House, I had decided to call in consultations using the animal's name; I thought it sounded friendlier. Dog #86324 doesn't have a name, only a number, so this time I just call out, 'dog warden?' and wait for someone to react.

At the end of the waiting room, a young woman sitting with a small, thin Staffordshire bull terrier looks up. The terrier sees me and starts wagging its tail. The woman smiles sadly, and stands up. My heart sinks, because this dog doesn't look at all aggressive to me.

I turn back to my consulting room as the woman walks towards me, and I wonder how long this is going to take. There has been a bank holiday at the start of the week, which means I have a busy day ahead. Consultations are, of course, fully booked, with a number of extras squeezed in. In the ward, a dog that I have seen this morning may or may not be bleeding into its abdomen from a ruptured spleen; tests are pending.

A very busy day.

Dog #86324 runs into my room, pulling on her lead, closely followed by the young woman, who closes the door behind her. I glance at the computer. Our consultations are colour coded: yellow for normal, blue for extra 'fit in', red for emergency. Dog #86324's consultation is dark grey. As I turn from my computer, the little dog jumps up at my legs, wagging her tail. I reach down to pat her, and she takes my whole hand into her mouth and sucks it, thoughtfully. I remove my hand and turn to the young woman, who is still trying to smile.

'Okay, what's the story with this little one?' I ask.

The young woman who works for the dog warden explains that Dog #86324 is a stray, brought in a few weeks ago. No owner has come forward. The dog warden in Bridgford normally has a no-destruction policy, but Dog #86324 has apparently been tested twice with other dogs, and has been deemed 'very aggressive'.

'I didn't see the tests myself,' the young woman says, as the terrier runs back and forth between the two of us, 'but I'm told they were pretty bad.'

I look down at the dog and hope that this is true. Because of these tests, Dog #86324 has been deemed unrehomable. Local animal charities can't take her in; they're already full with unwanted dogs that aren't aggressive. National staffy rescue charities are also completely full, and they have been for years.

The young woman places a form on the table. At the top is written Dog #86324's identification number, and her estimated age (no more than 18 months). Halfway down, there are a few notes on her behaviour. 'Care with other dogs!' one note says. 'Very mouthy.' I think of Dog #86324 sucking on my hand, and the fact that she walked obliviously past two other dogs in the waiting room on the way to see me. The young woman and I both agree it's a terrible shame. I turn back to my computer, and print off a euthanasia consent form.

We discuss the options; not of what we're going to do, but of how we're going to do it. We decide that sedating Dog #86324 first may be the best option. Sedation takes longer, and sometimes makes the animal feel a little sick, but the terrier is a bouncy little dog, and might get distressed with too much manual restraint. We don't know, of course. We barely know anything about Dog #86324. That isn't going to stop me, though.

I walk out into the prep room to draw up the sedation. It crosses my mind that I've been wondering about getting a dog. Maybe the aggression tests weren't accurate. I ponder this while I draw up the sedation, but I don't do anything about it, nor do I ask any of the nurses or support staff if they might be interested in another dog. We've all been asked the question before, and I know none of them are looking. Well, I think I know. It's a busy day. I don't want to bother people with difficult questions today.

Back in my consulting room, Dog #86324 is lying on her back, having her belly rubbed by the young woman who works for the dog warden. She jumps up, pleased to see me, and bounces over, taking my hand in her mouth again. Her teeth hurt a little, but not a lot. She doesn't mean it. It suddenly hits me, very hard and very raw, that in a few minutes this dog will be dead, and that I will have been the engine of its destruction. I want to run from the room, and hide downstairs, and get on with the business of saving lives, not taking them. I don't. There's a form on the table saying that I shouldn't. Instead, I ask the young woman to hold Dog #86324's head, while I inject the sedative into the scruff of her neck. The dog's tail stops wagging for a moment, and she looks at me almost reproachfully. Seconds later, my hand is in her mouth again, and the tail is back in action.

I ask the young woman if she'd like to leave Dog #86324 with us now. The woman shakes her head, clears her throat, and says that she would like to stay. She says she always stays. I want to hug her. While she lifts Dog #86324 onto the table, I walk out to reception to pick up my own form. On my way to the printer, Becky hands me the blood results for my critical inpatient. He has definitely lost a lot of blood somewhere. I'm going to have to scan the chest and abdomen to find out where. If we're lucky, it's the spleen, which can be safely (if messily) removed. I start thinking about my university notes on how to perform a splenectomy. It's a nice distraction.

Back in the room, the young woman and I each sign our respective forms; hers to acknowledge she gives consent for the humane destruction of Dog #86324, and mine to acknowledge to the dog warden that I have indeed put her to sleep. My signing is a little premature - Dog #86324 still has a few minutes to live - but it gives us something to do while the sedative starts to work.

I find that I can't stand to be in the room, making small talk whilst we wait. I escape, and begin to gather the materials I will need: some clippers, a swab soaked in surgical spirit, and ten millilitres of pentobarbitone solution. I tell Becky that I am going to need a hand with a PTS in a moment. She nods. She's seen the consultation on the list too. We all have.

I take a moment to run into the dog ward and check on my inpatient. His colour is much improved for the intravenous drip, and he's already quite a lot brighter. We have a little time. Hopefully the bleeding has stopped for the moment. While I am looking at him, my mind wanders back to my consulting room, and the inevitability that I have allowed to grow in my mind over what I am about to do. Just a few months ago, in a similar situation, I found a cat a new home rather than put it to sleep. That isn't going to happen today. I wonder if it had anything to do with the form from the dog warden. It occurs to me which way I would have probably reacted if I'd taken part in the infamous Milgram Experiments in the 50s.

It has been long enough. I head back up the stairs. Becky is waiting for me outside my consulting room door. I force a smile onto my face as I open the door carrying the clippers, the spirit, and the pentobarbitone-loaded syringe.

Dog #86324 is flat out on my table now, her third eyelids halfway across her eyes. As I enter, I try not to notice that her tail starts thumping from side to side again, weakly. The young woman looks up at me and sighs.

'This is Becky,' I say, comforting myself with my standard patter. 'She's just going to help me raise a vein on... er... her leg.' I falter a little because of the lack of name. Becky lifts Dog #86324 onto her front, and extends a small, thin forelimb towards me. The young woman tickles dog #86324's ears, not watching what I'm doing. I clip a small patch of fur over the forearm, and Becky twists her thumb around the crook of Dog #86324's elbow, raising her cephalic vein. Even with the sedative in her system, her vein is good. Of course it is. Dog #86324 is a healthy young dog.

I flex her wrist a couple of times, ostensibly to help raise the vein further, but there's really no need in this case. It's more of a ritual for me at this point. I take the needle cap off, rotate the bevel of the needle up so that the sharpest part will hit the skin first. I push the needle through the skin, and pull back on the syringe. A red flush in the blue liquid indicates that I have hit the vein first time, and there's at least some professional satisfaction to take as solace there. Becky releases the pressure, and I begin to inject the pentobarbitone.

Within a few seconds, Dog #86324 is unconscious as the general anaesthetic enteres her brain. I continue injecting. Dog #86324 gasps a number of times, and then her respiration, dulled by the overdose, stops. Her heart continues beating for a few more seconds but by the time I take the needle out of her leg, and place the stethoscope on her chest, it's already over. The young woman from the dog warden has started crying, softly, as we lower Dog #86324's head. I look at the small, thin body on the table, and wonder why I have just taken one life, and am about to attempt to save another. I try to remember taking my oath on the day that I graduated, when I spoke the words 'it will be my constant endeavour to ensure the welfare of animals under my care'.

Blessedly, I don't have time to think any more. There are already more people waiting to be seen. Within minutes, the heroic young woman who works for the dog warden, who always puts herself through this even though she doesn't have to, has gone, and Dog #86324 is being placed into a thick black plastic bag. I am consulting again, and thinking about how to perform a splenectomy.

I want to talk to Kate, to Becky, to anyone, to show that I am upset, even though how I feel makes no difference now to Dog #86324, who is as dead as she would be if I didn't care at all.

It strikes me that the drunken biochemist, years ago, was absolutely right.

Dog #86324. A small killing.

5 - Soul Searching

'Nothing you could have done, mate,' Cameron said, sitting opposite me in the Bridgford Arms - our standard venue for soul searching and woe-drowning. 'What else was there to do?'

I watched the bubbles rise to the top of my lager. 'I don't know. Try harder. I should have tried harder for her. I just let it happen.'

'What else was there to do?' Cameron repeated. 'What were you going to do, take her home?'

'Maybe,' I said.

'On the off-chance that she wasn't as aggressive as she was supposed to be, and Vienna got on with her,' Cameron said.

'It might have worked, though,' I insisted. 'If it was me, I'd want someone to fight for my life. Even if it had ended the same, I didn't try for her. I just did it.'

'You did what you could,' Cameron said.

'That's what you always say,' I said.

'That's because you're always bitching and beating yourself up, Alan,' Cameron said with a grin. 'You shouldn't take these things to heart. You can't. It's just... it's just part of the job.'

Cameron was right, of course. All of this was just part of the job. Maybe it was the job that was the problem.

It had seemed like a logical choice, veterinary medicine, a perfect match for the Quest, but it wasn't quite working out that way. I had learned that being a vet meant putting on a performance for the client. It meant being praised even when you made mistakes, and it meant being taken to the Royal College - whose judgement I was still awaiting - even when you didn't. Sometimes you tried your very hardest, and your patients died anyway. Sometimes you didn't try your hardest, and they died then, too.

Working as a vet in general practice meant being in the difficult position of making money out of pain and suffering; we were a business, after all. It meant that animals whose owners could afford better treatment got it, and animals that had no owners at all... well, their stories often ended in a different way. I had known all of this, of course, but in the aftermath of Dog #86324 - I had never learned her name, but I felt as if I would never forget that number - it felt very real.

The worst part was that even at the time, the case didn't have much impact upon me. It was only that night, waking at two am with a crushing feeling in my chest, that the knowledge that Dog #86324 wouldn't ever wake up again slid into my brain like a knife and kept me from the comforts of sleep. I longed to talk it over with Kate, but she was back in Devon visiting her parents, and Vienna, perching tensely at the bottom of the bed, was to comfort what George W. Bush was to diplomacy.

I had failed Dog #86324. Was this job really the job I wanted to be doing for the rest of my life? Every day I tried to go to work with the Quest in mind, and every day the mundane difficulties of the job squeezed those thoughts from my brain.

In the Bridgford Arms, Cameron said all the right things. Sue, David, James and him had shown me that there as many different ways of being a vet as there are vets. Maybe I could find a way that would work for me. I still had so much to learn, about the job, and about the clients.

Doubts aside, I was starting to feel more at home in my consulting room, but another aspect of the job was starting to challenge me: how to handle a clients that had a fundamentally different outlook on the world in general, and medicine in particular, than I did.

6 - T'aint Natural!

Squatting in the corner of my consulting room performing a rectal examination on a bouncy Labrador retriever was neither comfortable (for me or the lab) nor amenable to carrying out a conversation but, ever the professional, I did my best.

'I can't feel anything I'm worried about, Mrs Kane.'

Mrs Kane, a heavily made-up middle-aged woman, pursed her lips and frowned.

'Hm. Are you quite sure?'

'Absolutely, Mrs Kane, it all feels normal.'

I stood up, much to Bonnie the Labrador's relief. She immediately decided that, despite the indignities just perpetrated upon her, I was once again her new best friend, and she jumped excitedly at my legs to let me know while I removed my gloves and dropped them into the clinical waste bin.

'Could I ask, Mrs Kane, what symptoms made you worry that Bonnie had a problem in that area?'

'Symptoms?' Mrs Kane asked, puzzled.

'You said that you were worried that Bonnie had something wrong... up there,' I said, still smiling. 'What made you think that?'

'The horse whisperer,' Mrs Kane said.

I paused and considered this.

'Um...' I tried.

'I had my horse whisperer round last week,' Mrs Kane said. 'She's wonderful. She works magic.'

'On your horses?'

'Yes.'

'I see,' I said, not seeing. Bonnie jumped up at my legs until I gave in and cuddled her.

Mrs Kane frowned and continued. 'She told me that Bonnie had told my horse that she'd been uncomfortable recently. Bonnie thinks she has a pea-sized lump in her urethra.'

I looked down at Bonnie, who was now enthusiastically licking my hands. 'Bonnie... Bonnie told your horse?' Mrs Kane nodded. 'And then your horse told your horse whisperer?'

Mrs Kane nodded again. 'About her lump. I'm very surprised that you can't feel it.'

I tried to imagine the conversation that had allegedly occurred.

'All right, Dobbin?'

'Yeah, I'm all right, Bonnie. Lovely hay this year, I can't complain. How are you doing?'

'Well, Dobbin, as it happens...'

I studied Mrs Kane. She appeared to be perfectly serious.

'Well, good news!' I said. 'Nothing to feel, Bonnie's fine, aren't you, girl?'

Bonnie wagged her tail furiously in confirmation. Mrs Kane was not convinced. It was clear that she still believed the horse whisperer, rather than someone who had actually just felt the length of Bonnie's urethra.

'What did your horse whisperer recommend that you do, then?' I said, wondering if I might be able to work with Mrs Kane, rather than against her.

'She recommended that I bathe her Foo-foo twice a day; that should sort it out.[55]'

'In salty water?' I asked. I should have known better by this stage.

'Good heavens, no. She recommended that I use something natural! She gave me some there and then. Incredible stuff, it works wonders! That's probably why you can't feel the lump any more, I suspect.'

She didn't need to tell me anything more, because I could guess what was coming next; I had heard it a dozen times before. There was, it seemed, a substance on the Earth more precious than gold, and more magical than Harry Potter. If you or your pet had an injury, blemish, graze or scald, you merely had to apply it and all ills and pains would melt away. Tea Tree Oil. As well as Mrs

[55] A brief aside on the most common euphemisms I hear for pet's vulvas: front bottom, bits & pieces, Foo-foo, lady garden and, on one confused occasion, falafel. I've never really looked at Greek cuisine in the same way since.

Kane's mysterious horse whisperer, my clients had it recommended to them by friends, neighbours, and that nice lady in the health food shop who swore blind that it worked wonders on their irritable groin. It baffled me, because, as I had tried to explain to Bonnie's owner, science had already discovered such a miracle liquid: warm salty water. Pint of warm water, teaspoon full of salt, bit of cotton wool. Simple, effective, and a lot cheaper that tea tree oil.

The repeated praise I heard daily for the magical properties of tea tree oil began to bother me because, in my mind, it came to represent a larger issue. What was the reason behind the supposed majestic power of tea tree oil? Mrs Kane had already told me: it was because it was *natural*, that was why. And natural had to be good, hadn't it?

Except, what exactly was natural about tea tree oil? I couldn't remember the last time I had been walking through a forest only to be hit on the head by a bottle of tea tree oil shampoo falling from a ripe tea tree oil shampoo tree. Tea tree oil, like any other product, must be PRODUCED - extracted from the tree - via a commercial and highly mechanised industrial process. It was present in nature, true enough, but it was produced by a lot of machines, manpower and energy, and then put in a plastic bottle.

I had never understood the popular obsession with things being 'natural'. What exactly did that word mean? I heard the word so often that I ended up looking it up in my Oxford English Dictionary: *Existing in or derived from nature; not made or caused by humankind.*

It seemed that I had a different idea of what this meant than a lot of my clients. Here's what 'natural' meant to me: dying alone from septicaemia contracted from an infection you got from a thorn in the foot; watching your baby cubs be mangled to death by the new male lion who's muscled his way into your pride; or suffering from cramping diarrhoea and vomiting from taking tea tree oil internally, as it happens to be toxic.

'Natural' wasn't some mystical code-word for unlocking the secrets of the universe. It wasn't magical, or spiritual. It was horrible, because nature was horrible. The word natural might have conjured up an idyllic image of a picnic in a buttercup-strewn field on a summer's day, but I felt that you might have a different perspective if you tried spending the same in the same field as a field mouse. If you ended the day with some food in your belly and not dead, then you would be having a good day. Even then you'd probably get eaten by an owl overnight.

It was war out there. If, within a few hundred yards radius from where a natural food shop was, there weren't large numbers of creatures that were fearful, starving, killing or dying, then that natural food shop was probably sitting on Pluto.

My view was that nature meant pain, and death, and starvation. It necessarily followed from evolution - you're either the absolute best at extracting the necessary resources from your environment, or your dead. So the advice I wanted to give to clients, when they asked me if this natural remedy or that was any good, was this: please don't buy something because it's 'natural'. You may think your arnica cream is 'natural'[56], but so is getting your arm bitten off by a polar bear. Take your pills, and thank God for Western medicine. It wasn't perfect, but it was a bloody sight better than the alternative.

---

[56] It isn't.

7 - Red in Tooth and Claw

It wasn't only clients that I disagreed with from time to time. Of course, I had numerous fundamental differences with James in the way I thought that animals (and people) should be treated, but as time went on I started to discover areas where my views varied from my other colleagues, too. Wildlife, for example. David was passionate about wildlife work. He had co-written a textbook on the subject, and he did a tremendous amount of work for the local wild animal sanctuary, rehabilitating those unfortunates that had fallen by the wayside. He devoted a lot of his free time to his cause, and when he was away (often at wildlife conferences), the other vets, including myself, would visit the sanctuary instead, tending to hedgehogs, foxes, badgers, mice, and birds by the dozen. The people who worked there were incredibly compassionate, caring, and dedicated. They would feel the loss of every animal acutely, and they were, all in all, a wonderful group of human beings. I think that David hoped that I would follow him in his fascination and love for wildlife medicine.

I couldn't, though. I have already hinted at why. My attitude to 'the wild' mirrored that of the German filmmaker Werner Herzog[57]: it is terrifying, full of death, pain, hunger and horrors. When I saw creatures brought in from 'the wild', I didn't think of them as fluffy, cute animals. They were wounded soldiers. They had been on the front line. It was war out there for them - a literal life and death struggle every single day of their lives.

Several months into the job, I was talking to an acquaintance of mine who had only just discovered that I was a vet. This acquaintance had found a wounded sparrow in the garden, attacked by a neighbourhood cat. It was very small and weak. She and her daughter decided to take the sparrow in, and put it in the sink of their bathroom. They gave it a little water, trying to help it recover. It was too ill to drink; it was too ill to do anything. The

---

[57] As espoused in the excellent documentary about Timothy Treadwell, *Grizzly Man.*

sparrow died after a day or so.

When I asked her why they had not taken the sparrow to their local vets, just up the road, she said, 'I was worried that they would put it to sleep.'

Stop and consider that for the moment. Stop and think about what that sparrow experienced from the moment it was injured, until the moment it died. Put yourself in that sparrow's position.

I'm spelling this out because, if I had been the vet on duty in that practice, then my friend's worst fears would have been confirmed. I would, absolutely, have put the sparrow to sleep. What's more, I would have done it for about ninety percent of the wildlife ever brought to me. And if you can explain to me why doing that is worse than what that poor sparrow went through in my acquaintance's sink, then you have a different view of morals and ethics than I have.

The wildlife animals that were brought to me were not pets. They didn't behave like pets. They were scared of humans. They were scared of confinement. They were scared of everything in the world, because everything in the world was trying to kill them, directly or indirectly. If I saw, for instance, a blackbird that had been attacked by a cat, I had a few choices. One was to say, 'Let's just see how it goes overnight,' give it a few jabs, and not worry about it until the morning. The other was to put it to sleep straight away. One of these choices was immediately very tempting for me, because (despite what you might believe after reading the above few paragraphs) I didn't actually enjoying killing things. In fact, it would be fair to say that I bloody hated doing it.

That wouldn't stop me making the second choice, however. The overnight option was much easier, nicer for all concerned, and when I came in the next morning to find the blackbird has died overnight, then I could say 'Ah, well, I tried.'

Except that I couldn't do that. All I would be thinking about, all night, was that blackbird, alone in a cage. Terrified and dying. What kind of a night did it have? Any better than the sparrow in the sink?

What about the ones that wouldn't have died overnight?

Well, firstly, it's fewer than you might think. I didn't always adopt this attitude, you see. In my first few months, spurred on by David, I tried my best with the patients brought in to me from the wild. I had my fair share of nocturnal deaths. It's not a good feeling.

Secondly, as I saw it, these were soldiers. I was patching them up to get back in the fight. If I couldn't guarantee that this bird or mouse wasn't at the absolute top of its game when I released it, then I was condemning that animal to die, either at the hands of a predator, or from starvation.

A lucky few of these wounded warriors - some hedgehogs at the animal sanctuary, for instance - would be adopted by people, and become their pets. That was fine. If they were never going back to war again, then I did all I could to help them. Some species also seem to cope better with captivity than others - the aforementioned hedgehogs, for instance. But they were the exception, not the rule. And so I euthanised most of them. I felt sorry, but I didn't feel ashamed, because it was the right thing to do.

I was starting to develop as a vet, even if my worries about the job were growing. Then, one morning in the early spring, an envelope arrived at the practice with my name and professional registration number printed upon it.

It was from the Royal College of Veterinary Surgeons.

8 - Professional Misconduct

I thought about leaving the letter until I got home, but the idea of working the whole day at the practice without knowing whether the Royal College considered me fit to be a vet seemed more than I could bear. I tore open the envelope and pulled out the three sheets of paper.

'Dear Mr Reece'

Good start, I hoped. Friendly.

'RE: MR AND MRS JACKSON

Further to my letter from last year, I write to confirm that two senior members of the Preliminary Investigation Committee have now carefully considered Mr and Mrs Jackson's complaint.'

That chilled my blood. Two senior members, poring over their notes to see why a certain Mr Reece dared to call himself a veterinary surgeon.

'The Case Examiners found no indication of serious professional misconduct and accordingly the matter will now be closed.

For your information I enclose a copy of the letter we have sent to Mrs Jackson which sets out the reason for this decision.

Thank you for your cooperation and patience while the matter has been investigated.'

And that was it. No indication of serious professional misconduct. Off the hook. I felt that I had done everything I could to help Khan, and the Royal College agreed.

None of this helped Khan, though. I had no sense of victory, just a quiet relief that it was over.

I turned the page. Attached to my letter was a copy of the one that somewhere in Bridgford was presumably currently being opened by Mr and Mrs Jackson. It outlined, in brief, clinical language, why the college felt that I had done all that could have been reasonably expected to do at the time I saw Khan. It stated that there was nothing to challenge my fitness to practise veterinary surgery, and that there was no basis upon which a complaint could be pursued. It thanked the Jacksons for bringing the case to the attention of the Royal College. Finally, it offered sincerest sympathies for the Jackson's loss of Khan.

I put the letter down, and thought about the Jackson's reading through the letter. I wondered how I would feel in their position, having lost their companion having done everything right themselves, and receiving this letter telling them that I had done everything right as well.

The letter was worded carefully, and professionally - the only way it could be. If I had lost my dog in the way the Jackson's lost theirs, I didn't feel that it would offer me any comfort at all. I didn't think that I would believe a word of it. I wanted to ring them, to tell them how sorry I was that they had lost their friend, but I couldn't see how that could help.

Still, there it was - a resolution. Like everything in my veterinary life, it felt messy, and unsatisfying, but at least it was over. Kate, when I showed her the letter, was over the moon and wanted to celebrate, but she was working the night shift so it would have to be postponed until the weekend; that was fine by me. It didn't feel right celebrating. Maybe a quiet night in was the best medicine for me anyway. Maybe.

I managed to put dark thoughts to the back of my mind for the rest of the day. Nothing died, and that much was well with the world. I travelled home and sank into the sofa, opening a can of lager. I had started drinking at home a few weeks after starting the job. It had felt like a bit of a reward, a way to distinguish nights on call - where I couldn't drink at all - from all the other nights. It was a habit I hadn't quite shaken even though my relationship with Kate was going pretty well. No harm in it, anyway. Just one drink.

I was hunting for the remote control when an angry knock came from the front door. I could tell it was angry because the door shook under its power, and it was repeated twice before I had even got up from the sofa.

Who on earth would knock angrily? Kate would just let herself in, and she was stuck in the practice all night. Could it be the Jacksons? Had they tracked me down, desperate for something more than the clinical letter from the Royal College had given them?

It crossed my mind to turn the light off and pretend that I wasn't at home, but I suddenly felt very weary of running away from my problems. I stood up, and took the few brief paces to the front door. If it was the Jacksons come to beat me up, at least it might make me feel a little better about the whole thing afterwards.

I turned the lock, and swung the door open. Standing there, hand raised to batter the door once more, was an angry bespectacled Scottish surgeon.

'James!' I said, unnecessarily.

His cheeks were flushed red and he was breathing heavily as he looked at me.

'You got away with it then,' he said, in a worryingly quiet voice. 'At least someone thinks you're fit to practice.'

I opened my mouth, wondering if this was really happening. Could I have fallen asleep on the sofa?

James leaned across the threshold and whispered through gritted teeth, 'They're wrong.'

Terrified as I was, I was also tired, depressed, and not at all in the mood for James's craziness.

'What the fuck do you want, James? Have you really driven round here just to tell me that?'

James blinked. He used swear words like weapons, the harsh syllables shocking his prey into submission. He wasn't used to me turning them back against him.

He looked to one side of the door. 'I know you were there,' he muttered quietly.

'Where?' I asked. 'What the hell are you talking about?'

'The bedroom!' he said. 'New Year's Day! You were there, hiding somewhere, weren't you, you little rat!'

It was my turn to blink. James's face was so blotchy and red with fury that he looked like a human lava lamp.

'I saw your car,' James said. 'Do you think I'm a moron?'

'No,' I said, slowly. 'I don't think you're a moron. I think you're completely fucking crazy.'

'You were there! Admit it! I want to hear it!'

'Yes,' I said, heart racing, 'I was there! And so what?'

'I knew it! You fucking little rat, after I told you--'

James took a step into the entrance hall, hands curling up into fists, face twisted into a snarl. It looked like I was going to get beaten up after all. I hadn't been in a fight since primary school. James raised a fist, and I raised one in return. Suddenly, he began to make a peculiar screeching noise, a weird haunting yowl like a cat that has caught a mouse. I stopped in confusion, only to see that James had too, and suddenly I realised that the noise wasn't coming from James at all.

Vienna leapt out of the kitchen and straight onto James's face, a hissing black ball of wrath with legs and teeth flashing. James wailed in distress, trying to grab her, while she hissed and snarled and showed him exactly what she thought of him. James flailed backwards, tripping over the doorstep and falling onto his back. The impact with the ground shook Vienna loose, and she ran back to the house. James kicked her hard as she ran back into the house and she cried in pain. I was incensed. Vienna was a psychopath, but she was *my* psychopath. She ran up the stairs to the bedroom, apparently uninjured - unlike James, who lay dazed and bleeding from half a dozen scratches to his face just outside the door.

I looked down at him as he hunted for his glasses.

'Goodnight James,' I said cheerfully, feeling immensely happier than I had just a few minutes before. I closed the door and sat back down on the sofa. There were no more knocks on my door that night.

*

'Oh my God!' Kate said, mouth half-full of scrambled egg. I had driven round to her place first thing in the morning to cook her breakfast. 'He actually came to the house?'

I nodded. 'No problem. I fought him off.'

'You said Vienna jumped on his face!'

'I fought him off by proxy,' I conceded.

'Bloody hell, what a lunatic! What do you think he'll do now?'

I shrugged. 'Don't know. His pride was hurt as well as his face, but I think he'll just go into professional mode and pretend nothing happened.'

'That would be nice. Still, working with him is going to get even more uncomfortable, isn't it?'

I scratched my chin. 'I'm not sure that's possible.'

Kate paused, playing with a piece of toast. 'Alan,' she said, 'I want to move on.'

My face suddenly felt numb. 'Ah. Oh. Hm. I see. I... er... it wasn't... I mean, I didn't think that... I mean, I understand, but I--'

Kate frowned as I stammered, then grinned. 'Not from you, turnip brain! The breakfast isn't that bad. I mean the job, this place. I want to move on from Bridgford. I want to move south, closer to my parents in Devon.'

I didn't know whether to be relieved or depressed. A distance relationship?

She stopped, and looked at me. 'You want to come with me?'

I thought about James. I thought about Dog #86324, and about the puppy. I thought about the way Bridgford's weird chemical smell seemed to collect in my nose first thing in the morning, and I thought about the letter in my pocket from the Royal College. I thought about the Quest. It hadn't worked here. Maybe I could find the answers that I was looking for somewhere else.

I nodded. 'Let's start looking,' I said.

9 - Cabin Fever

Summer rolled over Bridgford like a blob-creature in a fifties B-movie, and the air once again thickened with plastic-factory fumes. All across the south west, Veterinary practice managers were opening envelopes containing Kate's CV for their consideration. Once the decision was made, I was inpatient to move on - James was behaving more obnoxiously than ever - but we needed to wait and find a job that suited Kate. Once we did, I would try to get locum jobs near her while searching for a new job of my own. In the mean time, my plan was to build up as much experience as possible at Beech House - although hopefully not in the way Oscar Wilde used the word - to prepare me for the wider veterinary world.

My first anniversary at Beech House brought with it a pay rise, and a new responsibility: occasional forays to the practice's mobile surgery in a village on the edge of the Cotswold Hills. 'Mobile' was something of a misnomer for the surgery - it was a large portacabin set in concrete and it would have taken the Hulk to move it anywhere[58]. Long before my time, when David was first setting up Beech House, the 'mobile' had been exactly that: a caravan filled with veterinary supplies that David drove around the various local villages. Many years ago, the caravan had burned to the ground in a mysterious accident that I never quite got to the bottom of[59] and so was replaced with the less-than-mobile cabin, but the name had stuck.

The mobile surgery ran intermittently throughout the week and on Saturday mornings, and it was an 'open' surgery; that is, no appointments were necessary. Clients turned up in the hour or half-hour slot that it was open, and the vet saw them one after another until they were all gone. Because we were on our own at

---

[58] Or a crane, I suppose. It's possible that I read too many comics.

[59] Although I like to think it was razed to the ground by Viking marauders (see my previous footnote).

the mobile, David and Sue left it a year before new graduates were sent to work there - although they actually sent me a few months earlier than usual.

Apprehensive about my first sole-charge, I found to my surprise that I actually rather enjoyed working in that dusty old cabin. The nature of it - the unpredictability of the appointments; the intermittent power supply which meant that I had to write my notes in a logbook rather than use a computer; the fact that no matter how well-stocked the shelves were, there was always something that I couldn't find or had forgotten to bring[60] - along with the spectacular backdrop of the Cotswolds combined to make the whole experience feel a lot closer to the Herriot books that had inspired me into the profession in the first place. I took pride in the fact that I never finished a mobile surgery late, no matter how many clients turned up or what cases were thrown at me - although much of the stress was reduced by knowing that if anything needing hospitalisation arrived on my doorstep, I would be sending them on their way to the main practice in Bridgford.

It wasn't all joy and laughter, of course. The mobile presented its own difficulties, and required learning new skills - such as one-handed blood sampling (friendly animal required). It also meant that I had to bill clients there and then, instead of happily sending them out to reception. Like most vets I knew (with one obvious exception), I was embarrassed and uncomfortable asking people for money despite the fact that I had just provided them with a service. At the mobile, there was a far greater proportion of the type of client that bristled at the first mention of payment, usually stating indignantly that they had 'known David for years, and he always sends me an invoice*/gives me three-months credit*/lets me buy him drinks at the golf club in payment*'[61] – excuses which would invariably lead to David rolling his eyes and sighing when I

[60] Vaccines, thermometer, stethoscope, and on one unfortunate occasion, rubber gloves, which instantly guaranteed that the next three consults I saw were all for anal gland emptying

[61] * Delete as applicable

trustingly repeated them to him on my return to Beech House.

The set-up of the mobile - one waiting room and one consulting room - also created problems. One Saturday morning, my very first task was to euthanise an elderly cat in kidney failure. Despite being hampered by the lack of nurse, and having to resort to the one-handed vein hitting technique, the procedure went smoothly. However, the cat had been so ill that the client had carried her in rather than bring her in a cat basket, and they wanted her body taken back to the practice to be picked up for cremation. After the client left, I looked at the cat on the table and realised that, this time, the thing I had forgotten to bring was a cat basket. The waiting room was starting to fill up and echo with the happy laughs of children who had come along with their rabbit to see it get vaccinated, and I couldn't help but feel that me strolling through with a dead cat in my arms on the way to depositing it in the boot of my car would spoil their trip to the vets. The dead cat spent the rest of the hour lying at the bottom of the only cupboard in the cramped consulting room - the cupboard that also contained the drugs, syringes and needles. By the end of what felt like a very long surgery, a trickle of cat pee had started to leak out of the cupboard and collect in a very obvious yellow puddle below it, steadily growing despite all my efforts to will it not to. Hopefully, any clients that noticed it merely blamed it on the lack of toilet facilities at the cabin and far too much coffee being drunk on my part.

Despite hiccups along these lines, working at the mobile made me feel more like a proper veterinary surgeon, as if I was in one of the stories I had read as a child. However, it seemed ironic that I found it enjoyable precisely because of its 'Herriot-ness', because the other facet of my job that remained close to Herriot's experiences filled me with dread.

House visits.

10 - Visiting Hours

Boil a small animal vet's job down into its basic components and you're left with three parts - the elementary particles of veterinary life: consultations, operations, and visits. Dreaded visits.

The problem with a house visit, first and foremost, was that I was out of my comfort zone. In the practice, I could always extract the animal from the owner, and pop it out the back for a quick second opinion from Cameron or Sue. At the mobile, I could send complicated cases back to the main surgery at Beech House. Not possible on a house visit. On top of this, the surroundings were different. Even though I had only been a vet for a year, I was becoming a creature of habit, and something as simple as consulting in a room different to the one I usually consulted in created enough cognitive dissonance to put me off my game for a few minutes. I found the mobile practice easy to get used to; it was my own space, even for only half an hour. In someone else's living room, it was harder to find the zone - the sweet spot where my veterinary notes were all present and correct in my head, and I was able to concentrate entirely on the case in front of me; not impossible, but harder.

Another problem: finding the place. People in Somerset lived in the craziest places - on top of hills, beside rivers, squeezed into the tiniest possible gaps on housing estates. They also pick the bizarrest name for their homes - why settle for '4' when 'The Azaleas' or 'Piffingsworth' will do? Why, indeed, unless you want anyone to actually find the place.

Coupled with many people's complete inability to give directions to their own home, this meant I often had problems before I'd even pressed the doorbell. This wasn't so bad if I was only heading out to clip a puppy's claws, but after a few visits I discovered a hitherto unknown physical law, which stated that the later the hour and the more urgent the call, the harder the client's house would be to find. I remember dozens of stressful middle-of-the-night calls attempting to drive with an A-Z on my lap, swearing at the car, the map, my legs and life in general (of course, now everybody has satellite navigation systems, so complaining about this makes me sound like someone moaning that there has been no good music made since 1994[62], but satnavs are neither infallible nor particularly good at calming you down when you're stressed so the problem still periodically raises its head[63]).

Successfully tracking down the evasive location usually led to the next problem, which was, and there's no polite way to put this, people. It probably isn't news to you that while the vast majority of humanity can be caring, compassionate, big-hearted, generous, grateful and charitable, it can also be, along with these laudable characteristics, just plain weird; and if they're weird when they're in the bank or doing their shopping, then that weirdness increases dramatically when they are safely back in their houses, away from the judging eyes of the rest of mankind.

This was, in part, the comfort zone problem all over again: I was away from my safe consulting room where I knew where the thermometer and hand wash was, and in a place where I didn't know what the sticky patch on the floor was, or what that peculiar smell was, or just *who* that person was standing at the back of the room, silently staring at me and wearing only a towel.

As well as people who were a little... well, different, I also encountered a number of people who were just plain unpleasant. I was personally threatened a couple of times on visits in Bridgford; on both occasions I had been called out to put an animal to sleep, and arrived to discover that some members of the family violently disagreed with that decision - emphasis on the violent. Sadly, in both cases it was the members of the family with the largest fists and the shortest tempers.

That last point touches upon another problem with house visits; what I was actually going out there to do. In most situations, people would bring their animals in to the practice, and visits

---

[62] But seriously, have you heard what they're listening to nowadays?

[63] I can't be the only one for whom the phrase, 'Turn around where possible' makes me want to cry.

usually only happened when people were housebound with no way of getting in to see us, or if the pet had such a stressful personality that it got in too much of a panic on the trip to the surgery. This often meant that the animals I was visiting were more skittish and sometimes more aggressive than those I normally encountered in the practice, and I would be going to see them with less manpower (usually just one vet, or one vet and a nurse). I was invading their home territory to boot. Not really a recipe for fun for owner, vet or pet.

The exception to this general rule was, of course, when it was the last visit the animal would ever receive. Some people chose to have their animals put to sleep at home, in familiar surroundings, avoiding the stress of being taken in to the practice, and the long, lonely minutes in the waiting room, surrounded by people whose world isn't falling apart. Absolutely understandable, but it did mean that a high proportion of my home visits were euthanasia visits.

Not long after I started working at the mobile, I received a call to visit an elderly woman who lived in a large house in a seaside village to put her Great Dane to sleep. It was a Sunday afternoon, which meant that it was just me, no nurses. The dog was *in extremis* due to heart failure, which meant that the procedure itself went smoothly, and the old lady was very grateful for his peaceful end, but then we were faced with something of a problem - although I am, of course, incredibly manly and strong, I couldn't lift an eighty-kilogram dog by myself. The old woman was almost bent in two with back problems, but she didn't seem too worried.

'Just a second,' she said, brightly. She opened the front door and hobbled out to a man who happened to be passing by. 'Excuse me,' she said. 'Could we just have a hand lifting something?' The kind stranger agreed, and it was only when he walked into the living room that he realised exactly what the 'something' was. His eyes met mine. I smiled apologetically, which seemed inadequate given the circumstances. He took it in his stride, though, only looking aghast for a few seconds before he helped me carry the dog. Magnanimously, I took the back end, and together we hoisted it into the back of my car, and he went on his way. I often wonder what he told his family and friends about that day.

A few months later, I received a call from a man asking me to visit him to put his canary to sleep. It was, of course, a Sunday afternoon again, and I was extremely busy, so I asked if there was any way he might be able to bring it in to the practice.

'I can't get near him,' he said, sounding nervous.

'Er...right. Is he somewhere you can't get to?' I asked, thinking it might have flown up into his loft or something similar.

'No, no, he's outside the front door, tied up, but he won't let me get past him. I can't even get to the car!'

The mental image of a massive bird, with wide-staring eyes and saliva-dripping from its beak, viciously pecking anyone who dared to step near it confused me enough that it took me several minutes to understand that the man was actually talking about a *presa canary* - an enormous mastiff-type dog several rungs higher than the Hound of the Baskervilles on the 'vicious bastard' ladder, and about as far from a tiny gentle yellow bird as it is possible to get. It turned out he'd bought it from his mate down the pub, and now it wouldn't let him leave the house. In the end we had to enlist the services of a vet with a blowgun, who darted it into unconsciousness so that the deed could be done.

Despite all these drawbacks, house visits were not without their perks. Firstly, they got me out of the mania of the practice for a little while, and it was always nice to have a breather. Secondly (and most importantly), it gave me a chance to be nosey - the same kind of nosey as peeking into people's living rooms as you walk past[64]. This interest, I think, stems from the nagging feeling a lot of us have that *we* are the weird ones; that there's something not quite normal about our own households, and that other people do it differently. Properly. Well, we're right. After an extensive study of other households over the years, I can reassure you all that you're right: you're weird. Everyone is. Weird is actually the normal state of affairs.

---

[64] Which, I thought, was the main reason that Kate rode horses - you can get a far better look inside someone's living room from higher up.

It's the normal ones that you've got to watch out for.

*

Meanwhile, seventy miles to the south of Bridgford, a practice in Cornwall had interviewed Kate, and offered her the position of Deputy Head Nurse that same day. Our days in the conveniently situated toilet were finally numbered. I would try to learn all I could before I left in all aspects of the job.

Well, all aspects except one.

11- Snakes... why did it have to be snakes?

I clicked on the next consult. 'Freddy'. What was wrong with Freddy, then? The brief description next to the consultation didn't give much away: 'unwell'. It could be anything from a cat-bite abscess to a... hang on! Freddy's details had appeared on my screen. He wasn't a cat, as I had for some reason assumed.

Freddy was a grass snake. My blood ran cold. [65]

'Oh pissing heck,' I muttered. I hurried out of my door to find Cameron leaning back against the pharmacy counter, reading the latest copy of the *Veterinary Times*.

'Hey, Cameron, I just need to go the toilet, maybe you could-_'

'No way,' said Cameron without looking up.

'What?'

'I saw that owl last night, didn't I? And that crested dragon thing or whatever it was the other day - sounded like something out of Lord of the Rings, anyway. It's your turn.'

'Aw, come on. I didn't even know it was a snake until I clicked on it.'

'Well then consider this a learning experience, my young apprentice,' Cameron said, pretending to be riveted by the article he was reading.

'I'll do the next three anal glands,' I said, desperately.

Cameron looked up and considered this for a moment. 'Hm,' he said. 'Five.'

I sighed. 'Okay, okay. Five! Done.'

Cameron raised an eyebrow as he considered the offer. 'Nah, you know what. It's not worth it.' He turned a page. 'Bloody hate exotics,' he muttered.

I turned slowly back to my consulting room, condemned. There was no escaping it now. A snake. An 'exotic'.

You see, doctors have one species to deal with. It's an odd species, I'll grant you, and tends to talk your ear off before getting

[65] Which was ironic, now I think about it.

to the point of exactly what is wrong with it, plus it has a tendency to mislead or just plain lie to you about what its symptoms are, but it's still only one species. All the others on the planet[66] are the domain of the veterinary surgeon - everything from aardvarks to zebras; at least, in theory. In practice, of course, it doesn't quite work like that. Back in Herriot's day, every vet in general practice saw everything that was thrown at them, from pets to farm animals, but that was changing by the early millennium. At Beech House, though I was in theory a mixed-practice vet, I spent almost all of my day job dealing with dogs and cats, but I was occasionally catapulted, blinking and surprised, onto a farm in the middle of the night. A lot of vets that graduated since my time have never set foot on a farm since they packed their wellies away after their final year viva.

This is not a bad thing. It means that the vets get more experienced and specialised in their particular field, and as a customer, you're likely to get better service. I was growing more confident and comfortable in my consulting room. Even for the cases I hadn't encountered before, I knew enough to go back to the first principles of veterinary medicine and work things out from scratch. Until, that is, an *exotic* entered the room.

Now, in the average person's mind, the word exotic may conjure a vision of cocktails, palm trees and hula skirts, but for vets it is a vague term for anything that they don't frequently encounter. Years before I graduated, the phrase had included rabbits, but by the time I entered practice, rabbits were increasingly house pets and edging closer to dogs as Britain's second favourite pet (after cats). At one time the 'small furries' - mice, rats, ferrets and so on could just about have been considered under the term, even though 'exotic' seems a very strange adjective to apply to a gerbil. Here's what we really meant by 'exotic' when I was in practice: feathers or scales. I suppose a carapace would do it too, as well as whatever an amphibian is covered with (which might give you some idea of the extent of my amphibian knowledge).

[66] It's a difficult thing to estimate, but somewhere over eight million.

It's not that we were afraid of them as animals (well, I wasn't; Kate had a different opinion on the matter. She saw *The Birds* at an impressionable age). I was fortunate, considering my job, not to have a phobia about any animals at all. If you took me to the top of the Eiffel Tower, I would scream and cower, shaking on the floor like Scooby Doo, but I wasn't scared of critters, just clueless.

Here was the problem: reptiles and birds are *very* different creatures to mammals. That's why they're in a whole different class (I mean this in the taxoniomical sense, though you can take that sentence any way you like and probably still get the right idea). Let's take a look at birds to make the point.

I don't know what it is about birds. I mean, they are fascinating creatures - they can fly, for heaven's sake! An animal adapted to doing what mankind could only, until the last century, dream about. They are the evolutionary successors of dinosaurs. What's not to like? But, for some reason, they just don't float my boat. I can't find myself excited by, or even especially interested in, birds. I don't actively dislike them, because I don't actively dislike any animal[67] but they simply don't do it for me. I'd watch an elephant troupe trekking across the savannah for hours, but I'd rapidly get bored watching a fish eagle hunt for its food. I can't explain why. Perhaps I just have difficulty relating to them, because they really are very different to mammals. Here's a few examples to give an insight into a tiny fraction of the differences that caused the assistants at Beech House so many prep-room arguments:

First (and foremost) - outward signs of disease, or lack thereof. Birds are really not good at looking ill, at least until they are so ill that they don't really have any choice. The practical upshot of this is that if a bird is taken to their local vet, they are normally very ill indeed. In the case of budgies, they are often so ill that merely the act of clinically examining them can be enough to cause them to squawk off their mortal coil; an unfortunate experience for both vet and budgie.

Second: diagnostics. Birds have a vastly different anatomical

[67] Except wasps. Bastards.

and physiological set-up than mammals; although they do have lungs, they are tiny and don't expand, and the principle means of air flow is via air sacs. They don't have a stomach, instead they have a crop[68], a proventriculus and a gizzard. They don't have external genitalia[69]; checking the sex of a bird usually involves an anaesthetic and a laparoscope.[70] They have a 'renal portal system', which means that anything you inject into the back legs ends up passing straight through the kidneys at much higher concentration than you would expect in another species.

It was hard, not experienced in looking at birds, to even know the difference between normal and pathological. Was that poo supposed to look like that? Are the eyes usually that colour? Does that air sac sound rough? The problem was compounded by the lack of interest in teaching about the exotic species at university. My lectures on birds were almost entirely about chickens, and the vast majority of them focused on the fifteen different types of ventilation systems used for housed birds, as well as what lighting protocol you should follow to pump as many eggs as possible out of them. Consequently, my notes on avian medicine consisted largely of unhelpful tips like 'If there's something wrong with the birds, sacrifice one and send it for post mortem to find out what it is': unlikely to go down well in a consulting room.

Thirdly: metabolism. Birds have a faster metabolism than mammals, and if I tried to use my drugs at a normal dose scaled down, I'd probably be underdosing. Add to this that almost no medicines were licensed for use in birds, and that different sources recommended different doses, plus the simple difficulty for an owner to get medicines into them, and I was still having problems even if I did manage to work out what was wrong with them.

[68] Well, some of them do.

[69] Well, most of them don't.

[70] Except for budgies which have nicely colour-coded ceres (the fleshy bit just above the beak) - blue for boys and pink for girls, satisfyingly. Actually, it's more brown than pink for girls, but let's not spoil it.

With reptiles, things only got harder. They are creatures that shed their skin, that only eat every third day or less, that don't bother with the trouble of keeping warm, just letting the environment do the job for them (which made me wonder quite what a tortoise's opinion of living in Britain in mid-January was). Also... how can I put this delicately? The average reptile owner was, and I'm only saying generally, not perhaps the most well-to-do member of society. Because I was a typical vet - i.e. a very poor businessman - I always cringed when I had to point out that people have to pay for our services, because we were a business. The sad truth of the matter is that reptile owners often couldn't afford any tests or diagnostic aids that might have helped me work out what was going wrong, and certainly couldn't afford to be referred to a specialist reptile vet.

The best approach to exotics work was, I quickly discovered, to be unashamedly honest with the owners when they brought in their bearded dragons. 'I don't claim to be a reptile specialist,' I'd say, 'but I'm happy to have a look!' I also made no bones about the fact that I was 'going to have a look in my exotics manual to see if it's got anything about this'. It might have made me look a bit dumb, but I'd rather the owner knew where they stood than try and pretend I was some sort of lizard wizard.

According to my trusty manual, the grass snake had stomatitis (an infection in the gum tissue, relatively easy to clear with antibiotics and antiseptic washes). I had made it through another exotic consultation.

Visits, the mobile surgery and exotic consultations were rounding out my experiences in the veterinary world, and almost before I knew it, it was time to step out into that wider world.

I hoped that somewhere out there I would find the answers to my many questions about the job.

12 - Water Under The Bridg

David shook my hand and smiled. For a moment the smile made me wonder if I was doing the right thing, but I knew that it was time. Kate had already started her job as deputy head nurse, down in Cornwall, and after just over a year at Beech House I knew that I needed a change if I was going to have any chance of resolving my turmoil with the job.

Beech House had been good to me - a great practice, with high standards of clinical care. David had succeeded in what he had set out to do when he started the place. I learned a lot of good habits at Beech House, as well as some hard lessons. Now, the wild world was calling me.

In thirteen months I knew that I had grown as a vet. I had surprised myself that I could actually do the job at all. David and Sue told me that they would be very sorry to see me go. I was sorry to leave too - they had been extremely supportive over that first year, and if I had any skills in veterinary medicine at all, I largely had those two to thank for it. In my first few weeks at Beech House, while attempting to scan a bouncy Staffordshire bull terrier, I had dropped the new and very expensive microchip scanner. The staffy, enjoying the game, had pounced upon it and kicked it into the wall, whereupon the tired LCD screen gave up the ghost and shattered. Feeling extremely low, I carried the now-deceased scanner up to David and humbly apologised. He nodded, and frowned, and sent me on my way. Today, as I handed my notice in, he told me that it was the first time in twenty years that he could remember anyone owning up for any of their mistakes in that way. He told me I was the most honest vet he had worked with, and that I should keep hold of that through my career. I thanked him, a little bemused, but determined to stick to his advice. I thought about the new vets that I was going to be working with, and about the people I was leaving behind.

David had been an excellent first role model. His paternalistic approach to clients may have been different to my more interactive relationship, but he was a great logical thinker, and a deeply caring, moral man. More than anyone else in the practice, David helped me understand that vets made mistakes, and that so long as they were honest, and learned from them, it wasn't the all-encompassing disaster that it felt like when it happened.

I was going to miss Sue a lot - her filthy jokes and filthier laugh cheered me through many evening surgeries that we worked together, and she was probably the most skilled medic I have ever worked with in my career. She was as compassionate a person I have ever met, and if she was the vet for my own animals, I'd consider myself a happy man.

I was also very sorry to be leaving Cameron. He had been a beacon of reassurance and confidence when I had neither of those things. If I asked him about a case, he might not know any more about it than me, but he would talk it through, and make me feel like there must be a solution; everything had a solution. Cameron was the living embodiment of the adage that there were no problems, only opportunities.

I was going to miss Becky and the other nurses a great deal. They had been my friends when I felt I had none, and helped to remind me that I was still a normal human being, despite the crazy career I had chosen. We had worked many nights together; they had seen me at my worst, and, just occasionally, at my best.

And James. James was a hard person for me to understand. He approached veterinary medicine from an attitude of total professionalism. He was extremely concerned to be up to date with the research, and the papers, and the evidence; extremely laudable traits, except that there never seemed much room in his worldview for the patients themselves. Rather than listening to what his clients wanted, he bullied them into doing what he wanted them to do. He did this because he always knew that his way was the right way, and he had the evidence to prove it. I have always favoured a more pragmatic approach - laying out the options for the clients, explaining what would be medically best, then discussing what they wanted for their own pet, and finding the best compromise in the middle. He was more interested in one client that would spend £1000 on their pet, than twenty that could only afford £50 – I was of exactly the opposite opinion. James's approach was arrogant, condescending and lacking in compassion, both for the pets and the clients. Then again, I suspect James felt that I was lazy, slapdash, a poor earner for the business, and allowed the clients to dictate the way I handled my cases.

One evening, towards the end of my notice period, I was agonising about whether I should have it out with James once and for all. Would it help? Would it diffuse the tension between us if I explained my point of view? We had barely spoken since his retreat from Vienna on my doorstep. Would I sleep better at night if I told him exactly what I thought of him? It wasn't just his behaviour about Kate. I wanted to confront about our fundamental differences in the way we viewed veterinary medicine.

With these thoughts whirring in my head, I stepped out of my consulting room to get an injection from the prep room shelf, and I heard a noise from James's room. Turning, I could see that his door was open. A dead dog was lying on his table; a Springer spaniel that he had just put to sleep. The dog's owners had left, and James was standing in the middle of the otherwise empty room, with his back to me. He had one hand on the dog's chest, and another over his face. His shoulders were shaking.

It struck me then that, whatever our differences, James and I were just trying to get through the day however we could. Although we had different takes on it, we both wanted to do the best job possible, for our clients, and for the animals. James was an extremely competent surgeon, and, in his way, he cared. He was overbearing and imperious, but he was also, more often than not, right. I was about to head out into a new world, and I was about to encounter many more vets. Some vets wouldn't care at all; vets that were purely motivated by money, or were lethally incompetent. Although I didn't know it, I had been spoiled at Beech House. I watched James, silently crying for a lost patient, and I couldn't find it in my heart to accuse him of anything. We all had our own Quests. I wanted to get back to mine, back to the reason I had wanted to do this job in the first place. The Quest had been hard in my first year.

It was only going to get harder.

13 - Land's End

Closing the door behind me, I walked down the short path and jumped out of the way of next door's violent Newfoundland dog for thankfully the last time. Vienna was perched on the front seat, boxed and yowling. My possessions[71] filled the boot and the rest of the back seat. I drove back to the practice, dropped the keys off, said my goodbyes, hugged my hugs, and headed south, away from Bridgford.

The car I was driving was Kate's old Peugeot; she had donated it to me for the journey, while I investigated getting a car of my own. Her new practice was in Newquay, somewhere in the middle of Cornwall, and she had rented a cottage that she said would have been characterful and quaint had it not been positioned directly on the main road.[72] However, it was at least twice the size of my home in Bridgford and the hot water tank worked, so it was quite an upgrade for me.

When I told people that I was moving to Cornwall, they smiled and said 'Oh, you lucky devil!', or 'Beautiful! Such amazing beaches!'. Everyone agreed that it was a lovely part of the world to be living and working; which is why it came as something of a surprise that it was, being blunt, a shithole.

Driving down the A-road (there are, of course, no motorways in Cornwall) with Vienna singing angrily next to me, my heart was full of excitement and possibility. I hadn't secured a full-time job yet, but a number of practices in the area had expressed interest in my doing some locum work for them. I was looking forward to the change. Cornwall was waiting for me. Anything could happen!

An hour and a half later I was driving through Newquay with a sinking feeling. I had just spent several hours on the road driving past spectacular windswept moors, the sea twinkling invitingly

[71] Except for my prized enormous telly, which had been sent on ahead - possibly with a police escort.

[72] And I do mean 'directly' - the front door opened right onto the road, with no pavement.

through the grey drizzle. I had now arrived in a small characterless town, full of litter, hotels, B&Bs and an atmosphere of bleak desperation. It appeared, in fact, very much like a malign deity had scooped up Bridgford as soon as I had left it, hurriedly carried it over my head as I drove, and plonked it down (none too carefully) on the coast in time for my arrival.

A little deflated, but unbowed, I parked the Peugeot in the road, and quickly unloaded the car. Vienna immediately disappeared upstairs (presumably in search of the most expensive thing she could find to piss on). Kate was at work, but Beattie, her greyhound, was overjoyed to see me. Over a quick cup of tea, I decided the best way to get Cornwall to win me over was to take the doggy for a walk of one of its famous beaches, the nearest of which, according to my trusty OS map, was just a few minutes' drive away (or a twenty minute walk up the main road, which didn't sound quite as appealing).

'Let's go and see these amazing beaches, then, shall we?' I said to Beattie, who wagged her tail in excited agreement. A few minutes later we were pulling into a grimy car park behind an industrial estate. I peered through the drizzle for the way to the beach. Eventually I saw a narrow, overgrown path between two six-feet high wire mesh fences. A small wooden sign above it had once proclaimed 'To the beach', but since then someone had helpfully spray-painted over it with the words 'Dog Shit Alley'. I looked down the path. The unknown annotator had not been exaggerating. Making sure I had an ample supply of poo bags for my own dog, and carefully watching my step, I headed down the path to the sea.

*

I suspect the problem with Cornwall was that Kate and I just had the misfortune to see some of the worst parts of it. First impressions are important. So are second and third. Kate was keen to impress her new employers, and was working so much that it was hard to get out and enjoy the surroundings for what they were;

a similar problem we'd encountered with Bridgford and the nearby spectacular Cotswold hills.

Kate's new job was friendly but very different to Beech House; there was no need for her to be on-site all the time, as the practice wasn't a veterinary hospital, but this did mean she occasionally got called out to assist the vets with large-animal work. I did my best to smooth the transition with her as much as I could; this mostly involved me making sure that the cottage was well-stocked with wine when she returned. Her constant worry was that, as she was working in a mixed practice, she would one night get called out to help minister to a pig - creatures which she had been terrified of ever since she had actually encountered some at Langford veterinary college and realised that they weren't small cute pink things that said 'oink', but enormous flesh-coloured animals that *screamed*[73].

On top of all the usual worries a new job brings, Kate had communication problems to deal with: she often took calls from farms deep in the Cornish wilds, where the accents were as thick as concrete porridge, and just as difficult to penetrate. One memorable night I accompanied her on a visit to help the vet look at a sick goat on a rickety old farm - the vet had asked the farmer to phone for assistance. She stepped out of the car, shook the farmer's hand and asked where the goat was. The farmer, stubble-chinned and flat-capped, frowned.

'Goats? Ain't no goats. They be gilts! Pigs!'

From the sanctuary of the car I struggled to keep a straight face as I watched Kate's face turn paler than a milk tanker. My straight face remained very much intact when she introduced me as a veterinary nursing student who was going to perform the

---

[73] Personally, I really like pigs - they're also very intelligent animals; which makes the way they are treated in modern farming (especially on the continent where they are very slow to take up the new welfare requirement) even more of a crime. Not that intelligence is a prerequisite for suffering; chickens aren't bright by any standards but they don't deserve the horrors of battery farms - but I'm creeping onto a different topic. See the appendix for some of my thoughts on animal welfare issues.

procedure for her. Thank you, Kate.

Home life was good, though. Living together seemed like a natural step for us. James and Beech House felt like a long way away, and we were sickeningly in love. Beattie and I became quite familiar with Dog Shit Alley and the local supermarket suddenly found that it was selling quite a bit more wine than it had been doing.

Meanwhile, I had secured a short locum position in a practice in the nearby inland town of St. Trewin. Locuming is the supply-teaching of the veterinary world; part-time jobs filling in for sick days, maternity leave, nervous breakdowns and other unexpected absences. The pay is much better that an average veterinary job[74], but you generally needed your own car and accommodation - both of which I was temporarily sponging off Kate.

I was excited and nervous - I had learned a lot at Beech House, but I had never worked anywhere else. Any hopes I had harboured that Newquay was a one-off centre of horribleness in Cornwall were dashed as I drove into St. Trewin; it was, at least, a two-off. St. Trewin was easily as grey, dark and unpleasant as Newquay, without the added attraction of being on the seaside (turd-lined alleyways to get there notwithstanding).

I was locuming for a relatively small practice, Daisy Hills. Beech House had been custom-built as a veterinary surgery, but my new workplace had been converted from (what else?) a hotel. this gave it a certain charm, but also presented practical difficulties; the x-ray suite[75] was adjacent to reception. This meant that anything that had been x-rayed and subsequently needed surgery would have to be carried unconscious through the waiting room, which hardly looked professional. James would have had a fit, never mind our old health and safety officer. The consulting rooms were scattered throughout the building, seemingly at random, and it wasn't uncommon to be interrupted mid-bitch spay by clients

---

[74] Back then, it was about £125/day, in Cornwall at least.

[75] Okay, room. It was a room.

who had been seen by another vet, and were now lost in the maze, trying to find their way back out of the practice again.

All the staff - vets, nurses and receptionists - were lovely, but were characterised by a kind of Blitz-spirit Keep-Calm-and-Carry-On attitude, which was world's away from the (in retrospect) proud professionalism of Beech House. The owner of the practice was John: tall, dark-haired, very friendly, and probably the least organised man I have ever encountered in my life. He was forever setting off on farm visits, only to return to the practice ten minutes later to pick up a forgotten mobile phone, surgical kit, veterinary nurse, or medicine box. On the rare occasions that he remembered everything he needed, he turned up at the wrong farm. The farmers, used to this sort of thing, smiled and sent him on his way to the right place. How he ever managed to turn up to his final exams and qualify, I would never know.

Despite this, he was a very popular and competent vet. In fact, he seemed to thrive on the chaos and the sense of near-crisis that pervaded the practice. All the surgeries throughout the day were 'open' surgeries, just as they had been for the mobile surgery at Beech House. There, it had seemed quaint and slightly exciting; here, it only added to the sense of panic. Working there, for me, felt like skating on very thin ice, wearing red-hot ice skates.

Here's how surgeries worked at Daisy Hills: client's notes - handwritten - were laid out on the side in reception in order of them turning up. When it was time for your next appointment, you headed out to the waiting room, grabbed the top set of notes, and read the name on the top of the card, whereupon a relieved-looking owner would stand up from the cramped waiting room and follow you through to the consulting room. There usually followed an awkward pause while you tried to decipher what had been written on the notes last time so that you could work out what was going on. This was particularly difficult if John had been the last person to examine the animal; his handwriting looked as if it had been in a head-on collision. Assuming you managed to understand anything (I found it easier, eventually, just to get the client to fill me in on the story), you would carry out the consult, work your way through the Byzantine twisting-corridors to the dispensary, grab whatever drugs were necessary, send the client out to fend for themselves in the maze of twisty little passages, and, mindful of the ever-growing crowd in the waiting room, scribble down your notes as quickly as possible - something you would always regret the next time you came to see the client and would reflect sadly upon your own indecipherable scrawl. Then you would do it again, and again, until the waiting room was finally, blessedly empty.

It was a tense atmosphere at Daisy Hills. I was going to write 'organised chaos', but I would struggle to justify the word 'organised'. The place always felt just five minutes away from utter, disastrous collapse, but it never came; at least, not while I was working there. The head nurse, Sharon, who doubled as the practice manager and so was the person who had hired me, had the twitchy, nervous look of an air-raid warden expecting the Luftwaffe at any moment. I think that John must have shaved five years off her life with his laissez-faire attitude to punctuality and planning.

Consulting at Daisy Hills was my first opportunity to meet the people of Cornwall. What was I saying about first impressions?

14 - Steamed Rice

One of my very first consults at Daisy Hills was with a small, furtive man, who shuffled his collie into my room as if he was smuggling contraband across the border. The collie, as it entered, was obviously significantly lame on its right hind leg, but I had learned not to make too many assumptions about owner's reasons for bringing animals in.

'What can we do for Olive today, Mr. Rice?' I asked, looking at the card. Apart from the owner's name and address, the card was blank. Mr. Rice hadn't been to Daisy Hills before.

Mr. Rice looked at me witheringly. "Is leg,' he said, in the kind of tone that suggested that any moron could see that Olive had leg trouble.

'I see,' I said, smiling and swallowing my pride, and kneeling beside Olive, who wagged her tail. At least someone was pleased to see me. 'And how long has Olive been lame for?'

The man glanced sideways around the room, as if to make sure no-one else was listening.

'Couple o' days.'

'Right,' I said, moving behind Olive to try to feel her leg. 'And how long... could you hold her at the front for me, please?'

Olive had immediately turned round in an attempt to lick my face. The man gave me one of his looks again. Obviously a competent vet would be able to examine Olive without her even noticing them. I continued smiling. It was going to be one of those consults, was it?

'Olive, c'mere,' the man said, tapping his thigh. Olive ignored him, far more interested in the nice man in the green coat. 'Olive,' the man growled, 'c'mere!'. Olive glanced at him, then back to me, tail swishing.

'I think you might have to hold her, Mr Rice,' I suggested as politely as I could. I took the opportunity to have a quick check of Olive's mucous membrane colour, eyes, ears and teeth while she was looking at me (all of which were normal), and so I didn't have to look at the man's withering gaze again. Finally tiring of gazing at me, the man eventually took hold of Olive's head. Able, finally, to feel my way down the leg in question, I immediately noticed a small swelling on the medial aspect of Olive's knee: medial buttress. A sure-fire sign that the knee joint is inflamed. The rest of the leg felt normal, so I grasped the end of femur in my left hand, and the top of the tibea in my right, and moved my right hand forward and backward. Olive gave a very slight whimper, and I thought I could feel a little bit of movement. The leg isn't supposed to move in such a way; the cruciate ligaments prevent it[76]. The fact that it could suggested one of the ligaments - usually the cranial cruciate ligament - was ruptured; a relatively common injury in older dogs due to the fact that the ligament degenerates with age.[77]

'I think her cruciate ligament may have been injured, Mr. Rice,' I said.

'Hn,' replied Mr. Rice, looking me up and down. 'Wassat?'

'It's a ligament in the knee that can get thinner and weaker over time, so it becomes relatively easy to rupture. I'm not one hundred percent sure but if that's what she's got, she might need surgery on the knee to repair it.'

Mr. Rice stood up, and let Olive go, who started sniffing her way excitedly (and three-leggedly) around the consulting room. He eyeballed me with suspicion.

'Surgery, eh?'

'I'm afraid so. You can try and manage it with rest and painkillers, but it's often not eff--'

'Not hunnerd percent sure, eh? How d'you get sure, then?'

'Well, the best way would be to sedate Olive, so that I can feel the leg with the muscles relaxed. If it's not obvious from there, I might need to take an x-ray.'

The man nodded, knowingly, if this is what he had expected

---

[76] So called because they are aligned in a cross-shape within the knee joint.

[77] Only in dogs - to be a human and rupture a cruciate you have to something very dramatic; you're usually attached to a snowboard when you're doing it.

all along. He looked at me for a long time, his eyes slightly narrowed. I got the uncomfortable feeling that he was deciding whether it would be a quicker end to the consultation to just slip a knife between my ribs. Eventually, he rubbed a rough hand across the patchwork stubble on his chin, and broke into an entirely unreassuring grin.

'Al'ight, vet'ry, take yer x-ray.' His grin widened, and he reached down to ruffle Olive's ears, who wagged her tail. 'Not'in's too good for 'er, unnerstan'?'

I thought I did, so I nodded, and smiled. I headed off to reception to pick up a consent form for the sedative. Mr. Rice signed it, disturbingly cheerful now, and I picked up Olive's lead as he reached for the door. With his hand on the handle, he turned to look into my eyes, and said:

'You take bloody good care of 'er, vet'ry. Ye foller?'

I assured Mr. Rice we would look after as if she was one of our own pets. He nodded, curtly, smiled at the dog, and then slipped out of the door.

A few hours later, another endless Daisy Hills open morning surgery finally finished, I was injecting sedative into Olive's vein. She licked my nose once, then stuck her tongue out, and dropped her head. Laura, one of the nurses, and I lifted her on to the table in the prep room. I picked up her right hind leg, and grasped it as I had before. The knee was very loose: the cruciate had definitely gone. We took an x-ray to make sure there was no other damage - fortunately there wasn't. John walked past as I was peering at the radiograph on the viewer.

'What's that?' he said. 'Cruciate?'

'Looks like it,' I said. 'Do you repair cruciates here?' The procedure was beyond the scope of my surgical skills, but it was relatively common for more experienced vets with an interest in orthopaedics.

'Yes,' John nodded, looking at the x-ray. 'I'll get on with it now, if you like, save waking her up again.' He patted the unconscious Olive on the table.

'Aren't you off to TB test somewhere?' I asked. John

shrugged, feeling Olive's hind leg. I wasn't sure if this meant he didn't know or he didn't care, but it certainly seemed like a nicer idea than waking Olive up for surgery on another day.

'Okay,' I said, 'I'll ring the owner, see if he wants to do that.'

John nodded, and wandered upstairs. I grabbed the consent form, and headed upstairs to the phone. While I was dialling the number on the form, I saw John's car driving up the main road.

'Where's he going?' I asked Sharon.

'TB testing, Quayle's Farm,' she said. 'Why, did you want him?'

I sighed. 'No,' I said, 'doesn't matter. Haven't spoken to the owner yet.'

The number on the consent form was for a mobile phone, but wherever he was, Mr. Rice didn't pick it up. I tried again with no success. I tried a third time. This last time I could have sworn I heard breathing before the line went dead. I headed back downstairs.

'Better wake her up, Lara, I can't get through to Mr. Rice, and John seems to have... y'know.'

Lara nodded. She knew; she'd worked with John for several years by now. I gave Olive an injection of a painkiller, and carried on with the rest of my day. By six o'clock, I still hadn't heard from Mr. Rice, and he still wasn't answering his phone. I was getting worried. Olive had recovered well in her kennel, but I was sure that she'd be happier at home. The end of surgery was approaching. I was working the night on call, and St. Trewin was too far from Newquay to work from Kate's cottage, so I was spending the night in the practice, in one of the old hotel rooms above the surgery. This meant that at least Olive wouldn't be left on her own (Daisy Hills didn't normally have a nurse staying overnight at the practice like Beech House had done), but I was starting to get concerned about Mr. Rice. As I finished up my last consultation, Lara stepped into the room.

'Alan, Mr. Rice has just been on the phone.'

'Oh, brilliant! Finally! Is he coming to pick Olive up?'

Lara frowned. 'Er... no. No, he can't.'

'Can't?'

'No. He's been arrested.'

My mouth opened and closed a few times. This hadn't been quite what I had expected when I knew I was coming to work in Cornwall. 'Arrested? What for?'

'I'm not sure,' Lara said. 'But he sounded... well, he sounded really drunk.'

Brilliant. My first night on call in Cornwall and my client had been nicked for being drunk and disorderly.

'Er... huh. Hm,' I said. There hadn't been any lectures on this at vet school.

'He said that if we keep Olive here overnight, he'll come and get her in the morning. I think.'

'You think?'

'*Really* drunk,' Lara reminded me.

We headed out to the waiting room, where the receptionists were just cashing up, and heading out into the car park. I suddenly realised that I really didn't want to spend the night here.

'Well,' Lara said as she headed out. 'Have a quiet night! See you in the morning!'

I smiled, locking the door behind her, and set the burglar alarm. Bridgford suddenly felt a very long way away.

*

Something that had never occurred to me before: a veterinary surgery, out of hours, is a very scary place to be. All that time at Beech House, stressed and sitting next to the phone while I was on call, feeling sorry for myself, I had never stopped to think about how lonely it must have been for the nurse on call. The old surgery creaked and groaned as its walls cooled in the night, and the water pipes, innocuous in the day, gurgled and spluttered as if they were about to spit out a Kraken. I checked on Olive (she was fine) then climbed upstairs to stand by the phone, miserably. I wasn't sure which was worse; getting called out or waiting stressed and alone in this terrifying practice.

The phone rang, and my heart attempted to escape via my oesophagus. Getting called out was worse, I realised. I lifted the receiver.

'Hello, Beech H... ah, that is, Daisy Hills emergency service?'

'Mnnghgfkerbasershid,' said a slurred voice on the other end.

'Er, hello?' I said.

'Sdbasserdgotmbldydog,' the voice said. Although it sounded like it was crawling out of heavily anaesthetised lips, I recognised the heavy accent.

'Mr. Rice?' I asked.

There was a grunt, and the phone went dead.

I hurried downstairs and checked that the door was locked. Then I rushed to check that the alarm was working. Then I went and checked that Olive was okay. After that, I had run out of things to check, so I paced anxiously along the corridor leading to my room, until, mercifully, the phone rang again and I suddenly had some normal veterinary work to deal with.

One cat-bite abscess and one canine gastroenteritis later, I had almost forgotten about the mumbled phone call from the inebriated Mr. Rice. Almost; until I tried to go to bed. I was exhausted from the stressful day, but the moment I lay my head on the pillow, that slurred voice crept out of my subconscious. I felt like one of those dolls that closes its eyes when laid on its back, except that I was in reverse - standing, I could barely keep my eyelids from falling shut, but the moment I lay back, they flew open as if they were on springs.

With some effort, I forced them closed, and tried to sleep. Thirty minutes later, finally starting to relax, a tremendous clattering from outside the front door made me shoot out of bed just seconds before the alarm started ringing. I ran to the stairs in my pyjamas, and peered down into the dimly lit reception.

Immediately in front of the window, there was a small dark shape swaying and staggering around the car park. It was muttering and shouting semi-coherently, so that amongst a stream of garbled invective I could make out phrases such as 'take my fuckin' dog' and 'burn the place' - none of which did anything to settle my heart rate. As I watched, the shape disappeared from view for a moment, then reappeared carrying the dog-poo bin that had previously stood just next to the practice. Mr. Rice (I think it's safe to say that I could positively identify the shape at this point) lifted the bin over his head, whereupon a flurry of foul-smelling plastic bags dropped out of it onto his shoulders. Ignoring this, he threw the bin at the practice window. It rebounded and hit him in the shins, spewing more of its contents across the tarmac.

I did what I like to think that any heroic young veterinary surgeon would have done at this point. I called the police, and hid in my room. Mr. Rice continued his one-man assault on Daisy Hills, fortunately hampered by his extreme intoxication, while Olive, who had realised something was afoot, barked enthusiastically in the background. She was probably used to situations like this. Given the Cornishman's mental state, it didn't really seem like a wise option to hand Olive back to him; I suspected that he wasn't in the right frame of mind to go through a post-operative recovery form. Instead, I cowered behind my door for ten very, very long minutes, before St. Trewin's finest finally turned up and carted him off to the drunk tank. The constable seemed bemused when I asked why they had released him in the first place - he hadn't been arrested; at least, not in St Trewin. Whether he had been arrested elsewhere and escaped custody, or whether he had simply assumed that he was going to be arrested because that always happened when he got as drunk as he did, I never found out.

Mr. Rice turned up at eleven o'clock the next morning without breathing a word of what happened the night before. Aside from the fact that he looked as if he had spent the night in a police cell, and smelled as if he had spent it inside a redneck moonshine still, he otherwise appeared perfectly normal, rational, and even friendly. Olive bounded happily up to see him, and he nodded patiently and politely when I explained what was going on with the knee. He took the bottle of painkillers, and he and Olive walked out of Daisy Hills never, as far as I know, to return.

My rebooted quest was not off to a flying start. Drunken

assaults aside, Daisy Hills was a very different practice to Beech House. I was starting to suspect that I had been spoiled there. Had I started in one of the best?

Was I now going to see some of the worst?

15 - On the Road

And so, at Daisy Hills, and other practices around Cornwall, I began my brief career as a locum. Locum work was, or at least *felt*, very different to being a veterinary assistant at Beech House. Although the bare bones of the job itself were identical - vaccinations, neutering, work-ups, euthanasia, and so on - the start of every placement felt like being a new graduate again; new buildings, new colleagues, new animals, new cases, new clients. I didn't know where the antibiotics were kept, or how to write a consent form, or even how to find the x-ray machine[78], so every day involved a lot of questioning and a lot of feeling stupid. One thing was different to those first days, though - me. I had learned the job. I could spay a bitch, and catheterise a cat's urethra, and even pop a cow's uterus back into place, if push came to shove.[79] Starting at a new practice for a day or a week was always mildly terrifying, but I'd find that I would run through a few consults or ops, and a couple of burst abscesses or extracted uteruses later and I'd be feeling far more relaxed.

There were a number of advantages to go with these disadvantages: the pay, of course, was far better than an assistant's salary. There was also the carefree and often unacknowledged cheerfulness of the locum that comes from the fact that if you encounter a very difficult case, client, or animal, it isn't going to be your problem for much longer. That doesn't mean that I took any less care with my locum cases; I just knew that sooner or later I'd experience the undiminished joy of handling an awkward case over to another competent vet. Disadvantages stem from this, of course: as well as never having to worry about your cases, you also never get to see them through to conclusion - professionally and personally unsatisfying. I had no bond with the clients, who are

---

[78] And certainly not how to switch it on if I ever found the bugger in the first place.

[79] As it frequently did on such occasions.

naturally a little suspicious of a new vet that they've never seen before and are never likely to see again, and so I tended to spend my days doing the more routine work whilst the rest of the vets in the practice got stuck in with the meatier stuff.

All this notwithstanding, I learned a lot in my time as a locum. I saw how other practices did things - the good, and the bad. Quite a lot of the bad. I rapidly learned to loathe filling in at single-vet practices; partially because every single client I would call in from the waiting room would stand with a disgruntled look that said, very clearly, why wasn't Donald calling them in? , but largely because I often had a great deal of difficulty following their lines of reasoning.

Working in a multi-vet practice is, to some degree, self-correcting. If you make an error in judgement, you'll probably find out about it - either because your colleagues will come and tell you about it or (more likely, depending on how polite your colleagues are), when the client sees someone else in the practice, you'll check their notes and see how they approached the case differently. You're always learning from each other. You'll tend to tell each other about CPD courses you've been on[80], or about interesting papers that you've read.None of that happens in one-man (or woman - but I must admit, the vast majority of the solo practices I have worked at have been male-run) outfits. Consequently, like long-time bachelors, these solo vets tend to get a little... set in their ways. They go to CPD courses too, of course - they want to learn. But they spend all day every day of their working lives without another professional opinion to bounce ideas off. I couldn't imagine working like that, and after locuming at a number of solo-vet practices myself, I vowed never to go down that road.

I frequently wouldn't be able to follow the logic behind the solo vet's medicine. Occasionally I was alarmed to discover that procedures and drugs that were long obsolete in mainstream veterinary medicine were alive and well in the one-man clinics.

There's a difficult truth that isn't spoken of too much in

[80] Continuing Professional Development - post-graduate training lectures

medical circles: our patients, one way or another, will eventually die whatever we do. If you never have anyone else looking at what you've done, it's very easy to convince yourself that it's nothing to do with your medical or surgical skills, or failures thereof. You had the right diagnosis, you convince yourself, but sometimes they just don't get better despite your efforts. Earlier, Oscar Wilde told us that experience is just the name we give to our mistakes. If you never even know that you've made a mistake, how are you ever going to learn from it?

Some of the worst veterinary blunders I ever saw were made by solo practitioners, and I don't think that's a coincidence. I remember one vet I was locuming for casually remarking to me once, 'You know when you've got a downer cow, and you accidentally give it intravenous magnesium instead of calcium, and it drops dead in front of you? Embarrassing, isn't it?' - as if it was a frequent occurrence for him. The one and only time I saw ether used as an anaesthetic was in a one-man practice. Ether was, basically, one step up from chloroform, and was notable for being highly flammable. It was being used, on the occasion that I encountered it, on a dental with an ultrasonic scaler - a procedure known for occasionally producing sparks when the water has run out on the dental machine. I considered the cat lucky to survive the procedure.

I dealt with the aftermath of animals diagnosed with cancer by hand[81] in morning surgery, started on their first dose of intravenous chemotherapy, then sent back home with a complicated tablet regimen, all in the space of ten minutes. I saw animals incorrectly diagnosed with bone tumours, and consequently having their legs amputated unnecessarily. I saw veterinary surgeons attempt surgical procedures far beyond their skill, and I dealt with the trauma they caused to the animals and to the owners. In all of these incidences, in the awkward position of a locum vet, I tried to explain my worries to the practitioner, to be met with disinterest or outright anger.

[81] As opposed to by a pathologist via a biopsy

These problems were not exclusive to solo vets, of course. A similar problem could occur if a vet had been working a multi-vet practice long enough that you get a lot of personal clients - clients who won't see any other vet - and if they've been around long enough to think that you know what you're doing better than everyone else; a lot of younger vets call it 'old vet syndrome'. In those days as a locum, I tried to keep two things in mind that I hoped would prevent, or at least slow, my trip up old-vet lane. The first was from Socrates - the only thing I know is that I know nothing. The second was the prime directive of the medical practitioner - above all, do no harm.

Working as a locum, I'm sure, made me a better vet. Maybe not quite in the way I was expecting it to, but it opened my eyes, and I began to see the sort of things that David must have seen that made him want to start Beech House. I encountered veterinary surgeons that were money-driven, careless, incompetent, lazy, frustrated, uncaring, rude, arrogant, ignorant, or a heady mix of all of the above. I'd like to pretend that such vets are a rarity, but I know that isn't that case. They're a minority, but not an insignificant one. Most of the vets I encountered were caring, compassionate, committed, competent, and very aware of their own limitations. Some of them weren't, and working as a locum made me desperate to never become the kind of vet who had stopped learning anything, because they didn't realise there was anything else to learn. It made me appreciate James a hell of a lot more than I ever had at Beech House.

I was also discovering that incompetent vets were far from the biggest cause of animal suffering, however.

I think it's time to talk about breeding.

16 - Breeding Difficulties

Heidi, the three-year old bulldog, waddled across the floor of the prep room. She tried to sit, but her hugely distended abdomen made that uncomfortable for her, so instead she stood, and panted. Her thick eyelids drooped with weariness. Sam and I lifted her onto the prep table with some difficulty. Heidi gurgled and spluttered as we set her down, then started panting again. Green viscous fluid dripped from her vulva onto the table. We didn't have much time.

Sam raised Heidi's vein with some difficulty. This was uncomfortable for Heidi too. Not because of her distended abdomen this time, but because her elbow dysplasia made it hard for her to stretch her leg forward. I looked sadly down at her. Her whole life was a struggle against her own body - whenever she tried to walk, or eat, or defecate, or breathe, she had to fight against her own bizarre anatomy. I injected the propofol into her vein. Her eyes rolled downwards, and she started to sink to the table.

'We'll take it from here, love,' I said, and Sam smiled. Placing an E-T tube was difficult too - Heidi's soft palate was too long for her mouth, and it took some searching before I managed to locate her epiglottis - but the moment it was in place, Heidi's tongue lost its alarming bluish tinge and turned a reassuring pink.

'Probably the best lungful she's had for a while,' Sam said, as she tied the tube in. We rolled Heidi onto her side and started prepping her abdomen for surgery. I didn't want to put her onto her back until absolutely necessary; her abdomen was so bloated I was worried what the weight of it would do to the spine, and the blood vessels that ran ventral to it. We couldn't support her blood pressure nearly as well as I would have liked - Heidi's owner had declined intravenous fluids on cost grounds - and so I just wanted to get on with the caesarean as quickly as possible.

It was late on a Monday night, and I was locuming for a practice in Truro. Heidi was booked in for an elective caesarean the following Thursday, which would have been her 63rd day of pregnancy - a sensible precaution, because fewer than fifty percent of bulldogs managed to give birth without the operation - but in the last few days Heidi's abdomen had swelled to alarming proportions, and over the course of the day it became clear that the pups needed to come out, ready or not, or Heidi wasn't even going to make it to Thursday. The green discharge, which started coming out of Heidi's vuvla the hour before, indicated that the placentas had started to separate from the wall of the uterus.

Sam and I carried the now extremely-heavy dog into theatre, and I only swore and complained about my back once; something of a record, as Sam, who was just over half my size, politely pointed out. I looked at Heidi's immense abdomen, and suggested that there was probably more swearing to come. I was right.

As I scrubbed, my mind wandered back to a consultation with a bulldog owner just like Heidi's, back when I worked at Beech House. That bulldog had been called Rosie, and I was seeing her for her first adult vaccination, when she was about fourteen months old. Rosie's owner, a short, likeable man, told me that he was thinking of breeding from Rosie, and wanted to know what I thought. I glanced at Rosie's clinical notes, and tried to hide the expression of dismay that must have crept across my face. Despite her tender years, Rosie had had surgery four times - twice to replace prolapsed tear glands, once to correct her entropion (a condition where the eyelids are so fleshy and folded that they scroll inwards, allowing the fur to press against the eyeball, leading to chronic pain and frequent eye ulcers), and once to surgically remove her tail, which was so deformed it had formed a tight corkscrew shape, leading to repeated severe infections around her back end and, again, chronic pain. I wondered how I could delicately state that Rosie was about the worst candidate I could imagine to have more progeny. I wanted to grab him by the lapels, and scream, 'No, no! A thousand times, no! Can't you see how much she is suffering, just trying to walk?' but I felt that wouldn't bet very professional.

While I was thinking, the hitherto likeable owner, who seemed slightly surprised that I was not immediately excited at the prospect of Rosie producing puppies, said, 'I'll have all the tests, you know. I want to make sure I'm doing the right thing.'

This gave me an in. I calmly, and, I thought, quite logically, explained that I didn't need to do any 'tests' to tell me that Rosie was a poor choice of mother, both medically and genetically. All the conditions that she had to have surgically corrected, as well as the many she had which couldn't be, were heritable conditions, and any puppies that she had were likely to suffer from them too. I further explained that the Kennel Club, finally drawing a line in the sand long after the country behind the line has been invaded and razed, wouldn't allow any pups to be registered due to the number of corrective procedures that Rosie had already endured.

As I talked, I saw Rosie's owner's attention start to wander. I wasn't saying what he wanted to hear, so he stopped listening. I said it again, in a slightly different way, and then again, finally ending with an extremely strong recommendation that Rosie was spayed as soon as possible. This last statement was too much for Rosie's owner. At reception, I heard him asking never to see 'that vet' again.

Now, in Truro, I was scrubbed up for a different bulldog with many of the same problems. I entered theatre and donned my surgical gloves. Heidi's abdomen already had a long scar along it; this wasn't her first caesarean. In fact, it was her third. Heidi's owner said he won't let her have another litter after this one. He said that last time, too.

I opened her abdomen with a large incision, cutting through the scar tissue of her previous surgeries, and eased the huge, bloated uterus out of the wound. Incising it, I removed the first puppy in its amniotic sack. It was enormous; there was no way this monster could have passed through Heidi's pelvis. I handed the puppy to Sam, who quickly broke the sac, clearing the fluid, while I started to milk the next puppy towards the incision in the uterus.

'Alan...' Sam said. I looked up, and understood why Heidi was so bloated. The puppy looked like someone had been at it with a bicycle pump, bearing more resemblance to a hippo that a bulldog. The skin was thickened and distorted with fluid, and had torn in a number of places around the mouth. As Sam gently shifted the puppy's position, its abdomen split open, and she gasped in dismay. Fortunately, it was dead before I ever removed it from the uterus.

'Anasarca,' I muttered. Also known as 'water puppies' or 'walrus puppies': a condition of bulldog pups that caused severe oedema in the days leading up to birth. Mild cases might, just might, survive. The pup I had so far removed was not a mild case.

So it went for the remaining four puppies that I extracted. All of them were severely affected. Two of them had weak heart beats, so I asked Sam to euthanise them for me.

Heidi's colour had improved dramatically now that we had reduced the load on her uterus. I wished, once again, that we had her on fluids, but she seemed to be doing well now that all the puppies were out. I started to suture up the uterus. When I admitted Heidi, I asked the owner if he would like me to spay her at the same time, as he already had suggested that Heidi wouldn't have any more litters. He declined.

Suturing up a caesarean was often done to the noise of puppies crying for their mum's milk, but that night Sam and I finished the operation in silence. Afterwards, Sam stayed with Heidi while I telephoned the owner with the news. He was annoyed and depressed. Of course he was: a single live pup would have recouped double the cost of the caesarean. He wanted to know how many of the pups were female. We didn't think to check at the time, and I did so now. Only one of the five was a bitch, which seemed to be some comfort to Heidi's owner. Bitches were worth more than dogs. Finally, with genuine concern, he asked how Heidi was. I reassured him that she was fine, and he sounded relieved. He thanked me for my help. I put the phone down, and sat down in the dispensary, looking up at all the medicines I had at my disposal to treat sick animals. I wondered just how complicit in Heidi's suffering I was.

17 - Crisis of Faith

Kate slammed her coffee cup down on the table. '...absolute arsehole!' she was saying. 'I mean, can you believe it? He wouldn't let us do anything. "Didn't want to put it through too much"? As if a tablet a day was too sodding much.'

'Too much money, I suppose,' I said, sadly as she sat down in front of me.

'Yeah, that's right. I wish he'd just have admitted it. Anyway, he made Karen put it to sleep, of course.'

I had been there too. Sometimes clients had made their minds up about putting their pets to sleep, and they really didn't want to hear that there was a simple, if ongoing, treatment that could restore them to normal. Kate was talking about an older cat with obvious signs of hyperthyroidism, but she could just have easily been referring to a dog with arthritis, or Cushing's disease, or inflammatory bowel disease. It was one thing putting an animal to sleep to end its suffering - it was quite another doing it to save the owner money, or hassle.

'It's all about relieving the suffering,' I said, 'that's how you've got to look at it. Without the treatment, they'll suffer, so you're helping them anyway.'

Kate looked at me across the table. 'We didn't pick our jobs for the money, Alan - certainly not me. I want to relieve suffering, of course I do, but I resent being used as a disposal service for clients that just can't be bothered with it all.'

I nodded. I wasn't really in the best place, mentally, to help. I had struggled with the same questions too.

'So,' I said, playing with my increasingly soggy corn flakes, 'do you ever think we did the wrong thing? With our jobs, I mean.'

'Moving down here?'

'No, I mean the profession itself. We both wanted to do good, didn't we?' I paused. The next question lay heavily on my shoulders. 'Do you think that we do?'

Kate winced. 'That's a hell of a question to ask someone at seven-thirty in the morning.'

'So?'

Kate pinched the bridge of her nose, her habit when trying to distract herself.

'I don't know, Alan. I really don't. Maybe you should ask me again tomorrow.'

*

Driving to work that morning - I was doing a week's locum work for a practice in Penzance - I felt it all running through my head: the puppy, Dog #86324, Khan, Heidi, Kate's cat, all the other cases I had seen that had ebbed away my confidence. How did it all get so messy? It had seemed such a noble cause, such a worthwhile thing to do. How did it all get so lost amongst the business of the job?

I had lost sight of why I was doing the job in the first place. Fortunately for me, it was the day that I was going to meet Lucy, and Mr Howe.

*

'Alan,' Carl, one of the receptionists from the practice was at the door, 'I've got an extra just come in. Some guy found a stray dog, it's in a bit of a state. Could you see it next?'

I nodded, sighing a little. Clients who had 'found' stray animals sometimes used the story as cover to try to get their own animal treated for no cost. I had known people drop animals in, wait until they ended up at the local rehoming centre when their treatment was done, and then go and 'rescue' them again. 'Sure, sure, I'll go and grab it.'

Carl smiled a thank you and headed back out to the reception desk. I followed him. A middle-aged man in an expensive-looking suit was sitting in reception, cradling a bundle of furry rags in his arms. The rags had rubbed on the man's suit, and so now the front it was covered in fur and oil and some other unidentifiable substances. The man didn't seem to mind. He was looking concernedly at the rags in his arms. The rags suddenly opened their eyes and blinked at me.

'Mr Howe?' I said. I didn't have a dog's name to call. The man stood up quickly, relieved, and hurried into my consulting room.

'I just found her,' he said, 'down on the industrial estate. She could barely move. I think she's cold. Can you help her?'

I took a closer look at the bedraggled animal in Mr Howe's arms. Carl was right - it was indeed 'in a state'. The fur was so matted with oil and grime that it had clumped into an almost solid mass, all over her back, and between her back legs, where the fur was soiled with urine and faeces. Under that fur, the flesh hung off her bones like a concentration camp victim. Her feet were freezing cold, and she looked very dehydrated. She was peppered with small puncture wounds, and my first worry was that rats had attacked her, taking advantage of her inability to fight back.

She could barely move her head to look at me as I examined her head, but that's where I found her worst injury. Her teeth were bared as I looked at her, and initially I mistook this for her snarling at me, but soon I realised the problem: a degloving injury; an injury where the skin has been peeled right off the underlying tissue. It's called degloving because if it happens on a leg it looks as if someone has pulled the skin off the paw just as if it had been a glove. I always felt some particularly imaginative and possibly disturbed individual had come up with the name, but it was a very apt description of how it looked. The stray in front of me had degloved her lower jaw. The skin hung down, a tattered black and crumpled mess, from the bottom of her chin, and I could see the white bone of the mandible almost to the back of her mouth. The few patches of tissue that remained covering the bone were yellow and infected. No wonder the poor girl was unwell - she may well have had septicaemia from the wound amongst her many problems. The jaw injury was at least several days old, probably more. I wondered how long it must have been since she had been able to eat or drink anything.

'Can you do anything for her?' Mr Howe asked. His concern

had been growing as I examined the dog, and read the expression on my face.

'She's very, very sick,' I said, sadly. 'The jaw injury alone is going to take weeks to heal, and will need some major surgery to put right. She's very close to death.' I sighed. 'I'll talk to the RSPCA, and see what they say, but I suspect they will just--'

'No,' said Mr Howe, firmly, looking at the dog. He looked at me. 'There's a chance for her, you think?'

I raised my eyebrows. 'She needs nutrition, and quickly. Intravenous fluids, as soon as possible. Bloods to check her internal organs, then antibiotics, painkillers... all to get her in a state for surgery, where we can clean her up, get rid of these matts, x-ray to check for broken bones... and that's all before we've even managed to start on the jaw injury. I'm afraid I don't think that the RSCPA--'

Mr Howe waved his hand dismissively. His eyes were red. 'I'll pay. It doesn't matter what it costs. Just... don't let her have gone through all this for nothing.'

He squeezed the paw of the poor crumpled heap on the table, then he looked up at me. 'Seriously, I'll pay. I can pay today, just tell me what it will cost.'

I stood, quietly, taken aback. It dawned on me that the man was serious, and that I was wasting time.

'Okay, then I need to get to work,' I said, gently lifting the stray dog from the table. 'Let's keep our fingers crossed. I'll get a consent form sorted out.' I paused on the way out of the door. 'Do you have an idea what we should call her?'

The man stopped, his eyes on the dog. 'Lucy,' he said, slowly, certainly. The name obviously meant something to him. 'She's called Lucy.'

*

I kept Lucy on intravenous fluids (and how I managed to find her vein, I'll never know) for two days. She slowly recovered to the point where she could lift her head. Her jaw was deteriorating, though, and so we had to risk an anaesthetic to try to improve matters. Under the general anaesthetic, I x-rayed her to check for internal damage. Another nasty surprise awaited me when I looked at the radiograph - Lucy was peppered with airgun pellets, ten of them, all over her body. The cause of the small wounds in her skin became clear; someone had been using her for target practice.

The pellets didn't need to come out - they weren't causing harm any more, none of the wounds were infected - but Lucy needed a lot of work. We almost completely shaved her so we could clear all the debris from her skin, and clean up her wounds. Her jaw was a mess - I removed all the dead tissue, and cleaned off what remained. There were only two options for Lucy's lower jaw - an advancement flap (much like a skin graft), or amputation of the lower mandible. All I could do at the moment was clean up the tissue and prepare it for a possible graft in the future.

We waited anxiously with Lucy after the gas. She woke up, blinked, and very weakly wagged her tail. I've had worse days as a vet.

It was the start of a long road of recovery for Lucy. I was only locuming at the practice for another few days, but I kept in touch to keep track of her case. Over the next few days she grew stronger and stronger, soon managing to eat on her own and come out of her shell. Within a week the granulation bed was ready for a skin graft - whereupon Mr Howe paid for and transported her to a referral centre where her jaw was grafted. Several months later, Lucy was a bright, happy dog, with a working (if slightly peculiar-looking) jaw. Mr Howe not only still had her as a pet, but he had set up a permanent account. which he paid into every month, to help any other stray dogs in need in the area.

It occurred to me that Mr Howe might have shown me a way forward. He hadn't whinged or moped about his lot when he saw an animal suffering. He did something about it, and then he kept doing things about it. I had helped Lucy, but I couldn't have done it without the heroic Mr Howe. He had enabled me to take a step forward in restoring my faith.

In just a few months, that faith was about to be shaken again. It was going to be a difficult start to the new year – the year that foot and mouth disease came to Devon.

18 - A Disease of Economic Importance

Early in 2001, Kate's dream job came up[82]. The practice in her home town was advertising for a head vet nurse. Kate had spent many years as a work experience and then nursing student at the practice, and she knew and liked all the people that worked there. It was also (and this was crucial for the two of us currently living in Newquay) not in Newquay. It was in Totnes.

Totnes is a strange little town in South Devon. Despite being situated in an extremely conservative (both small and large 'C') area, it is a bastion of new-agery, peace, hippyism, and love. I'll freely admit that makes it sound like a special kind of hell designed exclusively for Republican senators, but it had a peculiar charm that made it quite unlike anywhere else I had visited. On my first night out with Kate in Totnes, I saw a rather drunken and extremely vociferous argument taking place outside a pub between two shouty gentlemen. Coming from Manchester, I assumed that they were arguing about football, but as we got closer I realised that they were having a violent disagreement about the conclusions of Albert Camus's dark philosophical novel 'The Outsider'. A few minutes up the road, a middle-aged couple wearing nothing but a pair of purple Doc Martin's boots jogged down the hill.

This is the sort of thing that happens in Totnes all the time. I liked it a great deal, and Kate was very keen to get a job closer to her friends and family. She applied.

For myself, after more than eight months, the fun of locuming was starting to wear thin. I started to look into jobs at other practices near Totnes. After a few weeks, another position appeared in a practice just a few miles away. We put on our best blouses and/or suits, scrubbed up as nicely as we could, and went to our respective interviews.

A few days later, we both heard that we had been successful.

---

[82] Okay, it didn't actually involve being paid enormous amounts of money for sitting on horses all day, so perhaps it wasn't her *dream* job.

Cornwall could keep its beaches, its shitty alleys, its indecipherable farmers and its crazy drunken clients - we were going to Devon. Good things were going to happen in Devon, in the way that they continually and repeatedly failed to do in Cornwall.

A few days after our decision to head north, we were both sitting watching a news report about a disease outbreak on a farm in Essex.

'Foot and mouth disease,' Kate said. 'That rings a bell. Which one is that?'

I shrugged. 'Um... is it... it's the one with... er. It's notifiable, isn't it?'

Kate looked pointedly back at the telly. 'Obviously.'

I shrugged again. 'Well, I'm sure it'll be okay.'

Hitherto, my sole encounter with the disease that would cause such destruction in Devon was while I was failing my public health examination in the fourth year. On the next page from the fabled *'Write short notes on the process of cheese making,'* there had been an essay question on foot and mouth disease. In the exam I had wracked my brain to try to remember my crib notes, and splurged it all out onto the blank sheet in front of me:

A viral disease - a picornavirus, to be precise. Very stable in the environment and highly contagious - the virus can potentially travel miles as an airborne particle - possibly even across the English Channel[83]. Predominantly affects ungulates. Causes fever, followed by ulcers in the mouth and around the feet. Rarely fatal in adults, but can cause heart problems in neonates. Otherwise self-limiting[84] in a few weeks. Not present in the UK at this time.

I surrounded these bare bones with a fair amount of waffle, but that covered most of the things I knew about the disease - which is another reason I failed the public health exam. I had written my notes as if I was looking at an individual animal. I wrote (and knew) almost nothing about the economic implications of the

[83] I was very proud of remembering this point - it must have appealed to the SF writer in me; also, I honestly did remember that it was a picornavirus.

[84] a medical term, meaning 'it goes away by itself'

disease.

That was going to change in the Spring of 2001.

*

Events moved quickly from that first diagnosis. A few days after the disease was confirmed in Essex, movement restrictions were placed in a five-mile radius around the site - no one could move animals in or out of the zone. By then, of course, it was already too late. Less than a week after the restrictions were imposed, a case was confirmed in Northumberland. The EU imposed a ban on the UK exporting any meat or meat products, and shortly after that, foot and mouth arrived in Devon. Within a week, cases had been confirmed in Scotland, Cornwall and Cumbria. It was becoming clear that the country was in the grip of a full-blown epidemic.

The Ministry of Agriculture, Food and Fisheries (MAFF) appeared to be moving swiftly to combat the disease. They quickly instigated further movement restrictions all over the country - not just for cattle, sheep and pigs, but for horses and dogs and humans too. Very soon into the crisis, they adopted a policy known as the 'contiguous cull' - every time a new case of foot and mouth was discovered, every cow, pig and sheep within a three mile radius was to be slaughtered.

Kate and I watched the news unravel with some confusion. Foot and mouth (and, from here on I'm going to use the accepted abbreviation FMD) was, in my mind, stored in a category along with kennel cough - highly contagious, but low severity. FMD wasn't a zoonosis - humans can't catch it.[85] It wasn't a pleasant disease to suffer from - what disease is? - but it certainly wasn't in the same league as the horrors of rabies, or anthrax, or any number of other diseases that I could think of without even reaching for

---

[85] Not strictly true - there have been a few reports of direct transmission from animals to humans, but these cases are very rare, not confirmed, and (just like FMD itself), get better very quickly.

my large animal medicine notes. As for the contagion - well, there was a vaccine available, wasn't there? I was sure there was. Quite an effective one, as I remembered. Why was the government behaving as if the dead had risen from the earth to feast upon the living?

Nevertheless, with outbreaks popping up all over the place, and with us being repeatedly told what a dreadful disease the government was dealing with, we assumed there were good reasons behind all the measures. I had failed my public health exam, after all - I was hardly an authority on the subject.

Within weeks it became clear that two counties had been particularly badly hit by the disease - Cumbria and Devon. MAFF was rapidly running out of staff to help with the crisis, and the call went out for veterinary surgeons to assist in combating the disease. Locuming at the time, there was no reason for me not to help out - no reason, except that I was not an experienced cattle vet, and I was concerned that I wasn't the sort of person that the ministry was looking for. I really wasn't sure that I wanted to be involved in this 'contiguous cull', however necessary it was. I was, after all, a vegetarian, and so to some extent had opted out of the system already. However, I still drunk milk, and ate cheese, and I knew I was fooling myself if I thought that didn't make me complicit in a lot of the problems of modern farming. Nevertheless, it didn't seem like something I could help with.

A few weeks into March, I changed my mind. I would dearly love to recount here that it was out of a sense of patriotism, or wanting to do my part for the country. I would, more dearly, like to announce that the reason I became a Temporary Veterinary Inspector (TVI) for the Ministry of Agriculture, Fisheries and Food was because, if more slaughter was necessary, then I would do what I could to ensure the welfare of those to be killed was as good as it could be. There's some truth to both of these, but here's the main, rather depressing one: MAFF were so desperate that they announced they were doubling the pay of TVIs from £125 per day to £250. A fortune for me - a week's pay for a couple of day's work.

I applied, was accepted, fast-tracked, and within a few days found myself standing outside the MAFF building near Exeter, hoping that someone in charge would explain to me, in very simple terms, exactly what the hell I was supposed to do.

Soon, I was sitting in a large conference room, amongst many other vets: some large animal veterans, some dyed-in the wool small animal-types, some new graduates, and many, many Spanish vets, who were taking advantage of the sudden opportunity for work and pay far better than anything they might find in their home country. We were being given a very short induction lecture, explaining what FMD was, how to spot it, and what MAFF were planning to do about it. This was a hot topic by now; arguments were raging across the political landscape. The countryside had been effectively shut down by the movement restrictions. People weren't supposed to venture into it unless absolutely necessary. Tourists stopped coming to the UK. Opposition party leaders were asking why MAFF hadn't imposed restrictions as soon as they had confirmed the disease in the Essex abattoir - as reports on the 1967 Northumberland epidemic were very clear that speed was of the essence in controlling the disease. Meanwhile, many members of the general public started asking the same question that had crossed my mind a number of times - what was so terrible about this disease that demanded the extreme response of the contiguous cull?

As I sat, flipping through my induction pack, listening to the explanation of the disease control policy, a line from one of my favourite childhood films ran through my mind. In *Aliens*, when Ellen Ripley discovers that the colony on LV421 has been overrun by the terrifying creatures that wiped out her entire crew in the first film, her solution is simple but effective.

'I say we take off, and nuke the site from orbit. It's the only way to be sure.'

It occurred to me that someone high up in the ministry was a fan of the film too.

*

Despite my worries, the job itself was simple - far simpler than my normal day job. Every day we (myself and a technician) would be assigned a number of farms to check in Devon. We would drive to the farm entrances in our MAFF-assigned vehicles, park outside, then don disposable boiler suits, hats and masks, dunk our white Government-issue wellies into virucidal solution, and inspect every single animal on the farm for symptoms of FMD. If all was well, we would move on to the next farm. If we found anything suspicious, however, we would call in the back-up, who would slaughter the suspected animals and test them for the disease. If it was confirmed, then the contiguous cull would come into force - every cow, sheep and pig in a three-mile radius would be culled, and their bodies burned to prevent spread of infection.

By the time I started at MAFF, there were a lot of bodies burning in Devon.

If we ever found FMD, then we would be, from that point on, classified as 'dirty', and my veterinary services would then be required to assist with the culling, and the clean-up afterwards. By this stage, with up to fifty new cases being found every day, there was a lot of culling that needed to be done. The military had been called in to help, and 'clean' vets were becoming harder to find; hence the pay increase to attract new TVIs. Within a few hours of my training video, I was inspecting sheep on a farm near Okehampton, worrying that the few slides I had seen wouldn't be enough preparation for me to tell the difference between FMD and foot rot. A few days after I started, MAFF, increasingly desperate, had introduced a 'suspected slaughter policy' - no more waiting for confirmation of the disease. If I saw lameness, would I be confident enough to cry wolf, and thus potentially condemn every livestock animal within a three mile radius to death.

I was in a better position than some, however. A lot of the Spanish vets had never seen a case of orf - a relatively common disease of sheep in Devon, that caused blistering lesions around the teats, mouth and feet. If they saw something that they suspected was FMD, then it didn't matter how many times the farmer pointed out they were actually looking at orf. All the animals on the farm would then be slaughtered, and if the case was deemed suspect enough, everything within three kilometres would follow them to the pyres.

Visiting a farm as a MAFF official was a very different experience from visiting one as a normal vet. Some farmers were friendly and welcoming, but these were the exceptions. The majority were scared that we would find something on their farm, or suspicious that despite our extravagant precautions at their gate, we would bring the disease to them. Who could blame them? Farmers were compensated for the loss of their animals, but money doesn't go very far in alleviating the distress caused by watching every living thing on your farm get slaughtered and burned. Those were uncomfortable visits, farmers nervously showing you their animals, silently praying that you didn't suddenly order them to stop, to take a closer look at something, and speak the words that would mean destruction of everything they had spent their lives building up.

A couple of weeks into my work as a TVI, the Ministry for Agriculture, Food and Fisheries transformed into the Department of Environment, Food and Rural Affairs, or DEFRA. It must have been in the pipeline before the outbreak started - the wheels of government turn slowly - but at the time it felt like a response to the perception of poor handling of the crisis in the media: 'Don't worry - MAFF are no longer in charge of fighting the disease! DEFRA is on the case now!' What it meant, in practical terms, was that one day I went to work to discover that all the headed paper had been changed from one logo to another.

I worked for about two months as a TVI during the crisis, travelling from farm to farm - usually three or four a day, but some of the big units, especially large sheep farms, took up a whole day or more. I was lucky. The farmers I visited were lucky. I saw plenty of lameness; I saw footrot, and I saw orf, but I never saw anything that resembled foot and mouth disease. I made it through clean.

*

The final case of the outbreak was reported on a Cumbrian farm at the end of September. Movement restrictions were finally lifted in 2002, a year after the first case. DEFRA's contiguous cull policy had worked. FMD was once again eradicated from the United Kingdom, after the slaughter of around ten million sheep, cattle and pigs.

I kept turning it over in my mind. FMD was a relatively mild, self-limiting disease in adult cattle. That was a hard thing to reconcile with the huge pyres of blackened, burning bodies that I, thankfully, only ever encountered on the news. The contiguous cull policy had worked.

So would have taking off, and nuking the site from orbit.

Here's the reason that FMD was taken so seriously by the Government: the economy, stupid. Affected cows suffer 'milk drop' - a reduction in the milk that they produce. This milk drop is usually temporary, but it can be permanent.

There is, as I had suspected a vaccine available for FMD. It's very effective, and relatively cheap. However, once you've vaccinated an animal, it is then impossible to test for the disease itself - the animal will test positive if the vaccine worked. For this reason, the World Health Organization classifies countries according to their FMD status thusly: 1 - FMD present; 2 - FMD-free with vaccination; 3 - FMD-free without vaccination. The third and last group gets better access to export markets, so countries in this group work hard to stay there; in fact, it's fair to say that, in 2001, the UK worked very, very hard to stay in group number 3. There have been a lot of studies on the economies of the 2001 FMD outbreak - some of which say it was worth it, in economic terms, some of which strongly argue that it wasn't. It seems to be a close-run thing.[86] DEFRA has, since the outbreak, acknowledged

---

[86] Here's some figures for the interested: getting the outbreak under control cost £8-10 billion pounds. Lost revenue for allowing FMD unchecked across the UK (and so ending up in the 'FMD present' group) could be £1.2 billion/year. Vaccination of all herds in the country would probably cost about £150 million. I can't find any figures for what the UK

that vaccination might be a sensible policy move faced with such an outbreak next time - vaccinations are allowed in some circumstances by the WHO in order to bring an epidemic under control.

In case you missed it, I'll say it again - ten million animals were slaughtered during the FMD crisis of 2001 - the vast majority of them being sheep. It's since been confirmed that roughly one in three of the 'suspect' diagnoses were correct. Thanks to the contiguous cull policy, with the three-mile 'protection' zone, this means that something like ninety percent of those slaughtered were uninfected.

Now, there's an argument to be made that all these animals would have been slaughtered anyway - we breed them to eat them, after all. As a counterpoint to that argument, consider this: slaughter in an abattoir is tightly regulated and controlled in order to minimise distress and discomfort to the animals. I have visited a number of abattoirs in my time. When it goes smoothly, the killing is painless, and very quick. It doesn't always go smoothly.

At the height of the disease in Devon, ninety thousand animals were being slaughtered a day. Ninety thousand. On farms. By vets, by technicians, and by the army. If you think that it went smoothly there, then I would suggest you are a poor student of human nature. None of the abattoir regulations were in place. Animals were not stunned prior to slaughter. They were not insensible at the moment of death, nor were they ignorant of the deaths around them. They were distressed, they were terrified, and then they were killed. Vets did what they could. Farmers did what they could; but that stark number of ten million animals, I can assure you, blurs an immense amount of suffering, fear, pain, and death into an easy-to-swallow statistic.

Foot and Mouth is a disease of economic importance. I stayed clean during the epidemic of 2001. Somehow, I still feel dirty.

---

being downgraded to Group 2 would be.

19 - The Quest

'So,' I said, opening the front of the cat basket and peering inside. It's morose occupant, a cream-coloured Persian cat with a squashed nose, peered back morosely at me with his one good eye. The other eye was clouded over, fringed with red, with a pink crater at the centre of it. 'What can I do for... er... Bouncer today?'

Despite being saddled with a name that would have been more appropriate for an enthusiastic Labrador, or perhaps a bush kangaroo, it was obvious even from a distance what I could do for Bouncer. He had a corneal ulcer - a very nasty one by the looks of things. Persians were prone to them due to their sadly deformed facial anatomy that someone who didn't have to live with the suffering that caused had decided was the right shape for a Persian to be. I was already reaching for the cat to get a better look.

'We want it put to sleep,' the man who had brought Bouncer in said.

It was almost the end of my time as a locum. The next couple of weeks would be taken up with packing and moving up to Devon, and the week after that I was due to start my new job near Totnes. I realised, shamefully, that right up until the man had spoken my mind had been more on that than it had been on my job. I looked up at the man - mid-thirties, in tan jeans and a long sleeved shirt. I cleared my throat.

'Ah, okay. Right. Why did you want Bouncer put to sleep?'

The man had the decency to look ashamed. The cat was seven years old - roughly halfway through his normal lifespan.

'Because of the eye?' I asked, hoping that there was something else wrong with the cat.

'We can't afford to treat it,' the man said. 'Been there for ages. It's getting worse. We think he's in pain.'

There are times, as a vet, when it's hard to remain professional and detached.

'Yes,' I agreed, looking at Bouncer, who was still watching me. 'He is in pain. He will have been for a while. The eye ulcer may have been quite easy to treat at first.' The man didn't say anything.

'It's still treatable now,' I added. 'It will just take a bit more--'

'We'd like it put to sleep,' the man repeated. 'Is there a form I can sign?'

I took Bouncer out of his basket and examined him. The ulcer was very deep on his eye - almost down to the last layer of cornea. If that layer went too, the eyeball would rupture, and the cat would almost certainly lose the sight in his eye. Extremely unpleasant, but a long way from dying. I checked the rest of him. Bouncer sat quietly on the table, blinking passively as I gave him a clinical exam. He seemed otherwise normal.

Bouncer's owner's expression had changed from mild embarrassment to mild annoyance. Presumably he had wanted this done with a minimum of fuss. I wasn't going to make it that easy for him.

'There doesn't seem to be anything wrong with the rest of him. We could treat the eye and see how he responds--'

The man cut me off with a frown. 'We haven't got the money. I can barely afford--'

A ringing noise from his pocket interrupted the man. He fished a mobile phone out of his pocket and answered it.

'I'm there now,' he said to the piece of plastic in his hand. 'Yeah, I won't be long. No. No, he won't.'

He put the phone back into his pocket and looked at me.

'If cost is an issue with Bouncer,' I said, trying to remain polite, 'have you considered speaking to some of the cat charities? Or rehoming?'

'We don't want it to go through all that,' he said. He hadn't looked at Bouncer once since I had taken him out of the basket. 'We just want it put to sleep. Let me sign the form.'

Bouncer remained motionless on the table while we discussed the end of his life. 'Okay,' I said, mostly calm, 'I'd just like you to consider--'

He shook his head, very slightly, and crossed his arms. He didn't want to hear that his cat had a treatable condition, and he didn't want to hear that other options were available, because he had decided that it was time for Bouncer's life to end. I thought of Dog

#86324, and the form that said that it was time for her to die.

'Do you want to stay with Bouncer while I put him to sleep?' I said. It was an effort of will for me not to say 'kill him'. Again the man shook his head, and I felt a glimmer of hope. 'Do you want to take him back with you afterwards?' I asked, trying not to let any expression show on my face.

The man seemed to consider this. I wondered if he knew what I was thinking. Either he didn't, or he didn't care. 'I just want the basket,' he said, after a moment.

I nodded, went and got a euthanasia consent form, and watched as he signed it. He left the room. I squatted down to make eye contact with Bouncer.

'If you're going to come home with me,' I said, 'we've really got to do something about that name.'

Bouncer blinked. For the first time, he started to purr.

*

Kate and I watched the peculiar creature as he nervously crept out of the basket. Bouncer had stayed in the practice while I had packed my things up - we felt it might be easier to get him used to one new home rather than two. A week later, I let him out of my battered old cat basket to explore his new home in Totnes.

'Look at him, poor little sod, he's got such a strange walk!' Kate said. Bouncer's was bow-legged, another product of his breeding. He took a few more steps, nervously, across the carpet. Suddenly, a dark shape appeared on the back of the sofa. It slinked up to Bouncer and sniffed his flattened nose. Bouncer remained stock-still, paralysed with nerves. Then the shape let out a cooing noise, and disappeared back behind the sofa.

'Bloody hell,' said Kate. 'I think Vienna approves of him.'

'Well that's a start,' I said. 'She always did prefer animals to people.'

'Her and me both,' Kate said, grinning. 'Present company excepted, of course.'

Beattie, Kate's greyhound, lay on the floor a few feet away

from Bouncer. She looked up, blinked at him, and then closed her eyes and went back to sleep. She was well-used to cats.

Bouncer looked at her, then suddenly jumped up onto Kate's lap. Conditioned by Vienna, we both tensed, and I waited for Kate's howl of pain. Bouncer started purring. Kate smiled, and ruffled his fur.

'You know, I think he's going to fit in,' she said. 'His eye's looking better.'

I nodded. He was responding to treatment, but I had booked an appointment with a nearby specialist eye vet to see if there was anything more that could be done - she had agreed to help out for a few bottles of wine and any referrals I could send her way.

'So, what are we going to call him?' I asked. 'He really doesn't look like a Bouncer, does he?'

Kate laughed as she tickled his chin. He was purring like a train now. 'I'll tell you what he looks like,' she said. 'He's an Alan.'

'Alan!' I said.

'Yeah, look, you can see it in his face. Intelligent, noble bearing.'

'Ugly as sin,' I added.

'That too,' Kate said. 'Just like his dad, aren't you, Alan.'

Alan purred some more. He seemed to agree.

Kate looked at me. 'We do make a difference, you know. Look at him. He wouldn't be here if it wasn't for you. Or Vienna. Beattie wouldn't be here if it wasn't for me. There's lots of other animals, all across the South West, that are running chasing balls, or purring on someone's lap, thanks to us.'

I looked at the scruffy ball of fur on Kate's lap. Over the next few days, watching Alan explore his new home, listening to him yowl with delight as he chased laser pointers and mice on strings, I started to realise that she was right. Not everything we did was good, but a lot of it was. Maybe enough of it was. Mr Howe had saved Lucy, but he couldn't have done it without me. Kate had saved Beattie from the dreadful fate that awaits most greyhounds when they retire from racing.

I watched Alan flailing on the floor with a toy in his grip, fighting against his own anatomy to play, and I thought of the Quest.

Saving the world, one animal at a time. Wasn't that what I had done with him? The job was difficult in many ways. It was taxing in ways that I had never imagined it would be, but it was important, too. Even when it came to the end, the last moments - that was important too.

I had been through a difficult journey in the last two years. For a long time I had thought that I wasn't good enough for the job - then I had worried that the job wasn't good enough for me.

It certainly wasn't perfect. Sometimes it meant that I had to do things that I didn't agree with. But it put me in a position to help animals like Alan, and Lucy, and Vienna, and Beattie.

One animal at a time.

20 - The Circle

Finally reconciled with my difficulties with being a vet - or at least resolved to try to get over those difficulties when I encountered them - it was time for a new start. A new job, in a mixed practice in a small rural town, twenty miles from Kate's beloved Totnes. I had been wary of accepting the first suitable position I was offered, but the new practice was custom-built (unlike the modified hotel that Daisy Hills had inhabited) and the people seemed friendly and enthusiastic.

Greeb and Michaelson Veterinary Surgery, named after the founders of the practice (who had long since retired), was a mixed practice in every sense - a mix of the old and new, as well as the large and small. The partners were firmly either 'large' or 'small', rarely crossing into the other's territory if they could avoid it. The younger vets like myself slotted in where they were needed. I immediately discovered that I got on far better with Jon, the small animal partner - a wonderfully enthusiastic, jovial and incredibly hard-working vet, whose only real failing was a tendency to sing loudly, enthusiastically and atonally whenever he was operating on anything. Whenever I scrubbed in with him to help, he considered forming a duet with him part of the normal job of a surgical assistant.

I settled in nicely at Greeb and Michaelson; at least as far as Jon was concerned. I think he was relieved to have someone working with him who took the small-animal side of the job as seriously as he did. He was an excellent and popular vet, with an animal-first approach that I liked a lot. Despite a few problems with the practice, I thought that I would learn a lot from Jon.

As summer approached, and I entered my third working year, Greeb and Michaelson took on another vet - Rosie. She was young and keen, with a wide smile. She was also a new graduate. I saw her come through the door on her first day, nervous and unsure, and was immediately taken back to my first day - twenty-five months, and a thousand years, before. I thought of all the sleepless nights worrying about inpatients, all the those dreadful 'I've never seen this before!' consultations, and all those horrible sweaty, sticky surgeries, feeling lost and afraid - behind me, and ahead of Rosie. I thought of the learning curve I had been on in those two years, and what it had meant.

Rosie strode over to me and shook my hand.

'Hi,' she said, a smile on her lips not quite covering the terror underneath. 'I'm Rosie.'

'Good to meet you, Rosie,' I said, smiling back. 'I'm Alan. You'll mostly be working with me.'

We looked at the waiting room behind us, starting to fill up with clients. Rosie's eyes had grown a little wider, realising she was about to start her first morning of consultations ever.

'We'll look after you, Rosie, it'll be fine,' I said, a wave of sympathy washing over me for what she was going to face. 'Don't worry. It gets better in a few months. I promise.'

THE END

Appendix 1: Glossary (sort of)

Medical language has its own feel to it, just like any other foreign language. It sounds academic, enticing, and mysterious. It has an implicit authority to it, and that's no surprise; it was designed that way.

You see, many years ago, doctors didn't actually know very much. Sure, they could prod you, and prescribe leeches to suck your blood, but it didn't really escape the notice of the general population that their chances of getting better with treatment weren't dramatically better than the chances of getting better without. So, a poser: how could one make a living as a quack when it was patently obvious that you didn't know what you were talking about?

The solution: make it *sound* as if you know what you're talking about. Language is, and always has been, a useful tool for those in power to keep the masses subjugated; Orwell's Big Brother understood this, with his doubleplus sinister idea, NewSpeak, and the founders of the Christian religion understood it too. Latin survived as a language largely because it wasn't understood by the poorly educated masses. The bible was always written in Latin so that churchmen (who had a similar credibility problem to the proto-medics) would be able to interpret it for the poor - and thus control the poor.

In a similar spirit, early practitioners of the medical arts realised that suggesting to a prospective patient that 'I'm going to suck out a lot of your blood and hope that you feel better,' tended to garner a less-than-enthusiastic response. However, if you told them 'I'm going to perform a phlebotomy in order to balance the humours within your body,' people tended to nod, smile hopefully, and (most importantly) hand over their coins.

So, medical terminology developed largely as a way of keeping knowledge (or lack of it) from the masses. As medical arts slowly transformed into medical science, it became more than that, however; much of medical language has a very specific and precise literal meaning (unlike, ironically, 'literally', any more[87]) which can get across a lot of information very quickly. Nowadays it's an invaluable tool to precisely explain your thoughts on a case in terms that, in theory, mean exactly the same thing to any medically trained personnel who reads or hears them.

I touched upon the idea that it's been claimed that learning the medical lexicon is like learning another language. I'm suspicious of this claim[88], but I can't deny that I get a certain thrill from being able to say that I'm suffering from post-prandial narcolepsy, rather than 'I'm feeling dozy after eating'. However, as a writer it's my job to attempt to make my thoughts as clear as possible. In the spirit of this, I'd like to offer you up a number of medical terms, and explain to you what they mean, and show you how they're useful.

1. *Shock*

This is a word that arises often in emergency situations - 'Is he in shock, doctor?' (I do get embarrassed when clients call me doctor, but I'm far too polite to correct them. Okay, okay, I get a thrill out of it too.)

It's a good demonstration of the preciseness of medical terms - shock, in medical language, does not mean 'surprised' or 'pissed off that a car has just hit them' but, instead, that the patient's tissues are starting to run dangerously low on oxygen because there isn't enough blood getting to them. Shock is further divided into several categories which more precisely define why the blood isn't getting where it needs to be, such as: *cardiogenic* (the heart isn't

---

[87] And don't get me started on 'ironically'.

[88] Certainly there's nothing in medical terminology to compare to my excruciating second-year French classes, where Mrs McKee used to point at random suspects in the class room and utter the dread nonsensical phrase 'Eresbotty' in a low growl. Everyone else in the room seemed to know what she meant, and after a few lessons I was afraid to ask. Fortunately, fate never selected me for such punishment and it was only several weeks into term that I realised she was saying 'Error Spotting,' meaning they had to comment on the next pupil's French skills. I'm not sure why I was considered a bright child, to be honest.

pumping the blood around the body properly), *hypovolaemic* (literally 'low volume' - you've lost a lot of blood), *endotoxic* (the blood vessels have become leaky due to infection; you've still got all your blood, but it's leaked out of the blood vessels). It's a useful and descriptive word, and nothing at all to do with the emotional shock experienced when, say, discovering that your evil twin brother has been performing an elaborate decade-long revenge against you culminating in him stealing your job and knocking off your wife. For instance.

2. *Cranial/ caudal/ medial/ lateral/ dorsal/ ventral/ left/ right*

These are among the first medical terms I learned; they're all terms used to orientate yourself anatomically so that you can describe exactly where on the body you have encountered a lesion or abnormality. Fans of *Jaws* (and this will, presumably, include all my readers, as it is literally[89] the greatest film ever) may be familiar with 'dorsal', due to the terrifying image of that grey triangle slicing silently through the water, signifying the arrival of Bruce the shark. The triangle is Bruce's dorsal fin, named because 'dorsal' means 'on the same side of the body as the spine'. Ventral means the opposite - the side of the body opposite to the spine, so that your belly button is on your ventral abdomen (and if it isn't, a trip to the doctor's may be in order, if you haven't been already).

'Cranial' means, perhaps unsurprisingly, 'towards the head', whereas 'caudal' means towards the tail - so your stomach is cranial to your colon, but caudal to your lungs (unless you really are in trouble) - and you'll see that these terms can refer to internal as well as external anatomy.

'Medial' means towards the midline (i.e. towards the spine) and 'lateral' means away from the midline - so your thumb is (usually) medial to your little finger, and both your eyes are lateral to your nose.

I include left and right as an anatomical point of order - such

[89] Because apparently I'm allowed to use 'literally' like this nowadays.

terms are *always* from the patient's point of view, so 'left eye' means 'the patient's left eye'.

There's a whole load more of these, for more precise localisation - 'buccal' and 'lingual' for 'on the same side as the cheek' and 'on the same side as the tongue', for instance. Hopefully you can see these terms are very useful for medics, and can help you to understand such gobbledygook as '3mm ulcerated lesion approx 2cm caudal and 3cm medial to most cranial nipple right hand side'

3. *Acute and Chronic*

A little like shock, these terms are occasionally used correctly, but more frequently abused by, the general public. I often get acute and chronic used as descriptive terms for how severe a condition is, so let's be specific - from a medical point of view, these words say nothing about a condition's severity. All they tell us is how long you've had the condition.

'Acute' means the condition appeared suddenly, and has changed rapidly. This means, of course, that acute conditions tend to be more severe when we see them, and are more likely to be in some sort of crisis, but the term in itself merely means sudden onset, rapid change.

'Chronic' conditions are the opposite - slow to develop and cause symptoms. There can be mixing of the terms; often a chronic disease will arrive in our practice in an acute crisis, because that is usually when the owner notices something is going wrong.

4. *...otomy/ ...ectomy/ ...ostomy*

Ahh, now we're getting to the good stuff - the Greek. The above are suffixes that we apply to parts of the body to explain what we've done to them, only to do it in such a way that makes us sound clever.

'...otomy' means to cut a hole in something. So, instead of

saying 'I have cut a hole in your dog's stomach', we can instead use the far sexier 'I have performed a gastrotomy.' Works with anything you can cut a hole in - bladder (cystotomy), small intestine (enterotomy), large intestine (colotomy), chest (thoracotomy) and so on. To perform a phlebotomy, as mentioned above, you make a hole in your patient's vein so the blood can leak out - usually done nowadays with a collection tube to send the blood for analysis.

'...ectomy' - remove entirely. So, no languishing in the 'I cut your cat's kidney out' for us learned veterinarians - we performed a nephrectomy. Works for anything you can chop out, so enterectomy (section of intestine), hysterectomy (uterus), orchiectomy (testicles). The ancient Incas were, of course, skilled practitioners of cardiectomy, although this was not generally to improve the patient's health.

'...ostomy' means to create a permanent hole in something. We don't do this very often in veterinary medicine - possibly the most common operation (and it's not all that common) would be a urethrostomy, a procedure where we permanently open up a male cat's urethra (the tube that runs from the bladder down through the penis) to prevent it getting blocked, although you may be more familiar with a colostomy, performed in humans with damaged or blocked bowels.

5. *Hyperplasia/ Metaplasia/ Neoplasia*

These terms are all to do with tissue growth - or, more to the point, cell growth. If you have hyperplasia, then the organ in question is perfectly normal, but bigger than it should be. This is rarely anything to worry about, but occasionally this can cause trouble if you haven't got a lot of room somewhere. Prostatic hyperplasia - enlargement of your prostate gland, which is a common ageing change in men - is the reason is gets harder to pee as you get older, owing to the fact that the prostate gland is annoyingly wrapped around your urethra

Metaplasia is change from one type of cells to another type of cells, usually as a result of some kind of injury or stress. It's reversible (usually if the stress is removed), and benign, and we don't see it all that often; usually because by the time we find out about this, the cells have moved onto the next stage, which is...

Neoplasia - the medical term for cancer. This is similar to metaplasia, except that once they reach this stage, the cells aren't going back to their previous state. They're very different cells to the ones that should be there, and unlike normal cells, which know when to stop growing, they just keep dividing. This, as I'm sure you're aware, causes all manner of problems which we won't go into now. Neoplasia doesn't necessarily mean a malignant tumour - a wart is a form of neoplasia.

For the record, neoplasia, cancer and tumour are all synonyms - none of them mean malignant or benign by themselves, although 'cancer' tends to be used to mean malignant, nowadays.[90] The difference between a malignant and a benign neoplasm is not clear cut, but it's related to how they behave: benign tumours tend to stop growing when they reach a natural tissue boundary, and are not spread via the lymph tissue or blood. Malignant tumours, unfortunately, are less respectful of tissue boundaries.

6. Idiopathic and ...opathy

Now we really enter the realms of sounding clever without saying an awful lot. These are very helpful terms. Idiopathic means, effectively, 'we don't know'. More to the point, it means that the consensus of medical opinion is still unsure as to the cause of this problem. So, when I tell you that your dog has 'idiopathic vestibular syndrome', I might be sounding very knowledgeable, but what I'm really saying is that you dog has a condition that no one in the veterinary world quite understands.

---

[90] Being pedantic, tumour simply means 'swelling', in the same way that 'rubour' means redness, but almost no one uses it in this context any more.

That's not to say this term isn't helpful - just because we don't understand where a condition comes from, doesn't mean we can't treat it, or at least recognise the pattern of the disease. Idiopathic vestibular syndrome, for instance, has a well-understood course (i.e. it usually gets a lot better within a day or two) and, if I write it on my notes, other vets who read it will know what I'm thinking. I'm just telling you that it's a shorthand way of us saying 'Oh, it's that thing where their balance centre goes wrong, but usually gets better again'.

...opathy is along the same lines. It's another suffix, and when attached to a particular organ, it means 'something is wrong with it'. Brilliant, eh? Works with anything. Pneumopathy - lung disease. Dermatopathy - dodgy skin. If I tell you that your hamster has an 'acute idiopathic hepatopathy', I'm telling you that its liver has gone wrong. I don't know how, or why, but at least I can tell you it happened pretty quickly.

7. *Iatrogenic*

This is a favoured classic, and something of a face-saver. Iatrogenic means caused by medical examination or treatment. In other words - that thing that's wrong with your pet? I did that. So, iatrogenic Cushing's disease is caused by your vet giving your pet too many steroids. In you vet's defence, they may have had no choice, because the disease that they're giving the steroids for is probably more severe than the Cushing's disease they're creating.

Iatrogenic haemorrhage is a euphemism along the lines of a surgeon telling you 'I'm afraid he lost a lot of blood during the surgery'. He didn't lose it - the surgeon did. It's nice that we have a special word for our balls-ups.

8. *Borborygmi*

Finally, I wanted to make special mention of my favourite word in the whole of veterinary medicine. It's pronounced BOR-BOR-IG-ME. Say it with me, because this word is onomatopoeic -

which is to say, it sounds like the thing it's trying to describe.

Borborygmi is the medical term for the sound of stomach gurgles. Say it again out loud, and tell me that isn't the greatest word ever invented.

Appendix 2 - Breed-related Diseases

As a veterinary student, and as a new vet, I hadn't really thought much about dog breeding. Dog breeds, to me, meant a tedious list of predisposed diseases that I had memorised by rote as part of my training - something a little like this:

o *West Highland White Terriers: atopy, lens luxation*

o *Daschunds: lumbosacral disc disease, elbow dysplasia*

o *Pugs: globe prolapse, brachcephalic airway syndrome*

o *King Charles Spaniels: mitral valve insufficiency, syringomyelia*

o *Boxers: aortic stenois, neoplasia, idiopathic syncope*

o *German Shepherds: anal furunculosis, atopy, pannus, dilated cardiomyopathy, hip dysplasia, chronic degenerative radiculomyopathy[91]*

... and so on. Questions on this would pop up all the time in exams, so you needed to know this stuff[92], but I never really considered what this list meant. It was just something else to learn: parathyroid hormone is responsible for the regulation of calcium levels within the body, and greyhounds are predisposed to develop osteosarcomas.

When I was growing up, our family pet was a cocker spaniel named Silky.[93] I loved her dearly, as you would expect. She was a

[91] This is not, by any means an exhaustive list for any of these breeds.

[92] And why, due to a particularly stressful 'steeplechase' exam in my fourth year, I will remember to my deathbed that Belgian Shepherds are predisposed to gastric adenocarcinomas.

[93] This is what happens when you allow your children to come up with

harder dog for my dad to love; she was extremely protective of her bed, and would growl and snap at him whenever he approached. She did the same to all of us if she ever wriggled under the bed, and she once bit me quite badly on the finger when I tried to extract her. At university, I learned that this was an inbred trait of spaniels - rage. So, it turns out, was the heart disease that claimed her life. Still, these things never really connected; by the time I qualified, Silky had been dead a long time, and my parents had another spaniel at home. We knew the breed, you see. We liked them.

In practice, this knowledge of breed diseases was very helpful. Young Labrador, unsteady on its back legs? Definitely worth x-raying the hips for dysplasia. Westie with breathing difficulties and crackling noises on auscultation of the chest? Need to investigate the possibility of pulmonary fibrosis. Very helpful knowledge; essential, in fact.

In those first few months, I was living from one consultation to the next, terrified that I was just one slip of the needle away from making some colossal mistake. Eventually, though, as the terror of being a new graduate slowly settled into a dull, lurking fear, and I started to see consultations that weren't wholly new to me, I began to notice just how much of my time was being taken up treating diseases that were on that list. Even for someone as slow on the uptake as me, when faced with my third westie in the same week with severely inflamed and infected skin due to its chronic allergic skin disease, I started to ask myself questions about whether there might be a better way of dealing with this stuff.

*

Suffering. It's a word that's followed me through my life, and through my career. As vets, we use it a lot. We are, we like to think, its enemy. Our whole *raison d'être*, our vocation, is to reduce it

names for your family pets, of course. We all liked the name, anyway. Don't judge us.

whenever and wherever we can. It's the reason we can euthanise five animals in a day and still get to sleep at night - we didn't want them to suffer any more.

Working in general practice, it finally started to click with me - this Rottweiler with entropion wasn't helping me out by presenting me with a disease I knew it was predisposed to. It was in pain, because its eyelashes were pressing onto its cornea. That Springer spaniel with purulent otitis externa was yelping when I examined it because it *hurt*. That Great Dane I put to sleep last week due to its dilated cardiomyopathy wasn't just another tick box on my mental list of breed diseases. It was dead, because its heart gave out. Because it was a Great Dane.

That's when I started to wonder about that list. Breed predispositions. It meant that, genetically, these breeds paid a price for their long ears, or their curly tails, or their short, cute, forelimbs. It meant that they were more likely to get certain diseases - and, from my experience in practice, I was realising that this didn't just mean a *bit* more likely. Something like fifty percent of westies have atopy. The same proportion of bulldogs can't give birth without a caesarean. I was coming to understand that the price a dog pays for being a certain breed is that it *suffers*.

*

As an afterword to our discussion of breed-related disorders, I'd like to briefly discuss the people responsible (and I do use the term very loosely) for producing puppies - breeders.

You can, I think, break breeders down into several types (rather than, say, their component atoms, which, despite my feelings on dog breeding, I do not advocate). Let's start with the type most commonly encountered by vets in general practice: the 'responsible' breeder.

'Responsible' breeders

The reason we encounter this type of breeder more

frequently is, sadly, not because they are more common than any other type, but simply because these are the breeders who do everything possible for the pups that they produce - vaccinations, worming, flea treatment, nutritional advice, hip scores (or whatever test other the breed needs to pass to make it's suffering less than it otherwise would be) - and so they're the ones who come to the vets. Often. Very often. In general practice, we'll be on first-name terms with them.

'Responsible' breeders occupy a strange position in many veterinary practices; generally liked (or at least tolerated) by practice owners, and largely resented by all the other vets, nurses and support staff - and by resented, I mean that their faces are likely to be pinned to a dartboard in the coffee room.

Here's the problem in a nutshell: breeders bring in a lot of money to the practice, both directly and indirectly, because if they like you, they're going to recommend you as the vets to go to. They are well aware of this, and as a consequence of this they frequently feel (not entirely without reason) like specially valued customers, which usually translates into them behaving as if they own the practice.

Responsible breeders have a tendency to be impatient with (if not downright rude to) the receptionists, nurses, and junior vets who have the temerity to obstruct them in their quest to be immediately seen by the senior partner. They'll assume their particular problem is going to be more important to the practice than any other client's, and they'll be very ready to write a complaint letter if it isn't treated as such. They'll expect vets to drop everything to kowtow to their wishes, and they will usually hold the views of younger vets in disdain.

I can't tell you how many times I've heard some variant of the mantra, 'I've been breeding dogs for thirty years, young man,' with the strong silent implication that my own decade or so of treating sick animals every single day of my working life preceded by five years at university is worthless in comparison to this enormous achievement. Being my usual diplomatic self, at times like these I bite my tongue rather than point out that it's really not too difficult to produce a dog.[94] Even if the breeder hasn't personally been breeding dogs for very long, they will always be accompanied by a friend who has been, and with whom every single statement you make as a vet must be checked and verified.

Now, I'm being unfair here, because for every two obnoxious, rude and demanding responsible breeders, there is one that is extremely pleasant (and yes, that's the correct ratio as I have experienced it). Not only that, these are, and I mean this genuinely, people who care about what they are doing: they care about the puppies that they breed, and the mothers, and they want to see them go to good homes. They want to do the very best medically for their animals, and they would be horrified to think that they were causing any degree of animal suffering at all.

They are, though. However horrified they might be at the thought, they are most certainly causing suffering. Quite apart from the severe, dreadful misery caused by inbreeding, for every puppy sold to a new home, there is a dog in a rescue centre denied one. A dog that will either ultimately get put to sleep, or will spend the rest of its life in a kennel. Every single puppy. They don't mean to cause misery, but I am here to tell you that even the most caring, responsible, well-read and clued-in breeder is causing it nevertheless.

And these are the good ones.

Irresponsible Breeders

If responsible breeders are likely to find their faces on dartboards in vet practices, then irresponsible ones are more likely to find their way onto the toilet roll. Irresponsible breeders don't really care about vaccinations, or worming, or nutrition; all of those cut into the profit margins. They care about mum, in so far as they need the bitch to keep producing puppies, but when she's past breeding age they'll pass her on, or put her to sleep (and vets are

---

[94] If you're not familiar with the procedure, here's what you need: two dogs.

not commonly involved in this last procedure).

Irresponsible breeders are the type who lead to situations like my caesarean in Cornwall. They may attempt lip-service to the fact that they're dealing with a living creature rather than, say, a money-printing machine, but their actions belie their motives.

Breeders like this are frequently encountered for the first time in the middle of the night, having 'just moved to the area' or 'not registered the dog before', both statements being euphemisms for having run up a huge bill at one of the other vets in the area and having no intention to pay it. It's considered unprofessional for vet practices to inform other vets in the area that such clients haven't paid their bill, but we usually get the idea pretty quickly from the circumstances around that first phone call.

Despite the fact that a single puppy from a pedigree breed would generally cover more than double the cost of a caesarean, irresponsible breeders forget to bring their wallets with them surprisingly often - and frequently find them again very quickly when they are informed they must pay at the time they collect the dog.

Such breeders are the cause of immense amounts of suffering - principally to the deformed, unhealthy puppies that they produce, the females of which are destined to become dog-shaped money machines like their mother, but also to vets and nurses. Being faced with a client that simply refuses to pay and an animal that is in severe pain and in need of a caesarean is every vet's nightmare scenario. Yes, we can, in principle, simply offer to euthanise the animal on humane grounds, but if anyone else can do that and still get to sleep at night, I'd appreciate some tips.

Breeders of this type are far, far more likely to report your actions to the Royal College of Veterinary Surgeons - so for those people who have suggested me, after hearing the tale of my caesarean in Cornwall, that performing the surgery described without spaying the poor bulldog was unethical, all I can say to you is this: not according to the Royal College. Performing a surgical procedure on an animal without consent is very definitely going to get a vet struck off, and so is the 'whoops, the uterus broke so I had to take it out' strategy that has been whispered about behind closed doors.

As time goes on, and I become more of a fundamentalist about breeding in general, I am starting to include anyone who breeds dogs of such obvious anatomical unhealthiness as pugs, bulldogs, basset hounds and so on as automatically, and by definition, irresponsible. Yes, I know pugs are beloved by the internet. I also know that, because of their shape, they suffer; perhaps if you had treated several animals that had prolapsed their eyeballs because they had a nasty coughing fit, you might feel similarly.

Puppy Farms

It is with sorrow that I even have to include this category, as I would have hoped that these would have died out years ago, but nope, they're still going strong. Puppy farmers are, effectively, irresponsible breeders who have embraced the principles of battery farming, and applied it to dogs.

A lot of vets know very little about what goes on in puppy farms, because they never visit them, and they never hear from the breeders. The first they know at all about such places is when they are presented with a puppy that someone has bought from them. Even by pedigree standards, puppies from here are going to be in pretty poor states. Often these puppies are bought on the internet, and while it boggles my mind that anyone could be so stupid as to order a puppy in the same way that your order your shopping, it still happens. Thankfully, a recent petition requesting the banning of the such places by the excellent PupAid charity has very recently topped 100,000 signatures, which means the issue must now be debated in parliament.

I haven't got much to say about puppy farms at all, to be honest, other than to say that they are vile, evil places, which cause about as much suffering and death as anywhere I can think of outside of... well, outside of a battery farm. Which does spur me to make one last point about them - if, like me, you can't stand the thought of a helpless dog, trapped for its whole life and forced into repeated pregnancies to produce animals simply for profit - then please stop and consider what you're doing when you buy cheap eggs, or pork, or veal.

What to do?

So far I have, I hope, given a pretty clear indication of the suffering that is caused by the puppy trade. Is there anything that can be done to prevent it?

Well, fortunately for me, I've saved the easiest part of my long discussion of breeding for last. Yes. Yes there is. It's really very simple.

I could give some simple advice here about never, ever ordering a puppy if you haven't seen and visited it's mother, and made sure it's in comfortable surroundings, and healthy, and well. Never even think about buying a puppy online, and don't ever, ever get anyone a puppy for a present, no matter how good an idea it seems. But, I'll be honest with you, sitting here typing out the words 'ordering a puppy' makes me feel a little queasy. Here's my much simpler advice (and I warned you I'm a fundamentalist on the topic):

Don't buy puppies. Don't breed puppies. Get your animals from rescue and rehoming centres. Always.

That's it. That's the sum total of my advice. Follow it, and I can guarantee you'll be reducing animal suffering, and you will have a wonderful new addition to your family.

As to the rebuttals to that advice that may have sprung instantly to your mind, then I'll deal with them below:

But... if everyone did that, there wouldn't be any pet dogs! Is that what you want?

No, it isn't, but... don't be silly. Rescue centres are absolutely full. Animals are getting put to sleep right now. Read Dog #86324. If they ever get even close to emptying, I'll change my advice. I suspect that I won't ever have to do that.

But... I want to know what I'm going to get!

Well, I can tell you what you're going to get with a pedigree dog, but let's not go there. You can, and I hope I'm not sounding rude here, possibly get a reasonable idea of what you're going to get by *looking* at the dog you're rescuing, as opposed to assuming that a dog that you've ordered from a breeder and that doesn't yet exist is going to be fine.

But what if the rescue dog is aggressive?

What if the pedigree dog is? At least the rescue dog will have been screened for its behaviour. The pedigree one won't. I've met plenty of 'well-bred' dogs that took a disliking to my nose too.

But I want a dog that won't shed any hair, I'm sort of allergic to dog hair. Think of my children!

Well, labradoodles need to be rescued too, you know. Failing that, buy a better vacuum cleaner, or, if you and/or your child is allergic to dog hair then, and I'm only suggesting this, possibly a dog isn't really the pet for you. I'm extremely uncomfortable with this idea of getting a pet 'to order' - it's this sort of thinking that got dog breeds where they are today, which is to say, suffering.

But... my Brunhilde is amazing, I just want one litter of pups from her.

I understand this impulse. You love your dog. You don't want that to be it when they're gone. Listen, no one in the world loved their dog more than I loved Geri - but I wouldn't have bred from her, even if I had the option. Why? Because there are thousands of dogs like Geri, and yes, like Brunhilde, already waiting for a home. The world doesn't need more of them. It really doesn't.

Don't buy puppies. Don't breed puppies. Get your animals from rescue and rehoming centres. Always.

Nick Marsh

By the same author

Soul Purpose
Past Tense
The Ancients
The Express Diaries

www.nick-marsh.co.uk

Printed in Great Britain
by Amazon